A BOX of GARGOYLES

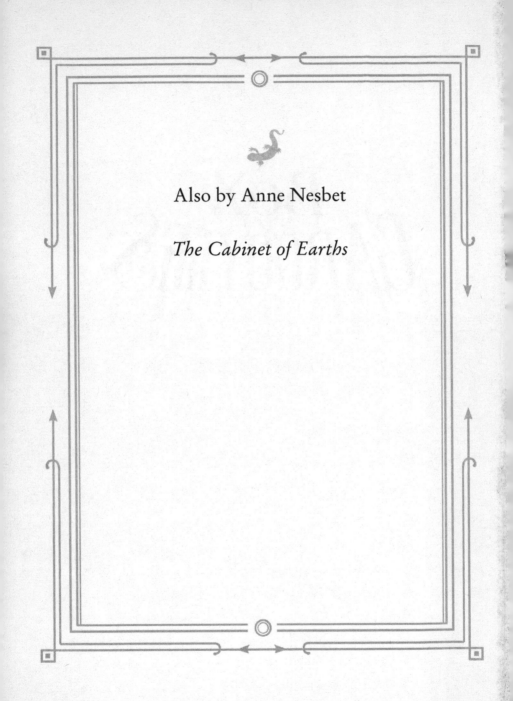

Also by Anne Nesbet

The Cabinet of Earths

A BÔX —of— GARGOYLES

Anne Nesbet

HARPER
An Imprint of HarperCollinsPublishers

Library of Congress Cataloging-in-Publication Data is available.
ISBN 978-0-06-210425-0

Typography by Andrea Vandergrift
13 14 15 16 17 LP/RRDH 10 9 8 7 6 5 4 3 2 1
❖
First Edition

For Eric

CONTENTS

0

THIS STORY STARTS WITH A . . .

*B*ANG. No, louder than that! It was the loudest sound any of the stones in that wall had ever heard. They hadn't been paying attention to the wrinkled man as he knelt on the ground fiddling with his parchments and beakers, despite the tang of magic all around him. People come and people go—that's the way stones see it. When you've been around for eighty million years, human beings amount to a cloud of noisy mosquitoes. Not even worth swatting at—if limestone could swat.

But this bent-over smoke streak of a man did something no mosquito ever does: he made the world explode. He put his wizened, tangy palm right up against the wall, he made clickety-breathy human sounds with his mouth, and the magic went BANG and blasted its way right into the heart of those poor stones.

And in that one awful moment everything changed.

Aeiiii! It hurt terribly.

The limestone did its best to yelp and pull away, but stone isn't good at either of those things.

So the change raced through the wall like lightning, like lava, like all of time squished into a single dreadful moment, and the limestone, shrieking silently, found itself filling up with weird poisons: a million pointy-edged words, a gazillion chattering thoughts.

I am no longer myself! thought the wall, and was horrified to find itself thinking. All of a sudden, for instance, it knew where it had been standing all this time: on an avenue in the city of Paris, a block away from the river Seine. On one side of itself was the avenue Rapp, a proud part of France, and on the other stood a couple of buildings, an embassy, which belonged, through the peculiar magic of diplomacy and treaties, to another country (with a long, pebbly name: Bulgaria) a thousand miles away. In two places at once! That was why this wall was such a good place for magic. It knew, furthermore, that its own stone had been quarried in faraway Bulgaria; it had traveled on barges and trucks and trains to get here; that travel had taken fifty-nine days, and at the end of the fifty-nine days, the squeaky, wispy human beings had slapped some mortar down in their hasty way and thrown the stone blocks on top of one another, and the wall had been standing here quietly, recovering from all that hullabaloo, all the forty-three years since. This very minute the air was dark and cold because the date was the twentieth of the month of October, and the hour was eleven p.m., and the day of the week was Saturday. . . . In short, it knew a thousand million things no wall should ever know.

Those were facts, and it's bad enough for a wall to know facts. Worse by far was the foul thing all those facts were dragging in with them: not just words all a-jumble, but a *mind*. That was what the smoke-streak man had been up to, the one who stank of magic. He was magicking up—rude man!—a hiding place for his mind. That mind spread now through the astonished stones like a miasma, like a sour mist hugging the face of a bog, a vile clot of purposes and intentions with a name tacked on top: *Henri de Fourcroy*.

Forty days, said the mind as it gloated its way deeper into the stones. It was full of instructions. *You will bring me the girl. She broke me; she will mend me. And you will keep me safe for forty days!*

That was the time it needed for the rest of the spell to work. The wall knew that now. The wall knew everything! The man's magic had reached into the tiniest crevice of What Is and opened a loophole there, to buy him some time.

He would be a shadow for a while. But he would mend. Once you have been immortal, you do not crush as easily as others do. No! Let others be crushed, yes. But not Henri de Fourcroy.

It all happened in a millisecond or two: the *bang*, the awful change, the mind rushing in. A moment ago the wall had been plain, quiet stone, and now—

Ptoooooie!

That is the sound of limestone having had enough. In less time than it takes to notice that the tasty morsel in your mouth has gone bad, bad, bad, the stone wall raced ahead of that mind and its loophole magic and spat it out.

And then the wall stood there, shaken to its very bones, and surveyed the damage. The wrinkled man was gone. There was smoke and shadow everywhere, and more of those mosquito-swarm people running up, waving their spindly little arms and squeaking the way humans do.

But oh, grief: there was a hole now in its own stone self. *I spat too hard*, thought the wall.

And was horrified to find itself *still* thinking.

It goes to show how hard it can be to spit out a mind, especially as sticky a mind as that of Henri de Fourcroy.

Everywhere faint tendrils of that mind still remained, and they whispered poison as they coiled and uncoiled:

Maya Davidson. Find her. She broke me; she must mend me. She will pay.

1

THE WALL THAT BLINKED

Trouble doesn't always start with a sudden sense of well-being and the smell of warm chocolate croissants—but then again, sometimes it does.

Maya Davidson, almost thirteen, was walking along the avenue Rapp under leafless Parisian late-October trees, and the croissants sang out in small sugary, buttery voices from within their twists of white paper, and with every step she took, those letters in her pocket that had just come today reminded her of their presence by crinkling a little. And Maya herself felt—

Well, how exactly did she feel?

She wrapped her arms around her wool-jacketed self and considered the question for a moment, smiling, while her breath made thin clouds in the air.

One thing was clear: she was not the same girl she had been three months ago. No. Things had happened. She had changed. In fact, so many things had happened that if an old, out-of-date version of Maya, the Maya from way back in June, were to show up suddenly, on this very sidewalk (probably looking pretty freaked out, thought Maya, to find herself suddenly whooshed all the way from California to this big French city), it would be pretty hard to explain any of it without sounding, to be honest, kind of loopy.

Dad took that laboratory job in Paris. . . .

That much would make sense to the old, out-of-date Maya. That was the kind of thing that happens sometimes to people, when their wonderful, beloved, misguided mothers (who have always wanted to live in France, who have always, *always*, so very much dreamed of spending time in that *magical old city*—what an opportunity for the *children*!) are finally getting better after having been so sick for way too long. Maya's father did take the job in Paris. It really happened. Paris, by the way, is very far from California, and when you are dragged six thousand miles from home and plonked into the local school, you notice pretty fast that in Paris, everyone in school speaks French.

So that was hard. *But not as hard as you think it's going to be*, said Maya-in-October to old-Maya-from-June. *You'll do okay. It's the other things that happen*—

Because it turns out that Paris really *is* an old and magical city, and sometimes the magic sneaks up and holds you tight and will not let you go.

Sometimes an evil, beautiful uncle will show up out of nowhere and try to trap you in some terrible spell, just so that he can go on in his wicked ways forever and ever.

Uncle? said old-Maya-from-June. *What uncle? And did you just say "spell," like in old fairy tales about princesses and frogs and stuff? Are you nuts?*

I know it sounds weird, said new-Maya-from-Now. *But listen—*

So this Henri de Fourcroy, who was sort of their uncle, had even had the gall to kidnap Maya's impossibly likable baby brother, James, so that he could drain him of his charm.

KIDNAP? said Maya-from-Then to Maya-from-Now. *JAMES? You let that happen? You're the one who's supposed to TAKE CARE of James—*

That made Maya stop in her tracks for a moment, remembering how it had felt that horrible, awful, terrible day, which wasn't, when you thought about it, very many days ago. Last Saturday! It took her smile right away, remembering that. Because Maya-from-Then was right: it was always Maya who was supposed to take care of James—

And I did take care of him, said Maya to herself, finding her footing again. *I found him. I rescued him. I saved him. I did. But of course it got pretty strange—*

7

It was the fairy-tale stuff again, only for real: she, Maya, had had to foil the plans of that wicked old Henri de Fourcroy.

She herself had reached through the glass into the Cabinet of Earths and pulled out that bottle of his, where everything that had been mortal in him had been hidden so safely for so many long years, and time had caught up with him again and made him old. So now he was withered away and gone.

The Cabinet of WHATS? Maya-from-Then was saying, somewhere in the background now. *What was that you just said?*

Maya-from-Now waved her earlier self away, though she tried to be nice about it.

Don't worry, she said. *The point is, it all worked out. You're okay. You're going to be okay! Really!*

Because she knew, better than anyone else could ever possibly know, about the knot of worry that Maya-from-Then was carrying around in her, always. How much it ached, that worry. How hard it was, sometimes, to be that Maya. But finally it was October, and life was back to normal, if you could ever call living half the world away from your home "normal." At least the French schools believed in a lot of vacation. Maya's school had just let out for ten full days—yes! It was true! She had survived the whole first quarter of the school year.

What's more, she had made a real, actual friend here in Paris, a dark-haired, quick-smiling boy named Valko Nikolov, who had lived for years in New York—

—and when she had just run up to her apartment for a moment after school to drop off her books, she had found a small stack of letters for her on the table in the dining room, so her friends in California had not forgotten her, after all—

—and then when she had stopped at the bakery to get something to share with Valko as they went walking across the bridge or along the Seine, the chocolate croissants had been *warm*.

All in all, what Maya, the former champion worrier of the world, was feeling at the moment was something she hadn't felt much of in the last few weeks (or months, or years): the tingling, hopeful feeling that is the *opposite* of worry.

Was there a single, perfect word to describe this particular feeling? She wasn't sure. If there were, it might have to be spelled like this:

(!!!)

Maya had to put a hand to her mouth to keep her smile from breaking loose as she crossed the last little street before the block where Valko lived.

At that point she paused for a moment to admire the interesting new hole, outlined in jagged scorch marks, that had appeared in the high garden wall of the Bulgarian embassy last Saturday night. A transformer must have blown, Valko had said with some relish as he showed off the flashlight he now carried everywhere. Medium-sized chaos! Embassies apparently didn't like their walls exploding, even if only partially, and they didn't much care for power outages, either.

There were lines of police tape marking off the part of the sidewalk directly under the hole, and an exceedingly bored policeman, whose job was to stand there all day in case some acrobat decided to spider-walk up the wall to the hole and then scramble through into the Bulgarians' private garden. Through the hole you could see bits of branches and greenery, and embassy windows that would ordinarily have been invisible. And what was that? Craning her neck to get a better look, Maya put her hand on the wall to steady herself—

and the wall JUMPED.

Well, not jumped, exactly: twitched; flinched; *blinked*. It was Maya who did the actual jumping, as she snatched her hand away from the stone.

Could a stone wall have some kind of electricity coiled up in it? A secret internal alarm system trained to yell when fingers touched it? Sensitive stone nerves?

None of that seemed remotely likely, but then her head was still ringing from the silent *twangggg* that had come shooting up through her fingers. It wasn't exactly like getting a shock from a doorknob after you've shuffled around a bit on the living-room carpet. No. That kind of jolt is, at least, impersonal. The thing about this one was—the wall had—okay, it was crazy to think like this, but this was what it felt like: the wall had *recognized* her.

Her, Maya.

Her heart began to skitter under her ribs.

Slow down, she told herself. *Slow way, way down.*

She surveyed the scene. The policeman was still poking away at a rough spot on his fingernail. The wall—she moved another inch away, just to be safe—was pretending to be a normal wall, if she ignored that sooty hole looking down at her from up there.

Really looking at her.

Not just looking, in fact, but *staring* at her.

The little hairs on the back of Maya's neck were prickling in alarm long before she realized what had caught her attention—caught it the way a hook might catch a fish.

An *eye* was gazing at her from that wall. The strangest eye in the world, an eye made up of gaps and stone and other even more peculiar things, all falling together into *eyeness* if you stood just where Maya was standing and looked up just so.

All right, all right, it was an illusion: the hole in the

wall was a sooty-edged oval turned on its side; an eye-shaped gap where stone wall used to be.

But then it got stranger, because framed by that gap the way a person's brown-green-blue-or-sometimes-purple iris is framed by eyelid and eyelash was a stone figure. It was far off and high up, hunched over itself in a round-iris way as it perched on its narrow, high embassy ledge, centered (if you were standing just where Maya happened at that moment to be standing) within the eye-shaped hole in the wall.

Maya squinted. Could that really be what she thought it was? Yes. The iris of the wall's impossible eye was a *gargoyle*. You didn't expect to see a stone gargoyle clinging to the side of the Bulgarian embassy, but there it was.

The gargoyle-iris looked directly down at Maya through the eye-shaped hole of the garden wall. The gargoyle's own eyes were piercing, shadow-black dots, and they were the pupil of the wall's eye, and it was all like one of those sets of Russian nesting dolls (eyes within eyes within eyes), only worse, because this eye was also a trap, and Maya was caught in it.

"Oh!" she said aloud, startled all over again.

She really must have touched a nerve or something in that wall. The gargoyle was staring at her as if it had been doing nothing since the day it was carved but waiting for her, *Maya Davidson*, to walk by. The air was still twanging in silent alarm all around her. In fact, a wave of strangeness was now—how to describe this?—rippling out from the eye in the wall, just as the church bells a few blocks away tolled four.

Maya had grown up in California, where there are earthquakes from time to time, so she automatically scanned the sidewalk for a nice solid table to hide under, but the sidewalk had no tables. And in any case, although her stomach pitched about a little as the wave of strangeness rolled through her, the ground was not actually moving, so this was weirder than an earthquake, whatever was going on now.

Something was ever so slightly wrong. But at first she could not see anything out of place. People were still walking along, still laughing and chatting or hurrying by in silence, as if nothing at all were the matter. It was like the sidewalk had turned into the deck of a very large ship, and a wave had just pitched that ship over onto its side, almost, and nobody but Maya even felt the slightest bit out of kilter.

And no railing to hang on to, not anywhere.

"Help," she said, in the tiniest of voices, because it is disconcerting to feel like the universe has just bent a little out of its ordinary shape when nobody else seems to notice. She was actually putting her hand against her forehead to see if maybe she might be out-of-the-blue feverish or something, when right in the sidewalk in front of her there appeared the slenderest vein of sand, a twisting miniature wriggle of sand, meandering out from the wall in a lazy curlicue.

She tested it with her toe, and it was really truly sand—dark sand, like lava ground down into grains of black salt. Not just a curlicue. No. It was zigzags and circles now, opening up in the pavement; she had to hop out of its way, it was scrawling about so fast, and when she hopped she collided with something that made a very displeased sound: the French policeman.

"Attention!" he said, his lips curled into a frown, but Maya was distracted by his pillbox hat, which was sprouting a small pair of blue canvas wings.

They were the tiniest of wings. The policeman didn't seem bothered by them at all. His hat lurched upward, almost free from his head, and he gave it a smart tap to settle it back down again, as if he had been having to deal firmly with this particular hat for years and years.

Maya moved well out of his way, and he strode on by, the policeman and his fluttering pillbox hat. Her own heart was still going tappity-tap, as if it had little wings, too.

She could see now that other odd things were happening in small doses all around:

The antenna of the car parked nearest to her had,

for example, quietly shredded itself into a frothy spray of metal and was now waving its thin stalks gracefully about in the air, like a skinny metallic sea creature. One single branch of the nearest sidewalk tree swelled up into a million little warty bumps, as if the bark had shivered itself into goose pimples, and out of those bumps burst the tiniest fuzz of new green leaves, completely out of place on that gray street.

Even the warm, buttery smell of the chocolate croissants was remaking itself right under her nose, becoming darker and mintier.

It was confusing, yes. The very air was confused; there was a bewildered hum running through it.

"Hey, Maya, listen," said someone very close by. "Something's gone wrong—oh, *gash*—it's so stupid. Listen—"

"*Gash?*" said Maya, but she could feel the smile (!!!) jumping back onto her face even before she had finished turning her head, because it was pretty much impossible not to smile when Valko showed up. If they ever invented a human-shaped cure for a world gone sideways, it would probably look a lot like Valko Nikolov. It would have tousled black hair and the friendliest possible gray eyes and a comfortable sort of voice.

But then she looked again and saw that even comfortable Valko was clearly bothered by something. The little lines that usually crinkled where much younger kids might have actual dimples were gone, for instance. And his eyes weren't really smiling either.

"Hi, there," she said, feeling the (!!!) fade slightly away. "It all started happening, like, maybe five minutes ago. Everything got weird. Did you really say *gash*?"

Valko did, on occasion, like to make up words. Or new uses for underappreciated words. But something was definitely, just now, not quite right.

"Everything got weird?" said Valko. He didn't sound like himself. He sounded distracted. "What got weird? Sorry I'm late—the power just went off again in there. Chaos. Bumping around. People looking for headlamps. But listen . . . "

Maya already was listening, but Valko let the sentence trail off instead of finishing it and then made the toe of his shoe stub itself pretty hard on the sidewalk.

"The power went off?" she said, finally, because it's hard to wait around as long as that for the rest of a sentence.

"*Gash*," said Valko with feeling. "Who cares about the power? There's a backup generator. The lights pop right back on again in a few minutes anyway. That's not the thing. The thing is, my grandmother called. Not the nice, sweet grandmother. The other one. *Baba Silva*."

He shuddered.

"She has a totally incredibly huge mole right there, on her cheek. I'm telling you. And she's *fierce*. When she frowns, you think that mole is just going to reach out and whack you or something. Anyway . . ."

And then the drama faded from Valko's expression, and he was looking right at Maya, more directly and simply than people usually look at each other on sidewalks where strange things are happening, beneath walls with holes in them that if you squint just so become a lot like eyes. . . .

"I'm really sorry," he said. "The thing is, it's bad: they're sending me back to Bulgaria."

For a while she just stared at him. The words hovered in the air like soot.

"Bulgaria?" she echoed.

"Happy first day of vacation, right? They want to send me back to live with my totally terrifying grandmother-with-a-mole."

If the world was a ship and the ship was already tilting, all unsteady, to one side, suddenly Maya was in the water, with the cold waves rolling right over her head.

She said, "Why?"—but she couldn't make the sound of that word very loud. The water was too cold, and she was sinking through it way too fast.

"Because I'm *not Bulgarian enough*," said Valko, with a flourish of despairing bitterness. "Because *I've been dragged all over the world*—that's my grandmother talking, right? She had a marathon conversation on the phone yesterday with my parents. My Bulgarian is *barbaric*. I have no understanding of the *great cultural traditions of my homeland.*"

He paused.

"Hey, really, are you all right? You look a little pale or something."

How was she supposed to be all right? You think things are finally getting to be sort of okay, and then the universe goes and pushes you right off the deck of the boat. And the water is freezing cold.

"Did you say something weird was happening out here?" he prompted kindly.

Maya, of course, was drowning in cold water and trying very hard not to do something stupid like cry, both at once. She shook her head to clear things up. The air was still humming all around them, but it's hard to care about things like random branches on random trees suddenly sprouting random fuzzy little leaves when your friend, your true friend, your *only* real friend in a huge, old city where you still don't really belong, tells you he's going to vanish—*poof*—because of some dreadful grandmother.

"But . . . Bulgaria! That's awful!" she said, trying hard not to sound too clingy and pathetic. Her voice was all wobble, though. And then she realized how close she was to that scary edge where you fall totally apart and are embarrassed about it, probably, for the rest of your life. *Haul yourself back, Maya!* She hauled herself back. She stood straighter. After all, she was the very same girl, the new Maya-from-Now, who had just been feeling all hopeful about the world a few minutes ago. Maya Davidson was the kind of person (right?) who looked dangerous people in the face and foiled their evil, evil plans. One Bulgarian grandmother was not going to do her in now.

Nor was one oddly seasick world.

And why didn't Valko look more seasick, come to think of it? He didn't seem fazed by the strange things happening to car antennae or sidewalk trees; to judge from the expression on his face, the only thing worth worrying about was Maya herself.

"I wouldn't have minded so much," he was saying, "back in August. But I was kind of a friendless loner, back in August. Now I'd mind. I'd mind a lot."

Those, by the way, are the kind of words a person can hug pretty close to her soul. Maya stashed them away and felt several notches' worth better about everything, strangeness or no strangeness.

"*Me, too*—but quick, look over there," she said (since kind words can melt if you stare at them too hard). "See how weird that is?"

She was pointing at the policeman's still slightly fluttering cap.

Valko looked. And then turned back to Maya, his expression friendly, but with a thin blur of puzzlement around the edges.

"The policeman? They've had someone posted here all week," he said. "You know that. Ever since the wall went slightly kaboom on Saturday. Don't want random strangers climbing into the embassy gardens, right?"

He paused.

"Listen, I'll try not to let them make me go. You know I'll try. It's just, my *grandmother*—"

Maya gave a thin-lipped nod, staying very strong.

"It wouldn't be right now—it would be in December." They already had a date!

Cold water in her lungs. But she did it again: she *hauled herself back*. She made herself point one more time at that policeman.

"His *hat*," said Maya in the weird, extra-quiet voice that was all she could manage just at that moment, "has *wings*."

"He's a *French policeman*," said Valko. He was trying to help her out of the water. That's what he was doing. There was a smile flickering there somewhere, deep in his friendly gray eyes. "That's his *uniform*."

Fluttering wings? Just part of the uniform? Maya

took another, closer look at Valko, and a new tendril of worry (distracting her from the cold water, thank goodness) brushed against her mind. Did he really not see how strange that cap was?

"And that branch over there has leaves on it, all of a sudden. Look! And the antenna there shredded right up into ribbons, and something weird was happening to the pavement, too, back by the hole in the wall—"

Valko followed the swoop of her hand (all those strange things!), but once his gaze reached the ground behind them, his eyes widened and stared.

"Wow," he said. He sounded impressed. "Writing on the sidewalk? You? With the cop standing right there? Wow."

"I didn't—," said Maya, but when she turned her head to look, all the rest of her thoughts withered up and died, just like that.

The looping black sand had finished its work. All those curlicues and angles turned out to have been busily spelling something, and the word they had spelled out there on the pavement, plain as smoke against a pale sky, was—

MAYA.

"Oh, no," she said. She felt wobbly again, looking at the sidewalk's bold, confident scrawl. "You think I did that?"

"What did you use, charcoal? Chalk?" said Valko, leaning low over the sidewalk to take a closer look at that elaborate, impossible MAYA. "Wait, that's not chalk. You wrote your name with *sand*?"

"I didn't write anything with anything," said Maya. It came out sounding a little testy, but that was because of her nerves. "I guess it wrote itself. After I touched the wall. I was just standing here, and I touched the wall, and the gargoyle saw me, and all this *stuff* started happening."

Little stuff, true. Small things. The leaves on that branch were as tiny as could be. But it was all wrong, wrong, wrong. And there was the hum in the air, too. It was hard even to think properly, with that hum in the air.

"Excuse me, but did you just say *gargoyle*?" said Valko.

"The one up there," said Maya, and pointed. She had to pull Valko back away from the wall so that he could see.

Valko squinted.

"No," he said. "There can't be anything up there. That's where my room is."

"Well, but look," said Maya. "On that little ledge outside. The *gargoyle*. Wait, no, *two* gargoyles. I didn't see the other one before."

They had just about stepped right into the street by now, trying to get a better view.

"Oh!" he said, and shook his head three separate times, like a dog confused by too much water.

"But gargoyles are heavy," he said. "Aren't they? There can't be a *sudden* gargoyle. It must have always been there. Even if it wasn't. I mean, I didn't see it before. There was never a gargoyle on my windowsill. But I must have been wrong. It must always have been there. Right?"

"What do you mean, *always*?" said Maya. Valko was really beginning to worry her. There are friends you go to when the world gets wobbly and you need someone to explain again that everything is logical, really, if you study it hard enough. That was Valko. That was always Valko. And now here he went sounding, of all things, *vague*. "I don't know about the gargoyles, but I told you, the rest of it just happened two minutes ago. When I touched the wall. Valko?"

"There's got to be an explanation," Valko was saying, more to himself than to anyone else. "There's always an explanation. All right. A branch with new leaves—why? It came from a tree from a warmer climate, maybe, and was just grafted onto that trunk today. Or a committee has been wrapping it in heating pads, maybe, at night? That could be. All those warm heating pads, fooling the branch into thinking it's spring already. Or a bunch of people with hair dryers—"

Maya couldn't help herself: she snorted out loud. It

23

came from nowhere at all, that snort. For one second she had forgotten the cold water entirely.

"Why are you laughing?" said Valko, turning to look at her (but she was already not laughing anymore, because as soon as he looked at her, she remembered all over again about December). "It's a *scientific explanation*. Hair dryers. Why not? Yes, that's what it must have been."

"Stop it!" said Maya. "Something's messing with your brain." It was beginning to creep her out, to tell the truth.

"Oh," said Valko, and he perked up a little, considering that possibility. "Really? Like seeing things that aren't there? Like that shadow thing following you?"

Shadow?

Maya spun around to look.

It was true. Behind them the wind had kicked up a little column of leaves—of dust—of something. A sack's worth of shadow, hugging the embassy wall. It paused, spinning in place, tasting the air, and then began slipping along down the sidewalk in their direction, feeling its way toward them *against the wind*. A silvery trickle of cold raced down Maya's spine.

"I wonder what the scientific explanation is," said Valko, "for that shadow?"

It was tempting, at that moment, to turn tail and run. To drag Valko away in a completely other direction.

But she had just been thrown from the tilting deck of

the world into a lot of very cold water, and one effect of that, it turned out, was that bubbling up inside the old, cautious Maya was a new, half-drowned Maya, a little bit furious with the unfairness of the world. You know? *Gash!* So this is what she did instead:

She took one reckless step toward that shadowy, lurching column—and she *barked.*

2

BARKING AT SHADOWS

It's a useful talent, being able to bark like a dog. The shadow fell back, quavering, and Valko made the small gasping sound of someone finally waking up.

"Maya?" he said. "Did you just *bark* at that thing?"

"Let's get across the street," said Maya. But she couldn't help feeling flattered by the look on Valko's face: he was plainly impressed.

"You did! You *barked* at a *shadow*!" he said. "You're as crazy as those French ladies back there. I mean, the ones singing."

Ladies singing? Maya turned to look, and there they were, a small group of swaying, singing women farther down the sidewalk, their briefcases and shopping bags slumping carelessly to the ground. A wave of thin, nasal harmony was already rolling across the square. The words did not sound French.

Maya and Valko looked at each other.

"What's going on?" said Valko. "I mean, really. I didn't think so at first, but something really happened out here, didn't it?"

"At four o'clock," said Maya. "The bells were ringing when I touched the wall. I don't know where that creepy shadow came from, though. Oh, no—"

They turned their heads around, and sure enough: a dark column of leaf meal and dust was still picking its way along the street behind them.

The shadow lingered for a time in that cluster of singing women, threading itself through and around them almost as if it were whispering to them or longing to join in their dance, but now it was hunkering lower to the ground, the shadowy parody of an animal trying to catch a scent. It made the little hairs along Maya's shoulder blades prickle with fear.

"This way," said Valko, pointing down one of the side streets there. It was more or less an ordinary-looking Parisian alleyway, if you ignored the fact that one of the vast iron feet of the Eiffel Tower was planted just behind a building at its end.

"Valko," said Maya as they walked (pretty fast) down the next bit of sidewalk. "You know what I don't get? How could you not have noticed you had actual gargoyles perched outside your window?"

"Um," said Valko. "I don't. I didn't. I mean, there

aren't—no, what I really mean is, they weren't there before."

Maya gave him a gentle punch in the arm, just to keep him from fading back into vagueness again.

He blinked. "What I'm saying is, I know they weren't there last Saturday, because that's the last day I put a barometer reading in my weather log—"

"*Weather log?*" said Maya politely.

Valko shook his fist at her, in a friendly way.

"Okay, some people keep diaries, right? Huh? Maybe you used to have a diary? Ha! Thought so! Anyway, so I have a weather log. I've had it since I was six, thank you very much—"

"Wait," said Maya. "Did you just say that gargoyle wasn't even there before *Saturday*? You're sure?"

"I look out that window just about every single day. Like I said, to check my barometer. So yes, I'm sure. Nothing today makes the slightest bit of sense: those women singing, the cars going all confetti-like, that bizarro shadow thing following us—"

For a moment they had forgotten the shadow.

They spun around both at once, just to check, and there it was. Maybe thirty feet behind them, a vague pillar of dust and leaves and darkness, shuffling along the pavement. Valko's shoulder was so close to Maya's that she could feel his heart jump at the exact same moment as hers.

"Okay," said Valko. "The barking thing. How do you do it?"

"What? Come *on*!"

It wasn't the shadow that bothered her. It was the way it kept *moving toward them*.

Valko nudged her.

"The barking thing. How do you do it?"

"Valko!" said Maya. He folded his arms and waited. "All right, then. It's easy. Say *ruff* really loud while sucking your breath in. Please let's hurry."

"*Ruff*," said Valko, experimenting. "*Ruff!*"

"Valko, *please* let's keep moving—"

"*RRRRUFF!*"

Everything happened at once: Valko jumping out at that column of shadow and barking as loud as he could (*pretty good*, thought Maya, *for his third bark ever*); the shadow almost losing its balance—if losing its balance is something a whirling column of dust can do—falling back, straightening up again, stretching tendrils of darkness—*arms*—out in front of itself, reaching, reaching past Valko, feeling for something else or someone else—

Then . . .

M a y a, it said, in exactly the sort of ghastly dry whisper a column of leaves and dust would use if it was trying to learn to speak.

They turned and ran.

It wasn't far to the end of the street. At the corner

Maya took a chance and looked back.

"Hey, wait," she said, panting hard. "Look at that."

The shadow seemed to be stuck a ways behind them. They could see it pushing against the air, almost as if it had hit a wall.

"Stay here," said Valko, and he walked back a bit to look. He always had to investigate things properly. Maya shifted her weight from one foot to the other. Her feet were eager to keep moving.

"The air's different here," Valko called back over his shoulder. "Notice that?"

He was keeping his eyes glued to that shadow, though.

Maya took an exploratory breath. The air *was* different. It was like something chaotic in it had vanished. The hum was gone.

She saw Valko take another few steps and then pause. The sack's worth of shadow pressed against that invisible wall, but the wall didn't yield.

He went closer. The shadow just eddied there, waiting.

"Careful," said Maya.

"Don't worry," said Valko. He crossed over to the other side of the street. The shadow stayed where it was. It didn't seem to notice Valko coming closer from the side; Maya could have sworn it had its nonexistent eyes fixed entirely on her. Not such a good feeling.

"It's like there's a shimmer in the air here," said Valko. "Like an edge in the air. Or a wall. Do you see it? Look,

I can just slip my hand right through—"

"Eep!" said Maya. It came out more as a sound than a word.

"I know," said Valko, without turning around. "I saw that, too."

When Valko's hand had gone past that edge, the shadow thing had moved a little (*turned its head*, suggested Maya's mind, ignoring for a moment the point that columns of shadowy dust don't actually *have* heads). That was creepy.

A biologist who has just run into a grizzly bear will move with great caution; so did Valko. He seemed to be carefully fishing something out of his pockets. Maya squinted: oh, a pencil. Was he going to stop to take *notes*? How completely crazy could one person even be? She walked a few paces in his direction, just in case she needed to grab him by the sleeve and haul him away.

But now Valko was running his hand across the wall, right to the very place where the shimmer started.

"Um, what are you doing?" said Maya, trying not to catch the shadow's attention. "Seems like we should just leave, doesn't it?"

Valko was making a careful line of *X*s right there.

"Marking the edge," he said. "Got to be dark enough to find later, but not so big the graffiti police come and wipe it off."

M a y a, said the shadow thing.

"Enough," said Maya, shuddering slightly.

"Definitely enough," said Valko, stuffing the pencil into his pocket. Maya and Valko trotted back to the far end of the alleyway, and then one block farther from the river, because Valko wanted to see if they could see a boundary there, too.

They could. Valko ran down that street to the very edge of the shimmering air and left some more Xs on that wall, too.

It was five long minutes before the shadow appeared in that street, so at least (said Valko to Maya) it was *dumb and slow.*

"Dumb, slow dust that's walking and talking is still way smarter than it should be," said Maya.

It came out a little sharper than she meant it to, but having your name wheezed into the air by columns of leaf meal and shadow can give a person the grumps.

They left Xs on other walls in other streets, until Maya lost patience with the process and pointed out that they hadn't seen the shadow for a while, so maybe it was time to walk away somewhere where they could breathe a little.

"It's a circle," said Valko. "I'm pretty sure it's a circle, the strangeness. See how the marks are moving toward the embassy end of the street each time? So that's good."

"Good?"

"To be outside of it is good," said Valko. "I didn't realize it, at first, but it was making my head ache in there. Until you did whatever you did. Pinched me awake. We've got to figure this out, Maya. This is too weird."

They were trotting through the park now, with the enormous leg of the Eiffel Tower pushing its way into the clouds behind them. Even in October, it managed to feel like a park: bare-limbed trees and still-leafy bushes and elegant benches dotting the gravel paths.

"I forgot about the croissants!" said Maya, looking down almost in surprise at the crumpled paper sack she had just found in her jacket pocket. "Want a kind-of-squashed pastry? They were warm when I got them."

"Whoops! You're losing things," said Valko, and he raced ahead of her on the path to gather up papers there. Her letters! They had come out of her pocket with the pastry bag and gone flying.

By the time they had chased down the last of the unruly envelopes, Maya and Valko were truly ready for croissants, squashed or no.

"Mm," said Valko, licking a stray fleck of chocolate off his finger. "I'm tasting mint. Minty croissants! Bizarre. Good, though. So, who still writes letters? I mean, apart from my grandmothers, of course."

"Yes, well," said Maya (a cold shiver going through her as she remembered all over again about dreadful

Bulgaria). In fact, it felt a little embarrassing, to be brushing the dust off her cards. She hadn't meant to share them. Just to carry them around for a while. Just to have them close by. "Mostly they're cards, not letters. The thing is, it's my—"

"Birthday!" said Valko, who was extremely good at filling in gaps. "No, really! You weren't going to tell me?"

"It's not today," said Maya. "It's Wednesday. Halloween. I guess my friends were just being cautious."

It was so nice, that word: *friends.* Plural! Jenna, of course, but not just Jenna: there was a card from Eleanor Markowitz, who had been her best friend in third grade and then moved to Montana, and one from Ada Kwan, who had drawn the cutest little smiling people up and down the edges of the envelope, and then—

"What's that one?" said Valko.

Heavy, creamy-green paper, the sort of stationery you might see lying about on desks in a palace. And her name scrawled in elegant but hasty loops.

"That's real ink, not ballpoint," said Valko. "That's like calligraphy, almost. Who's it from?"

Maya turned the envelope over—no name on the back.

Something about it made her uneasy. It was so much weightier in her hands than the cards from her friends in California; that was one thing. It seemed to get heavier the more she stared at it, the more she turned it over and over in her hands.

"And look at the stamp," said Valko. "It's French. It's from here. Open it, Maya."

"I wasn't going to open any of them until my actual birthday," said Maya.

A bit of Valko's croissant apparently went down the wrong pipe: he had to pause for a moment to cough into his sleeve.

"You mean, your plan was to carry all these letters around in your pocket for days and days?"

Yes. That was her plan, exactly. Some people might call that *savoring* things. She was just about to say something sarcastic about people who keep weather logs not having legs to stand on when she looked over and saw that Valko wasn't smirking at her at all: no, he was smiling the nicest possible smile.

"Open just this one, then," he said, all sweetness. "Aren't you curious? *I'm* curious."

When he put it that way: yes, she was curious. But it was a curiosity that was sprinkled with dread. Unreasonable dread, of course. Nothing that made any sense.

Her fingers, however, were already loosening the fancy flap of that envelope, already pulling out that gorgeous piece of thick, regal paper and unfolding it, while Valko angled his head closer for a better look.

"Well, that's odd," he said.

And Maya's heart was going *tippetty tippetty*, as if she'd turned right into a rabbit. Still for next to no reason, because her eyes had hardly seen anything yet. And in any case, there wasn't all that much to see:

a monogram engraved at the top of the sheet (*H de F*),

a letter that apart from the salutation—*For Maya, my dear niece (or cousin)*—and the closing—*Fondly, your affectionate cousin (or uncle)*—consisted of exactly one word: *Félicitations!*

and under that strangest of one-word letters, an elegant scribble of a signature,

and under the signature, a smudge.

For a moment neither Maya nor Valko could find anything to say.

Then Valko said, quietly, "Wow. H de F. Wow. But I thought you said that Henri de Fourcroy was dead."

"Almost dead," said Maya. "Shriveled up. Gone. I said he was gone."

"I thought *gone* meant 'dead,'" said Valko.

"I guess it just meant gone," said Maya. Inside, she herself felt what you might call a little bit *gone*. Cold and alone. Not here, not there, not anywhere. None of this was supposed to be happening, not in real life.

"Not nearly gone enough," said Valko. "If he's sending you letters."

And then his hand shot out like lightning and he

36

grabbed back the envelope to take another look.

"Postmarked this Monday," he said.

Maya shivered. *Gone!*

"So he could have shoved it in a box on Sunday," said Valko, making a kind of calendar out of his fingers. "Or even Saturday night, right after he shriveled up or went away or whatever. Nothing gets postmarked on Sundays, you know."

There was a pause.

"So he gets caustic powder thrown at him—"

"Earth," said Maya. She always had to correct this part of the story, when Valko told it. "His own earth, coming back to him."

"And he creeps away, in really bad shape, and he sends you a *birthday card*? Am I missing something here?"

"I don't think it's a birthday card," said Maya. "It's a—I don't know what it is. Nothing good. The paper's very heavy, did you notice? And that smudge!"

"Yes," said Valko. "The smudge."

They both stared at the smudge. The more you looked at it, the less like a mere smudge it seemed to be. It had depth and detail and purpose, somehow, despite being nothing more than an inky blur.

"Wish I had my magnifying lens," said Valko.

Then something hazy happened. Either Maya thought of her necklace, or Valko thought of her necklace, or they

37

both did at the same time. It was hard, afterward, to figure out exactly whose fault it all was. That was also a kind of smudge, come to think of it.

The reason they thought of Maya's necklace was that it was a round puddle of glass, all that was left of the formerly beautiful and dangerous Cabinet of Earths. That Cabinet had held the secret of Henri de Fourcroy's long, long life, until Maya had taken a hammer to its beauty and destroyed it. Now she wore the Cabinet glass around her neck on a string, and there was a tiny magical salamander swimming in it, which was one reminder that this was not ordinary glass. Another reminder was the way it sometimes melted in Maya's palm, became liquid, and then hardened again. Ordinary glass stays glassy unless a furnace's worth of heat gets to it.

But that necklace did look a little like the lens of a magnifying glass. That is true. And so it ended up in Maya's hand, with the last feeble rays of October sun trickling through it and onto the mysterious page, the letter, the smudge.

"Aha!" said Valko, his head almost bumping into Maya's, he was so intent on getting a glimpse through that glass. "See that?"

Seen through Maya's necklace, the smudge was, indeed, not actually a smudge. The blur resolved itself into lines and loops and dots, into whole strings of writing.

The Reader of these words, it read, *is absolutely and irrevocably bound to do all that is necessary, no matter what the risk or cost, to make me, myself, Henri de Fourcroy, once again WHOLE—*

"Whatever that means," said Valko.

"There's more," said Maya.

And should the Reader doubt the binding nature of this message, would he please hold this paper up to the light.

"Oh, don't!" said Maya, but Valko of course already had. The sun was weak, but in the face of that light a whole picture welled up from within (*deep within,* thought Maya, but that was illogical) the paper: a terrible face, scowling, with a bunch of writhing worms where most people have hair.

"Snakes," said Valko. "I've heard of something like that before. Snakes for hair. Nice."

"That was Medusa," said Maya. "That was the one who was so terrible, just looking at her would turn you into stone."

Valko gave her a little poke in the ribs.

"But hey, look at that: we're not stone," he said. He was making a joke, but the heavy feeling in Maya's chest made her wonder, *Is it true? Stone?*

"Shh, give that back," she said. "There was more."

The smudge went so deep: layer upon layer of smudge. Maybe (thought Maya half sensibly) that was why the paper seemed so heavy. A tremble had gotten into her fingers: she had to work extra hard, this time, to keep the necklace-glass steady.

That, Reader, is the international symbol of Absolutely Binding Documents. You thought you had triumphed over me, perhaps, little cousin-niece? But you are reading this, so now it is you who are bound. So then: your first task is to present yourself to the memory stone*—it will hold your instructions. It is waiting for you. It knows who you are.

"Memory stone?" said Valko.

The smudge deepened again. There was an asterisk, but it wobbled terribly. Valko had to add a hand to the edges of the glass for the image to settle down.

*THAT IS, TO BE PERFECTLY CLEAR: you will go put your hand on the stone wall of the embassy and wake up the mind I am about to leave there. THEN: you will make your way, without delay, to my writing desk—

40

"Seriously?" said Valko. "This is the bossiest letter I have ever read in my life. Are we done yet? What's that last bit there?"

The last bit there was

You may find its contents useful. Here's the key.

And then a very tiny squiggle.

"Well," said Valko, leaning back against the bench. "One thing's for sure: your old uncle Fourcroy was stark, raving bonkers. A lunatic. Mad."

Maya still had her head bent over the image in the Cabinet glass. There was something about that squiggle. When you looked closely, it organized itself: round inky flourishes at one end, blocky inky shapes at the other. Of course! A key.

The ink lines of that key, moreover, were straining away from the paper it had been penned into. How could that be? Maya squinted. Yes, there was a gap between ink and paper—she was almost sure there was a gap.

When her own curious fingertip entered that magnified world under the glass, it looked so unexpectedly enormous that Maya trembled again, and all the writing became a tipsy blur for a moment. But she held her breath and steadied herself and the Cabinet glass, and soon her gigantic fingertip was inching toward that writhing, inky key again, worrying at the space between ink and paper. Could there even be such a space?

Really, now: could ink have a life of its own?

Could a great, big human fingertip really feel the thin edge of a scribbled key?

It could, it could. The key felt like an eyelash, like the thinnest thread. And then the inky key was no longer on Henri de Fourcroy's pale-green stationery at all: it was firmly attached to the tip of Maya's own finger. And it would not budge, even when she gave her hand a sharp shake, the way you do when an almost-invisible insect sinks its tiny, tiny, ink-black teeth into you.

"Hey!" she said, jumping up. "It bit me!"

At the same moment the Cabinet glass twitched in Maya's other hand, pulled itself away from the creamy-green menace of that paper, and softened and cowered in her palm.

"What?" said Valko. "What? What bit you?"

"That stupid key," she said. "I poked it, and it bit me. Look—"

On the very tip of her index finger, the smallest, smallest, smallest of black keys.

"You've got to be kidding," said Valko. He took a long look at her finger and then tried to flick the key off the top of it with his free hand, but nothing happened.

Nothing happened when they blew fierce puffs of

breath at the key on her finger or when Maya wiped her fingertip across the cold wood of the bench or when Valko took hold of her finger and rubbed it against the rough wool of his sleeve. The tiny key was there to stay.

"Like a tattoo, almost," said Valko. "Well, *that* is definitely weird-and-a-half."

For a breathless moment, the two of them just watched the wind play with the edges of the letter in Maya's lap, while their brains chased wild galloping thoughts down a thousand different endless corridors.

"And how does your necklace even do that melting and unmelting stuff?" said Valko finally. "Not to mention the magnifying thing. That is the strangest necklace I've ever seen."

Maya hardly heard him. All of a sudden she was so eager to be gone. She leaped up off the bench, stuffed the necklace into one jacket pocket and all those letters into another. She wasn't just awake again: she was furious. She had one word to say, and that one word filled every nook and cranny of her, drowned out all the other thoughts and worries that might be there, pushed everything else aside as it exploded out into the world.

That word was "*No!*"

3

GARGOYLES GETTING IN THE WAY

The more she thought about it, the angrier she got. Henri de Fourcroy binding her, Maya, to bring him back to life! Sticking tiny keys on fingertips where they definitely didn't belong! When it was his own fault, everything that had happened to him! You don't just kidnap small children and drain them of their charm and then go around expecting those children's older sisters to *fix you right back up*! No!

"Slow down a bit," said Valko, loping along to keep up with her angry feet. (One of the first things Valko had ever told Maya about himself was that his name came from the Bulgarian word for *wolf*. He wasn't, at first glance, much like a wolf—no big, sharp teeth; no beady yellow eyes—but he certainly could *lope*.) "You're not making sense, you know. There's no such thing as Medusan stationery—there can't be!"

"What do you mean, 'can't'?" said Maya as her bitter

feet continued to slap, slap, slap at the sidewalk beneath them.

Cabinets can't hold people's mortalities in bottles, either, can they? Bronze salamanders can't turn their heads and chat with you. Glass can't melt in your hand and then unmelt again, just like that. The whole concept of "can't" had taken some serious hits over the last month or so, as far as Maya could see.

One of Valko's talents was patience, however. He just loped along, trying to wait out her anger and think things through.

"I mean, a piece of paper can't *make* you do anything it says. That's just craziness, to think it could. Where are we rushing off to right now, anyway?"

Maya stopped short. They were back in the street where the shadow had come creeping after them, but the whole place looked different now. That edge in the air had faded away. Things felt normal again. The wound-up spring in her chest relaxed a little.

"I don't know," she said. "Anywhere. I just don't like being told I'm trapped, that's all."

Valko grinned.

"Listen to me, then: *not trapped, not trapped, not trapped*! There, better? Give that letter to me a second; I'll fix it for you."

It was unfairly difficult to stay glum around Valko.

Maya fished the envelope back out of her pocket and handed it over. Valko already had his favorite black pen in his hand. He propped the letter against his backpack and made a preparatory flourish in the air.

"V-O-I-D," he said. "That's what we need!"

Ha! Why hadn't she thought of that? If the paper's super-powerful, just make it say something else!

But Valko was already staring, a bit puzzled, at the letter he had been scribbling on. He gave his pen a shake, and then rummaged through his backpack again, looking for another one.

"Won't write," he said. "Weird. I'm sure it's got ink in it, too."

The next pen wouldn't leave a mark, either. It skittered right off the page. They tried out the pens on other scraps of paper, and they worked fine. They just couldn't manage to leave a single trace on that inscrutable creamy-green letter. The paper wouldn't let itself be torn up, either, even when Valko tried to be extra wolfish about it and use his teeth.

"Well, never mind," said Valko, rubbing his jaw. "So it's stronger than steel, and the ink he used is super special—who cares? You can still refuse. Just don't do any of those things in the letter. Keep your hands off the embassy wall—"

"Oh," said Maya. She had forgotten the wall. "Oh, no.

That's how this all started, remember? I already touched that awful wall. Just like the letter told me to. Do you think that's what started all the weird stuff happening?"

"Excuse me," said Valko. "But I'm pretty sure you hadn't read that letter before you touched anything. Right? It's hardly like you were following instructions. And so what, anyway? Touch any wall you want! Does this place look like anything awful happened? Look how normal everything is now."

Everything did seem very normal. No shadows rustling after them. No more clusters of swaying, singing women. Sometimes you'll be walking along a green ridge in the fog, and the air will catch its breath and the fog will lift, just like that. As if fog had never been invented. Maya and Valko were standing on the fogless corner of the avenue Rapp, the broken wall of the Bulgarian embassy off to the left and the intricate façade of bad old Fourcroy's Salamander House to the right, and the air was its normal, unhummy self again. It was enough to make a person feel slightly embarrassed, if that person hated to think of herself as *overreacting*. Maya took a deep breath and walked ahead to take a closer look.

The hole in the wall was certainly still there. So (she checked) were the gargoyles. But the MAYA written in black sand on the pale cement of the sidewalk had faded to a thin, weathered, friendly gray. You could miss it entirely, if you were walking past at a brisk pace, with your eyes not glued to the ground. The mark left on the world by the strangeness was already fading. It was as if this whole part of Paris had been a lump of unbaked bread, and some ill-behaved magical giant had stuck a thumb into the dough. Marks don't last long in bread dough, do they? The dough stretches itself and yawns, and soon enough the dings and dents have faded away. There, then: at this rate everything in the nieghborhood might be back to almost normal by evening.

So it struck Maya now as rather unreasonable, how upset she had felt earlier.

"Okay," she said, letting herself relax into another notch's worth of relief. "I won't let a stupid letter boss me around."

"That's right," said Valko. "You tell 'em!"

Once a person starts to stand tall and be brave about one thing, all that courage can slop over into other parts of her being, too. Maya stopped in her tracks and gave Valko the sort of look that someone who has learned how not to drown, even when dumped into very cold water, might give a person.

"And there's no way we're going to let you be sent back to Bulgaria," said Maya, with more definiteness than was even remotely reasonable. "You're staying. We'll find a way. It's a plan."

"It's clear you've never met my grandmother," said Valko. "But thank you five million times over for wanting to rescue me. You are very brave."

That was when one of his quick grins rose up and took over his whole face.

"And you know what else? It's vacation! Liberty for all!"

Ten whole days without school! The wind was chilly as it curled around their liberated legs, but it was the brisk chill of freedom. They were strolling down the once-again ordinary street, and there were ten days of vacation stretching ahead of them, and the knot in Maya's chest loosened a little more with every step.

Soon it would be her birthday, after all! Even far, far, far away from home, birthdays mean something, don't they?

"Hey!" said Valko. "Look where we are! Your favorite old Salamander House!"

The cold air licked her neck when she raised her head—oh! How had they let their feet bring them here and not even notice?

Stone vines twined their way up and down the front of the building, and tangled up in those looping vines were the stone echoes of every kind of creature: broad ferns and docile cows, bold little people with their hands on jaunty sandstone hips, a woman's sad-eyed face, looking down at Maya from above the door. That façade always came as a shock, no matter how many times you had seen it. It was the sort of enchanted cliff that might loom up in front of a person on a jungle path, all of life's secrets crawling and twining and wriggling across it.

What was more, for all its stillness, the Salamander House had certainly noticed *them*. Stone eyes everywhere turned like mute spotlights on Maya herself, frozen on the sidewalk stage. Even the door had eyes to stare with—looping webs of iron and glass squinting past a pair of phoenixes at anyone bold enough to come close, reckless enough to let her fingertip drift across the cool bronze head of the salamander door handle.

The door clicked and opened.

Maya snatched her hand away. What was she doing?

"You want to go in?" said Valko. He sounded not shocked, but rather mildly curious, as if wandering into buildings where bad things had happened (and not that long ago) were a perfectly logical and normal thing to do.

"Of course not!" said Maya. She made her voice extra sharp, to get the point across. Her finger was still sort of itching to run itself across the salamander's head again, however. The bronze was so smooth and cold, and she could feel the little patterned ridges above its inscrutable eyes.

"Lots of interesting stuff in there still, probably," said

Valko. It sounded very convincing, when Valko said it. "Some pretty cool items . . ."

"Valko!" said Maya sternly. "That's where he lived. That's Fourcroy's own house. You *know* what's in there!"

Valko more or less laughed, but Maya thought she saw the faintest trace of cloud in his eyes, a few curling tendrils of fog.

"Oh, it's so ridiculously obvious!" she said. It really was. She couldn't believe they had been walking around a minute ago as if everything were completely normal. "The *writing desk*! His writing desk! Just the number-two thing the letter wanted us to go find, and here we were about to slide through the door and march right up to it. Sheesh."

"We weren't going in for any desk," said Valko. "We were going to look at all the other neat stuff—"

"The letter thinks it's got us," said Maya. She had to give Valko an impatient tug, away from the iron eyes of that door, away from the watching, waiting head of the salamander, but when she stepped away, the itch in her fingertip flared up for a moment. She stuffed that hand deep into her pocket and frowned. "I mean, it almost did have us. And you said letters couldn't boss us around. Ha!"

"All that weird laboratory equipment up there," said Valko with longing.

"That's it," said Maya. "We're leaving. Look at me, I'm leaving."

Her feet didn't very much want to go, but she kicked a leg forward and made herself take a step. Away. And then the left leg. Away. The hand pulling Valko along behind her felt strange, too, for that matter. Was he really that heavy? And the finger on her other hand sat there deep in her pocket and itched and itched.

"We would need," said Maya, and then stopped to catch her breath and force her leg forward again, "a *really good reason*"—take a breath/move a leg—"to go anywhere near"—breath/leg/tug on Valko—"that desk!"

They were ten feet away from the door. It was getting easier to move again.

"A really, really, really good reason," she said. She was exhausted.

Valko blinked and shook his head, his smile slowly coming back as he did so.

"You know what, Maya?" he said. "It's too much. You totally need a vacation. I can tell."

Twenty feet away, maybe more. They were walking like human beings again, not like underwater divers or people stuck in nightmares where the air has turned to sludge.

"Yes, I do," said Maya. "Without shadows, please. And no more letters making me do stuff."

"So far, nothing's actually made you do anything," said Valko. "Just pointing that out."

Maya looked at him.

"You were ready to close your eyes and dive in through that door," she said. "Still feel not trapped, not trapped, not trapped?"

"Just because I wanted to do some intelligent exploring—"

"You saw the shadow following us. You felt how weird everything got."

"But we didn't go in, did we? We walked right on by. We did. All the rest is just—I don't know—us getting sort of hysterical, maybe. Like kids telling each other spooky ghost stories."

So there it was. It turns out that there is something quite maddening about the very person who has just been at your side while you were chased through Parisian streets by a shadow and then hypnotized into potentially dangerous behavior by a letter on snakes-for-hair stationery then insisting that . . . nothing much had happened. That it was all in your mind.

It put a bad taste in her mouth the whole rest of that day. The first afternoon of fall vacation, ruined by a shadow, a snake-haired watermark, and a smudge! Really, life was not very fair.

That night Maya lay in bed, staring up at the ceiling

and worrying away at the itchy spot on her fingertip. There was something she was supposed to be figuring out, but she was too tired to remember what that was.

The letter. The writing desk.

The wind had kicked up that evening, and there was enough faint clattering outside her bedroom to make it hard to fall asleep, what with the leftover adrenaline and worry wandering her veins.

The writing desk. The letter. There would have to be a really good reason. . . .

But sleep she did, because suddenly it was midnight and she was awake again, sitting straight up in her bed, her heart pounding in her chest and her ears assaulted by a crashing, grinding, gritty sound—not "faint clattering," no, nothing faint about it: *What was that?*

It was all over so fast: by the time she reached for her lamp, the world had fallen quiet again. Still, it was a while before she could relax enough to think about sleeping. She thought maybe she had been dreaming about a writing desk with an old-fashioned sphinx statue perched on it, and the writing desk had fallen over with a bang. Pens everywhere! What else was in a writing desk? Pens and stamps and envelopes—

She sat back up again.

Special ink! And writing paper!

It had shown all sorts of signs of working, hadn't it, that letter? It had made her want desperately to go into the Salamander House, even though she knew that might be, from all sorts of perspectives, a bad idea. And Valko had been pretty much acting like a person under a spell, too, come to think of it, when they were standing in front of that door.

So that was what her brain had been trying to tell her all night: Medusan stationery was actually extremely effective stuff. All right. But poisons often had antidotes, right? So—what if a person who had been trapped by magical stationery into doing all sorts of things *found more of that stationery and wrote herself an antidote letter?*

Oh, she was feeling clever now! She even had a pretty clear idea of how that letter should look:

Dear Maya,

No, you will NOT do anything to bring that horrible old Fourcroy back to life. You may IGNORE all the commands in the previous letter, no matter what kind of magical paper it was written on. Please have a great vacation and a very happy birthday, and I guarantee that everything from now on will be absolutely A-OK.

Love, your friend and self, Maya

It was amazing how much better she felt, right away: worry just up and left her, looking for another home. The sheer and obvious *rightness* of this plan, of this antidote letter she had just composed so carefully in her head—it was as comforting as the warmest, thickest quilt she'd ever snuggled under, on an otherwise cold and windy night.

And when she woke up in the morning, she found she was still feeling oddly at peace. The wind had quieted, too. She remembered the dreadful crashing that had startled her in the middle of the night, and smiled to herself.

Something must have fallen outside, or been blown over by the wind. A flower pot on the fire escape, probably. She opened the window to take a look.

Old French apartment houses often have quite grand fronts, all carved stone and elaborate window decorations. Maya's building was like that: the Davidsons' living room, which was on the front corner of the building, looked across proudly at an equally grand apartment where a famous writer had once had an even more famous film director over for tea in November 1929 (there was a little metal plaque on the wall saying so). But all the building's grandness was saved for the front. The back of the apartment, where the bathrooms and the kitchen and Maya's bedroom were hidden, had windows with the kind of textured, ugly glass that is supposed to let in light while keeping your life private, and those dull-eyed windows looked out at a little courtyard. Not the romantic kind of courtyard with a secret garden and a lovely old hidden tree, either. Nope, this courtyard was all hard-working concrete slabs and trash bins.

Usually, then, there was not much to see out of Maya's window, and, to be honest, she hadn't opened it very often to look.

But now—

Urk!

A shock can knock a person right off her feet, it turns out. Before her mind had even gotten as far as words (*beaks, claws, wings*), Maya's arms had slammed the window shut again. And then her legs gave way under her, and she found herself sitting down very hard on her floor, her mind scrambling about like a crazy thing, trying to put itself together properly.

Gargoyles!

Somewhere far away the phone was ringing. Feet were hurrying along the hall.

Her mother stuck her head in through the doorway.

"What *was* all that racket?" she said. She looked worried. "Maya, are you all right?"

Maya tried to make a reassuring noise and more or less failed, but fortunately her mother had a phone in her hand, and was distracted.

"It's for you, dear," she said, and put the phone into Maya's still shaky hand.

"Um," said Maya.

"Hello?" said the phone, while Maya's mother, who believed everyone deserved a little privacy, backed tactfully out of the room. "Maya, you there? Hey, guess what?"

"What?" said Maya. That was progress: a whole entire coherent word.

"No more gargoyles!" said Valko's voice, all delighted. "Of course, my barometer's gone, too. But I really think—"

"Escape," said Maya, sounding hollower than she meant to.

"Excuse me, what?"

"Fire escape," she said, putting some extra effort into it.

"Did I just wake you up or something?"

"There are gargoyles on the fire escape," she said. "Right now. Outside my window. Gargoyles."

"No way," said Valko. "Really? Wait—"

There was a rustling sound on the other end of the line.

"Okay, got my notebook," he said. "Go ahead, tell me. What do you see? They appeared when?"

"What I see is my door," said Maya. "I told you, they're outside, on the fire escape. I just saw them right now."

"And they weren't there before that."

"Oh, come on," said Maya. "You know they weren't."

"Well, I haven't ever actually seen your fire escape," said Valko. "But that's all right. I've got my pencil. Just describe them as carefully as you can."

"They're gargoyles. A whole crowd of gargoyles."

"I mean, what do they look like?"

"They look like GARGOYLES."

The voice on the phone sighed, and then became very, very patient.

"See, the reason I'm asking," said Valko's patient voice, "is that I wonder whether these are the same gargoyles or different ones. Maybe somebody—all right, it's hard to imagine how, but never mind—picked the gargoyles off my window ledge and carried them over to your house. I mean, who knows, right? Maybe they're really made out of some kind of plaster that just looks like stone—I tried to get a sample last night, but I couldn't reach."

"Tried to get a sample?" echoed Maya.

"Yeah, like a little bit of an ear or a wing," said Valko. "You know, with a hammer. But they were too far away from the window. So I just wrote down a really careful description. That's all I could do. So now you describe yours, and we'll find out if they match."

"But I can't even see them," said Maya. "It's the kind of window you can't look through. I didn't see them until I opened it."

"Maybe you could even get that sample!" said Valko. Was he listening to her at all? "How close are they, exactly?"

"What do you mean, how close are they? They're *on my fire escape.* They're *right outside.* They are way, way, way too close."

Valko cleared his throat.

"But in centimeters," he said. "How far—"

"Valko!" said Maya. She kept her voice low, though, so as not to be worrying her mother, out in the hall. "I told you: the window is shut. And I'm inside."

Huddled on the floor by her bed, actually, but she didn't add that information.

"And if you want to go climbing around measuring those things with a ruler, you can come over here yourself," she added.

"I can't," said Valko. He sounded genuinely disappointed about that. "Today's all math problems, apparently."

That was the backward way things worked in Valko's family: if you were good at something, you ended up having to suffer through tons of extra lessons.

"Open the window and look," Valko was saying now. "Go ahead. They're just statues. They can't do anything to you."

He had a point, right? Gargoyles are carved from stone. Even if they appear out of the blue on your fire escape, even if there's a whole crowd of them, that doesn't mean they aren't *carved from stone.* Maya stood up and opened the window and took a long, brave look.

For one thing, there wasn't actually a whole *crowd* of gargoyles waiting out there: only two. That was a little embarrassing, but two unexpected gargoyles surely equal a crowd of other more normal animals, like, you know, squirrels. Each of them looked like a half-dozen different creatures, somehow spliced together. The one closest to Maya (its stone gaze fixed on her in a most unsettling way) had an eagle's beak, the horns and beard of a goat, feathers that turned to scales halfway down its stone belly, and a pair of carved wings curving back from its bony granite shoulders. The other one, over there blocking the ladder down, had the crumpled-up nose of a bat and little round ears poking out from an elaborately bumpy skull. And in its froggy front paws, it held something round and glinty—

"Ah!" said Valko over the phone. "Glinty, like made of brass? Round like a clock, sort of? With numbers around the outside, you know, and a needle?"

Yes, that pretty much described it. Only the whole thing was embedded thoroughly in the gargoyle's stone paw. Clever work on the sculptor's part: like a ship in a bottle, only stranger. Why did a gargoyle need to be hanging on to a clock, anyway?

"Not a clock," said Valko. "That sounds like my barometer."

"Oh," said Maya. What even *was* a barometer?

"And they *are* the same gargoyles we had. One all bumpy headed, right? So how did they get over there, anyway? And my barometer! Can you reach one of them?"

"Um," said Maya, eyeing the fierce frozen gaze of Gargoyle #1. "Sort of."

"What's it made of? Can you pick it up, I mean? Is it secretly made of foam or something?"

Maya thought about it for a moment and then stretched her non-telephone-holding hand right out the window toward the hunched gray shoulder of Gargoyle #1, keeping a cautious eye on his stony beak.

"Okay now, okay, there you go," she found herself murmuring, as if she were about to pat a strange dog. ("What?" said Valko's voice, far away, from the phone in her other hand. "What do you mean? What's okay?")

It was just stone, right? Her hand already knew before it got there what that stone shoulder would feel like: cold and grainy and maybe a little damp around the edges, just the way a stone gargoyle on a fire escape should feel, early in the morning in October.

But instead: *twannng!* She had snatched her hand back before she realized what had just happened. No, not just *snatched her hand back*: she had pulled her arm inside, slammed the window shut, thrown the latch, and slipped, shaking, down to the floor.

"What?" said an alarmed little voice from the phone. "What was *that*? You all right? Maya? Maya?"

It was that feeling all over again. She couldn't figure it out. It didn't make sense.

"Maya?"

"They've come here for me," said Maya. Maybe Valko could hear her, maybe he couldn't—she didn't really have the energy to lift the phone up to her ear. "They recognize me. They know who I am. And what if there's a *fire*?"

"Excuse me?" said the phone. "Fire?"

There was a lovely thought for you: fire on one side, gargoyles on the other.

"No escape!" said Maya. Even as she hung up the phone, though, something in her woke up, rebelled, and pulled her spine straight again. That was what that letter's gloating smudge wanted her to think, wasn't it? "No escape"!

Well, she had news for all of them (smudge, strangeness, gargoyles): it was going to take more than gargoyles on her fire escape to squash the spirit of Maya Davidson.

Maya's mother had a saying she liked to use when life closed in on you and got a little frightening: *Even when there's no way out, there's always a good way through.*

And now Maya knew where the path *through* was

63

taking her. She had figured that out in the middle of the night. She would go *through* by being *brave*. She would go back to the Salamander House to find another sheet of that horrible, magical paper, and she would scrawl her own commands all over it, the perfect antidote letter, and that would be that.

Just as well that Valko would be busy with his math. He had almost been sucked in by that doorway, hadn't he? Apparently, if you don't believe in magic, you are at extra-special risk of falling right into every one of its traps. Perhaps because if you don't think it exists, your mind doesn't work very hard to resist.

It'll have to be me, resisting for both of us, thought Maya. And then she went out into the hall to get her coat and sneak off, since she had such a very, very good reason, to the last place anyone would have thought she would ever, ever, ever have wanted to be.

4

A BILLION LITTLE DOMINOES

Going back to the Salamander House was as easy as floating downstream. Too easy, probably, but sometimes floating downstream is such a comfortable thing to do that a person can't bring herself to turn around, face the current, and swim. *I'll be very quick about it*, thought Maya as she eyed the wild front of the Salamander House. It was such a clever idea she had had in the middle of the night. *Pop in and pop out. Grab some of that magical paper and go.*

It still made all kinds of sense in her mind. As soon as her itchy finger touched the bronze head of the salamander, the front door clicked itself open, just as if it had been waiting for her for ages and ages. And maybe there was something strange going on with the atmospheric pressures in the neighborhood that day, but as the door opened, Maya felt the air around her grow tense, felt an odd suction going to work on her bones, pulling her through the door and into the shadowy lobby.

The apartment where that horrible Fourcroy used to live was a few floors up. Some resident had helpfully propped the lobby door open with a catalog. Good! Maya was free to keep floating up those stairs, all the way to the landing in front of the apartment door. She was trembling a little by this point, but the one time she tried to turn around and go back downstairs, the weird suction of that house tightened its hold on her a notch or two, and she found she *could not* turn anymore, *could not* go in any direction but onward.

That's apparently what it feels like, to be doing what you are bound to do. To be behaving well, from a bossy letter's point of view.

At the door of Fourcroy's apartment, still blocked off by a couple of neon strands of police tape, Maya tried to pause to catch her breath, but even pausing was a challenge, this close to the goal. If she could stay focused, it would all be all right. *A blank sheet of stationery. That's all. Grab it and go.*

The police must have struggled with that door. When she looked past the tape, she could see a blank gap where the door's lock must once have been: they hadn't been able to tease that lock open (guessed Maya), but had had to cut out the entire mechanism, lock, stock, and barrel. The weird feeling of being pulled forward, pulled forward, hadn't let up for a second. And her finger was itching again. She gave the door a gentle push, and it swung right open. All she had to do was duck under the yellow tape, and she would be in the purple-eyed Fourcroy's abandoned apartment. Where a week ago she had found her brother, slumped in a blurry puddle, all his charm gone.

She had had a very good reason to be here a week ago (rescuing her brother), and she had a very good reason to be here now (saving herself). *Go on,* she told herself, and she ducked under the police tape and went in.

The place was dim and huge and quiet. One long hall stretched off to her right, the hall that led to Fourcroy's laboratory rooms, his sinister tubes and flasks, the chair that had held poor James while his charm dripped out of all that hideous machinery into a simple beaker. It was too awful, remembering that afternoon. It made Maya's heart pound in her chest simply to think about any of it. She turned and looked down the main hallway, the one that led to the large living room at the far end. Other rooms opened out of this hall, too. One, she remembered, was a kind of library or office. Where better to keep a writing desk? It felt right to start there.

The fewer minutes she was in this place, the better. The quietness of it was giving her the creeps: side tables and old clocks and elaborately carved chairs, all completely still. As if frozen in place. Or waiting.

She stepped as lightly as she could manage, took small, quiet breaths, and kept her sleeves well away from the furniture; some part of her was still hoping she could come and go before the apartment even noticed she was there. The boards of the floor whimpered a little underfoot, however, as old parquet floors will do.

It was only a moment later that she slipped through the doorway of the room she thought of as the library and stood just inside the door, taking a quick inventory of the furniture: a desk, with a great big chair behind it. Another chair over on the right. The walls lined with bookcases. And a rather large statue of a big black bird in the corner, glowering down from its perch on an alabaster column.

The desk's larger drawers were open, probably because the police had forgotten to tidy up after doing their rummaging, but after a few minutes of careful searching, Maya took a step back in frustration. No pens, no paper, not a single sign that writing had ever happened here. Plus the itchy place on the tip of her index finger was getting impatient. It didn't seem to think there was anything for her here.

She straightened up and (feeling foolish) tried holding her itchy finger out in front of her, like a dousing wand.

"Over here?" she said—right out loud, to encourage herself—and she pointed her finger at the desk. The words echoed a little in the empty room and then were soaked up by the books or the carpet and vanished utterly, leaving Maya feeling very alone again. Her finger seemed uninterested in that particular desk. It itched in a bored and impatient way. It wanted to go somewhere else.

Not to mention that no matter where she moved in that room, the bright black eyes of that bird in the corner were fixed—like glue, like pins, like alien spaceship rays—right on her. It was completely unsettling. It was enough to send her back out into the dim entry hall, but as soon as she left the library, the nature of the itch in her fingertip changed (from *bored* to *exasperated*—it was amazing how many emotions a simple itch could convey), and that suctioning feeling pulled at her again. It had to be here, then.

She tried running her itchy finger along the backs of the books on those huge shelves, and although no book stood out, as far as the itch was concerned, there was definitely a pull toward one end of the bookcase, the end closest to the corner where that bird perched looking at her. Maya didn't like those glassy black eyes, so she whipped across to the shelves on the next stretch of wall and tried the finger trick on them, with similar results: the itch pointing toward the statue in the corner, even though nothing ever seemed less related to writing letters on fancy creamy-green letter paper than that beady-eyed bird staring her down from its column.

All right, Maya told her itchy finger, just to shut it up. *Let's take a look at that thing.* It was just a statue of a bird, after all, carved of a very dark wood. Perhaps ebony, like the black keys on a piano. (Although at least black keys on a piano didn't *stare* at you.) Up this close, Maya could see how much time the artist had spent perfecting every little feather. And there, high on its ebony chest, was a very small, very circular bump with a wiggly indentation in its middle. Maya went up on her tiptoes, trying to see the thing clearly. Her fingertip was practically screaming with impatience, so she let it take a look.

Not just a bump, said her eyes and her fingertip at about the same moment: *a keyhole!*

And by the time her mind had registered that word, the tiny, inky key had already peeled itself off the tip of her finger (a very strange feeling, like the smallest but stickiest Band-Aid you ever saw being torn off too early) and flung itself into that smallest of locks. And from inside the ebony bird's chest, there came a strange mechanical shudder, the surprised *click-click-click*ing of numberless little gears—and the bird's wings began to move.

Even as caught by surprise as she was, Maya managed to jump back, well out of the way. Something very old and deep in the human brain knows that when statues of black, black birds begin to click and tick and *move*, it is time to pick up your club (or equivalent) and back away carefully.

It was like nothing she had ever seen, what was happening to that statue. It had seemed so immutably, perfectly still! But now the wings were spreading—out, out, out to the sides—and the chest of the bird opened forward, fanning out as it went, revealing little cubbyholes and thin drawers—and then she could see how it all fit together, the gently tilted surface that had once been a chest and the angled insides of the wings and the intricate array of small shelves and drawers and sorting slots within and the piercing gaze of those glassy eyes still looking down from above—

because the ebony bird was a writing desk.

And resting on its gracefully angled surface (held fast by a delicate sliver of tape) was a letter.

As her mother used to say (her mother collected old sayings the way other people's mothers collected ceramic puppies), "Once bitten, twice shy!" Maya certainly felt bitten—by the letter she and Valko had read in the park, by the inky key, by the way the whole universe had conspired to make her come back here this morning, when any unbewitched person would have known it was Not A Good Idea.

Quick as quick, Maya put a hand out, making a slightly trembly wall between her eyes and the words of that letter. She would not look down. She would look quickly, quickly for stationery and pens in the drawers and cubbyholes, and she would not give this new letter the slightest chance to grab her.

But a minute later the drawers had proved themselves empty, except for a few very ordinary-looking paper clips and an exceptionally ordinary matchbox, and the cubbyholes had no stationery in them at all. Nothing. Just a soft, dusty heap at the bottom of the largest slot. She craned her neck forward to see better, and a ray of weak autumn sunlight sprang through the room's windows to help: a blue-green heap of— What was that, anyway? Her no-longer-itchy finger poked again at the pile, and she knew: ashes. Creamy-green magical ashes.

She imagined the ancient, crumbling Fourcroy standing in this very spot, a week ago, writing all his demands into that awful letter, folding it carefully and addressing the envelope—and then striking one of those ordinary matches and burning the rest of the stationery to ashes. Was he just being extraordinarily extra-careful? Or had he known somehow that Maya would come to this very place, looking for her antidote, for her piece of blank magical paper, and find only those creamy-green ashes laughing up at her?

Ugh! Maya scowled at the desk, but of course she was really scowling at herself. All of the beautiful logic that had brought her here this morning looked a lot less beautiful now. Like the fancy stationery with its gloating, snake-haired watermark, her plans had pretty much all caught fire and burned away to an ashy heap of nothing. She had been a fool all along, thinking she was being clever even as she walked right back into the patient maw of the trap.

"Stupid bird!" said Maya, glaring back at the raven's glassy, triumphant eyes, and she must have clenched her fist or fallen forward against the writing desk or something, because the whole thing trembled a little, the motors *click-click-click*ed again, and the ebony bird looked down at her and said—

No, of course, it couldn't *speak*—

But it was almost speaking, it was; it was trying to open that awful wooden beak—

A choking, metallic gurgle came from the bird's throat, as if something had gotten caught up in its mechanism, and there was another sound, of some crucial little gear cracking under the strain, and the whole lower section of the bird's glossy beak broke loose and dangled there on its broken hinge.

At which point something round and shiny (a button?) came spitting out from that breaking beak so quickly that Maya's hand couldn't help itself; it caught that button right in midair.

So what happened next was the button's fault, really. Of course, Maya's hand had to grab it, and of course, Maya's eyes had to look to see what kind of thing this was, that she had all of a sudden caught in her hand, and so of course what she saw instead were the words of the letter, so patiently waiting for her on the desk all this time, and even as her brain was shouting, *Don't look,* it was already too late: she *had* looked.

And once she had looked, she could not stop looking.

Well done! said the letter.

If you are reading these words, then the clockwork is ticking, and we are well on our way. Let's think of it as a TREASURE HUNT, Maya, my cousin-niece-and-apprentice, and the treasure at the end is (as treasures should be) incomparably great: my life, restored. You broke me; you will mend me. I think you have to agree, it is only fair.

The spell you must work is both difficult and simple. Magic is like cooking, some say. Here, then, are the ingredients you must gather, my young chef-in-training:

(1) A remnant of my physical self (there is a drop of blood soaked into this very paper, do you see? That will do, I think, in a pinch);

(2) My memories (reasonably transportable, I

hope: I will have placed them in the stone for safekeeping);

(3) An apprentice willing to sacrifice her life for that of her master (this is you, dear cousin-niece, and believe me, I am most grateful);

(4) All brought to a most Suitable Magical Place (follow the guide);

(5) Where the willing apprentice (still you, dear Maya) will prove her magical worth by combining the various ingredients within a spell that makes me whole. Then the apprentice will herself, for one glorious moment, be a sort of master, you see, before her life force transfers to the other (who is, of course, in this case, if I may remind us, with full grateful humility, Me). If you look at it properly, dear girl, you can't help but see the advantages all around: life for me; a well-earned, if fleeting, sense of accomplishment for you. In any event, you are henceforth on the clockwork path, and nothing can halt what you are now most fully bound to do.

With most cordial affection,
Your uncle—or cousin—and mentor,
Henri de Fourcroy

Maya read this letter a number of times, with the hairs on her neck standing up as straight as they could manage, and her hands clenched firmly at her sides. She could see the little splotch that must be Fourcroy's blood, but she did not let her arms so much as twitch, and the letter stayed where it was on the writing desk. The trick was not to do anything before thinking it thoroughly through, never ever again.

But so far that trick wasn't working so well, was it? Because here she was, and that wicked Fourcroy had *known* she would be here. He was so full of smug confidence: his letters had bound her; she was now *on the clockwork path.* And where did that lead?

Ice slid down her spine. But Maya Davidson would not be squashed so easily.

She was *not* his apprentice. She wasn't about to sacrifice herself to bring that selfish, selfish, wicked Fourcroy back to life! Was he kidding? The clockwork could tick itself to death, as far as Maya was concerned: *she was not willing.*

She backed away.

The writing desk shuddered a little.

Another small step. It was not as hard as she had thought it might be: the awful suction was gone. That made her think (all the while backing up, step by step, to the library door): the letter had said she should go to the writing desk, and she had done so. All right. She had been bound (not good), but the binding wasn't perfect, was it? He had written those letters in a rush, probably, knowing the police would be coming and his mind full of desperate spells and magics. He wouldn't have been able to think of everything. He had forgotten, for instance, to *command* her, just now, to take the page with his blood splotch on it. That was an important ingredient, wasn't it?

Just look at her, leaving it behind now! Ha!

But the other half of her mind was still moored in ice, facing that cold, cold thought: Maya, *on the clockwork path.*

As she went back through the doorway, there was a resounding crash: the writing desk had slammed itself back together again, the wings slapping back into place, the glassy eyes of the raven still glaring and glaring and glaring.

It made her jump, that crash; her breath caught in her chest, and then Maya turned and ran to the door and, stumblingly fast, down those winding, fancy stairs. It was two floors before she realized the button the raven had nearly choked on was still clenched in her hand—and she was all the way at the bottom of the stairs and already pushing herself out through the front doors of the Salamander House (so desperately eager to get back *home*), when Maya finally remembered the rest of that peculiar morning, the noises last night on her fire escape, and the silent, staring gargoyles still sitting in wait for her there.

She tumbled out through the door and—"OOF!"— barreled so hard into the person standing right there that she and the person both went sprawling to the ground.

"So sorry!" said she and the person she had barreled into, both at once.

And then they both said, "Oh!"—both of them with fairly sheepish looks on their faces—because this was the Salamander House, where people trying to, um, avoid Fourcroy's writing desk were definitely not supposed to be, and yet here they both were: Maya (climbing to her feet a little unsteadily because the breath had just been knocked right out of her) and Valko (looking rather shocked and surprised).

"Hey, I thought you were doing math," said Maya.

"Grandmother called from Bulgaria, so I was able to scamper," said Valko.

Maya frowned, remembering all the reasons she had to hate, hate, *hate* Bulgaria, but Valko was still chattering at her, his hand on her arm.

"Maya! You went in there without me! Are you okay?"

She considered that question. She didn't feel extremely wonderful, that much she knew.

"You see how stuck we are?" she said. "Every time we turn around, we're doing what he told us to do in that letter. Even when we think we're doing something different. It's awful. I don't want to be on a clockwork path."

"What? A what?"

"A *clockwork path*," said Maya, with more bitterness. "Ticktock. Like the whole universe is dominoes falling over, or something. I *hate* being a domino. You said a letter couldn't boss us around!"

"Oh," said Valko, and his eyes lit up a little, as they did whenever the conversation veered into ideas he particularly liked chewing over. "But. Well. I mean, a *letter* can't make you do anything, all right, but as far as dominoes go . . . The world really *is* sort of like that, right? Everything's caused by something. Billions and billions and billions of little dominoes, falling all the time. Don't you think about that, sometimes—you know, when you're about to open your mouth and say something? Don't you kind of wonder what it is the dominoes are going to make you say?"

Maya looked at him. *What? Wonder what the dominoes were going to make you say?*

"Nope," she said.

But the word felt strange in her mouth, all of a sudden— sort of rectangular and full of extra corners and—well, to tell the truth, ever so slightly like . . . a domino.

5

MISCHIEF NIGHT

Later that day Maya sat at the dining-room table with an open notebook in front of her and a pen in her hand. Her hand had more or less stopped in its tracks, and it was all Valko's fault. Billions of dominoes everywhere! So what did that mean? It was already fixed in stone somehow, what word she was about to write? If she paid careful, careful attention, could she catch that particular domino before it fell? Could she figure out what her brain and hand meant to write—and then do something completely different? Or would the different thing just be the domino falling, all over again? Her eyes had glued themselves to the tip of her ballpoint pen, and now they refused to budge.

She had sat there over her notebook, completely frozen, for a few minutes already, when she noticed her parents had stopped working on their jigsaw puzzle at the other end of the table and were now both staring at her in amused concern (or possibly just plain amusement; hard to tell).

"Maya, dear, are you stuck?" said her mother, who probably thought Maya was trying to do a bit of extra homework over vacation.

"Yes," said Maya in relief. "I can't figure out whether I can write anything surprising or if every time I write a word, a gazillion little dominoes have already decided what that word is going to be."

"Oh!" said her parents, and (freaking Maya out a bit) they gave each other particularly warm and loving smiles, as if the topic of little dominoes were for some reason near and dear to their hearts.

"Determinism! Physics! The great machine!" said her father to her mother, the way other people's parents might mention the national parks they visited on their honeymoon, and her mother laughed and patted him on the hand.

"Wiggle room, dear. It's all about the wiggle room."

Maya stared at them in growing disbelief.

"Hello?" she said. "Darling parents?"

They remembered themselves then, turned back to Maya, and included her in their smiles.

"Sorry, Maya," said her father. "It's just that we first met in this English class, you know, long long ago, right after the creation of the world, when we were in college—"

"Where they made us read *Oedipus Rex*," said her mother. "It's a play."

"Greek tragedy," said her father. "Oracle says baby will grow up to murder his father and marry his mother, so naturally they send the baby off to be left on the hillside to die—"

"Poor little thing!" said her mother.

"But instead," Maya's father continued, "a shepherd takes him in, and other stuff happens, and he ends up being raised by another family—"

"Yes, he does," said Maya's mother. "And then little Oedipus grows up and *he* goes and talks to the oracle, and it tells him he's going to kill his father and marry his mother, and so he does everything he can to avoid killing or marrying the people he thinks are his parents—"

"Which means, ha-ha, that he blunders right into killing another man, who of course turns out to have been his birth father, and marrying another woman, who of course turns out to have been his birth mother—"

Maya's parents were relishing this story all too much.

"That's seriously gross," said Maya.

"So the oracle was right all along," said Maya's mother. "That's the way Greek tragedies are. And then we got into a big argument in class."

"With the teacher?" said Maya.

"With each other." Her mother laughed. "I said it was

awful to think of life being all planned out in advance that way. It was so unfair! And how I was very glad I did not live in ancient Greece, if that's how they saw the world. And your father went on this long tear about deterministic theories of the universe, meaning everything is part of some kind of huge mechanism that just chugs along like a clock. And I said, *What about free will?* And he said, *No such thing, if you're a determinist.* And I said, *Then I'm not a determinist, that's for sure.* And he said, *Not that you have any choice about that.* And then I threw a notebook at him, and the other students clapped."

Maya's father grinned.

"They did. They were awful. Then, after class, I took your mother out for coffee and confessed."

"Confessed what?" said Maya.

"That I knew better. I was studying physics, right? There's all this stuff in modern physics that shows us that on the very small scale, on the quantum level, all sorts of strange things happen all the time. You can't even say A will cause B; you have to talk about what's probable, not what's certain, and sometimes even the very most improbable things happen."

"Oh," said Maya. She was still a little too caught up in the idea of her long-ago very young mother throwing a notebook at her long-ago very young father to follow the details of all of these As and Bs.

"So I said things might have worked out better for poor old Oedipus," said her mother, "if he had just managed to move from Greece to the quantum level."

She smiled.

"More wiggle room there, apparently."

"Um," said Maya. "So if someone now is, like, caught up in some kind of magic that makes her do all these different things, just like the Oedipus guy, then what should she do?"

"*Oedipus* was just a story," said her father, wagging his finger at her. "Stories are a different case entirely."

"Look for that wiggle room," said her mother. "There's usually more wiggle room than you think, even in stories."

Meanwhile, however, the wiggle room in Maya's life seemed in many respects very much limited. When she was getting ready for bed that night, something clinked onto the floor and wobbled there for a while like a flattish brass top. It was the clunky old button the ebony bird had spit out into her hand—she had forgotten all about it. She reached down to pick it up, and it gave an extra wobble in her palm, like a dog turning in circles before curling up in its bed. It was stamped with an old-fashioned crest: an elaborate *F* and a salamander curled up on a rock—

Oh, yes, thought Maya. *Of course. It* would *have to have a salamander.*

On the back were engraved a few words in French, *"Au point d'origine."* To the Origin Point. That made her think of graphs in her geometry textbook, but why geometry terms should be showing up on a button was not entirely clear. She put it up on a high shelf, out of sight.

And outside on the fire escape, the gargoyles sat waiting for her. That's not all: every day they sat *differently.* In the middle of each night Maya would be woken up by another brief eruption of clatter, and every morning when she cracked open the window to peer out, those gargoyles would still be there, but no longer exactly where they had been the day before. They would be clustered together looking at something, or one would be lifting something (a twig?) into the air, examining it, or their wings would be spread out wide to catch some nonexistent breeze, as if they had just landed back on the fire escape after a bit of aerial gallivanting when time froze for them again.

But stone is way, way heavier than air. Stone things can't fly.

Maya gave up. She could not think about these problems the way Valko did. "You just didn't notice the wings before"—that was what he had said yesterday on the phone. "They're *statues,* Maya. I know someone apparently dragged them from here to your place, which is really weird and hard to imagine and doesn't make any sense, but they can't really be moving around on their *own*. I mean, like we were saying the other day: it's hallucinations, maybe. Your brain is playing tricks on you."

But Valko wasn't the one who had to crack open the back window every morning and look at what the gargoyles were getting up to now.

At least I'm not as frightened as I used to be, she told herself. After three days of gargoyles on her fire escape, a person can find herself almost getting used to the idea. By yesterday, they were beginning to look what you might even call familiar: good old Beak-Face and Bonnet-Head (she even had names for them now), frozen in the middle of whatever their big project was, over there on the far side of the fire escape. And she would be thirteen tomorrow, anyway. She had always liked the number thirteen. It was a magical and courageous number: unique, prime, and with an individual approach to life.

She swung her legs over the edge of her bed and walked over to the window with quick, determined steps, the kind of steps someone almost thirteen should use, and opened the window with a quick, determined twist of the latch. And then ruined the effect by being so startled all over again that she squeaked out loud and took a hasty step back.

The thing was, he was so close to her window today,

old Beak-Face. His monsterish, craggy face was staring straight at her from about ten inches away, and his front claws were right there in front of her nose, almost as if that stony-bony index finger had been petrified just at the very moment it had decided to give his own carved chest a tap.

Once she found her balance again, she got mad, even though what use is it, really, to get mad at statues? So what she said was "What the heck do you *want*?" and it didn't come off as all that brave, either, because she was still trying not to make any sounds loud enough to tempt James or her mother into this room. They didn't know anything about the gargoyles, and she was absolutely determined to keep things that way. The gargoyles were her problem, hers alone.

And that's when the cold little wind kicked in, whipped right over her shoulders and through the room behind her, rustling through her birthday cards. In fact, one of those envelopes went flying right out the window—and ran right smack into the solid wall of the gargoyle's chest, while his stone eyes kept staring ahead at Maya in the most disconcerting way.

The letter was plastered against him now, like a beauty queen's sash or one of those "Hello, My Name Is" stickers, and his stone claws gripped the edges of it as if that was what they had been meant to do all along, the one sharp-clawed digit now not tapping his chest so much as pointing. She thought at first it was pointing at nothing, but the nothing changed as she looked, as if ink from the letter inside the envelope were leaching out through the creamy-green fibers—squiggles and lines—no, actual words from that awful letter, a whole phrase:

the memory stone—it will hold your instructions

It lingered there under the gargoyle's emphatic claw for a moment and then faded away again, leaving only that one word—

INSTRUCTIONS

—against the faintest, most delicately inked-in background of Medusa's scary-face-with-snakes-for-hair.

Maya found she had reached some kind of limit.

"You know what?" she said aloud to the stone gargoyles, to the old Fourcroy's Medusan letter, to the world. "That's enough. Forget it. I'm not doing any of it. Go away. Stop it. He can bring himself back to life, if that's what he wants, that stupid old shadowy Fourcroy. Good-bye!"

But even while she said these things, she wasn't moving safely away from the gargoyle, or closing the window, or anything like that. No, what she was actually doing was noticing that each letter of the word INSTRUCTIONS was growing larger and larger in its own right, as if the ink were still spreading across the paper. And now she could see that the letter *I*, for instance, actually contained (how clever!) whole microscopic sentences. Not lines of ink: lines of *words*. She couldn't help tipping her head a little to see what they said:

Once on the clockwork path, no foot can stray. . . .

Oh, good grief, what was she doing? Her eyes felt as if they had just been scorched. Was she really being that stupid, all over again? She snatched the letter away from the gargoyle's chest and crumpled it in her hand.

"NO," said Maya, outglaring the gargoyle as best she could. "I said no. No way. Stop it. I quit. And you know what?"

She ducked back into her room for a moment and came out again brandishing the button in her hand.

"It's all going away now," she said to the gargoyles. "Watch this!"

And she broke one of her father's cardinal rules about life in tall buildings: she threw the button and scrunched-up letter right out of that window, right over the gargoyles' heads and down into the debris of the courtyard below.

"Done," said Maya, and she slammed the window shut and walked away.

Had it been her imagination? Possibly. But it seemed to her that as the button had gone whistling out over his head, the gargoyle on the fire escape had looked for a moment—strikingly so, for a monstrous stone creature—not so much threatening as *amazed*.

There was a secret about Maya's birthdays. It went back to a night long ago, the thirtieth of October in the year she was turning seven. She had fallen asleep after the usual stories and teddy-bear kisses and tuckings in, and then, right in the smack-dab middle of the night, suddenly there her parents were again, waking her up with whispers and laughter.

"Mischief Night, Maya!" they said, and wrapped a blanket around her to keep the chill away. "We're going to watch your birthday come in this year: what do you think about that?"

Maya thought that made birthdays sound like a wonderful, silvery tide flooding in across the world; maybe it was the moonlight spilling over the lawn outside that made her think that. She sat on the front step with her parents, watching her birthday come in, and then when it was after midnight and her birthday was all safely arrived, her father carried her back to bed and pulled the quilt up around her and kissed her on the top of the head, and that was a magical birthday, for sure. In the years after that her parents were too busy with little baby James to do crazy things like wake up a birthday girl in the middle of the night, but what they didn't know was this:

Maya had always remembered. She had gotten up in the middle of the quiet night before every single Halloween since that first one long ago, and she had watched her birthday come in, every year.

Even in France, even with gargoyles parked outside her window, Maya was determined to be up in the dark middle of Mischief Night to watch her birthday roll in. She set her alarm before going to sleep, and then had the traditional hard time actually falling asleep (since knowing an alarm is going to ring soon makes even a very tired person jumpy), but when the bell did go off, a muffled jangle from underneath her pillow, she woke up in a flash, remembering right away who she was, and where she was, and what she was waking up for.

It wasn't like being at home, where there was that front yard she could go out into for a few minutes. Paris is a big city, and she didn't want the trouble of going all the way downstairs and past the door of the concierge and out onto the chilly sidewalks of the rue de Grenelle. No, she figured it was less trouble to face those gargoyles for a moment, and the third of a moon that was hanging about somewhere in the sky above the back courtyard.

So she took a deep breath and opened the window. Sure enough, the nearest gargoyle glittered dimly in the little bit of moonlight.

"Hey there, Beak-Face," she said under her breath. It made her feel braver. "Don't mind me. My birthday's on its way in."

She could feel how cold the air was, but she was still warm enough, with the blanket pulled around her shoulders. It must be just about time. She had set the clock for 11:55, not wanting a long wait.

There were scattered windows with lights on, far away across the courtyard, but their shades were drawn. Everything was chilly and still. Hard to believe a whole city was out there, beyond these quiet windowed cliffs of buildings.

And then the universe turned some tiny corner, and the fire escape exploded into clattering, chattering motion.

It caught Maya so much by surprise that she froze instead of flinching, her hands just clenching the blanket, her jaw trembling, her eyes stuck wide-open in disbelief.

A whirlwind of gargoyles!

Clattering tornado!

Stony, cacophonous blur!

She had an impression of wings, claws, motion: something happening over on the other side of the fire escape.

The blur was deepest there.

The whole world on fast-forward, that's what it was like. The gargoyles, who had been unmoving statues all day long, had suddenly jumped into life at racing speed. *To catch up with the rest of us,* thought Maya, and she leaned a little forward on the windowsill to get a better view of exactly what they were doing. This must be the clatter she had been waking up to the last few nights.

After all, it made some kind of sense. If you were a gargoyle and moved at normal human speed, you'd be caught pretty soon at it, wouldn't you? And people would fuss? So doing your living all at once, maybe that was a good way to go about things, if you were a gargoyle. Or maybe gargoyles didn't like moving around, since they were made of stone and all, so they tried to do all their motion in one quick burst, just to get it over with. (See how logical she could be at midnight? Maya felt almost smug, and then noticed the cold beginning to get under her skin.)

"Guess I'm really truly thirteen now," she said to the stony blur that was the gargoyles at work on whatever they were working on. "Hey, there! You hear me?"

To her surprise, they turned around and actually looked at her for the tiniest fraction of a second; they bobbed their stone heads, spread their wings, jumped up in the air (the sound was a cross between sticks breaking and a small avalanche)—and vanished.

She waited another minute, which must be worth an hour or more of gargoyle time.

Nothing.

They were gone. A pile of debris on the far side of the fire escape—that was all that the gargoyles had left behind.

And the quick staccato of her heart (because the whole thing had been quite a show, to tell the truth) was the only sound left.

"Well, happy birthday, me," she said to herself. She hardly knew how she felt: Relieved? Abandoned? Both?

She decided, since it was her birthday, to stick with *relieved*. And then she closed the window and went to bed again.

The next morning, with end-of-October sunlight filtering in, like weak tea, through the mottled glass of her window, it was hard to believe she had been watching a pair of statues race about and then fly away only a few hours earlier. But when she opened the window and looked out across the fire escape, the gargoyles were still gone. Just that mess in the corner of the fire escape—a pile of sticks and rubbish, that was all that was left.

Then she leaned out of the window to take a closer look at the mess, because really, why would a pair of stone gargoyles leave little piles of trash?

Already, now that her attention was focused on it, the trash looked distinctly less trashy. There was organization to it. The sticks piled up in a roughly doughnutish heap, and there—

There was something rounded and shiny, there in the middle. She could see that now. It would mean climbing out through the window onto the fire escape, though, if she wanted to take a closer look.

It's my birthday, thought Maya, and she brought the chair over to the window and climbed out over the windowsill, keeping her eyes on the shiny thing (she was not the sort of person who enjoys looking down through metal grids at the hard ground four stories below).

With one hand carefully gripping the metal railing—and not looking down—she bent her knees and leaned forward—not looking down—and stretched her right hand out, out, out, until she felt that smooth shininess under her palm.

She was doing fine, not looking down, and then a voice came from deep inside the apartment and broke right into that spell:

"Maya, good morning! Are you up?"

Oh, her mother would not be pleased to see her clambering around on the wrong side of the window! Forgetting all the rules, Maya *looked down* through the grating she was perched on, yipped with fear, and rebounded into her room like a yo-yo. In fact, she backed up over the sill so fast that she tripped and hit the floor of her room with a rolling splat.

"Maya?"

Her mother looked in through the bedroom doorway. A familiar, loving, worried face.

"Did you fall *again*? Happy birthday, sweetheart! Or is that some kind of violent yoga you've taken up? Close the window, don't you think?"

Maya got up off the floor to close the window; that was when she realized her hand was full of rounded, shiny stone.

"Birthday breakfast in five minutes," said her mother. Her face was especially pale today, Maya couldn't help but notice. "And what have you got there?"

"A rock?" said Maya, still somewhat dazed.

"How nice," said her mother. "Come as fast as you can."

And she was gone again.

Maya hardly noticed, however. As soon as she had opened her mouth, she had realized what it really was, the thing in her hand.

That hadn't been a pile of twigs and trash, after all, out there on the fire escape: it was a *nest*.

Of course! How obvious!

Which meant, if you thought about the thing logically,

that in her hands at this very moment was something pretty rare, something Maya had never heard of before, something rather incredible: a gargoyles' egg.

And the egg was large, for an egg. Not quite as big as an emu egg, but almost (Maya's science teacher back in California had kept an actual emu egg on her desk, next to the frog skeleton and the plaster model of a cell, so Maya knew what emu eggs looked like: gargantuan dark-green avocados). It was heavy, too, but then again, ordinary eggs weren't made of stone, and certainly not made of stone that warmed up so eagerly in your hand that you thought you might have to put it back down in a minute, or risk getting singed.

Like it's coming to life, thought Maya, and the surprise of it almost made her drop the poor egg on her toes. It was disconcerting to feel rock growing warm and shifting about under your own fingertips. She looked closer and saw it was the surface that was changing, in response to her touch. The stone the egg was made of had white, gray, and black flecks in it, and those flecks actually seemed to be shifting around from place to place, recombining, feeling their way toward new patterns of some kind. *Like an inside-out kaleidoscope*, thought Maya.

It was beautiful.

It was lovely.

It was the most perfect birthday present anyone could ever hope to have.

"Wait," said Valko, when she called him on the phone to explain (in half whispers, so the family wouldn't come nosing in) how gorgeous this egg was, how special and unprecedented and unique. "Wait, excuse me, Maya, but are you sure this is something you should be handling? Do you think it's safe?"

"Safe?" said Maya. Sometimes Valko had no spirit of adventure at all. "It's got *pictures* on it! It just spelled out something in *actual letters*! Only I can't read what they say. I think they're maybe Greek."

"That doesn't sound normal at all, not for a rock," said Valko. "It's not ticking or anything, is it?"

"Ticking!"

"Tuck it away somewhere, and I'll look at it when I get there."

Valko was coming to what Maya's mother kept referring to as *Maya's birthday party* that afternoon.

There were plenty of good reasons for Maya to be worried about this particular party.

For one thing, can you really have a birthday party in a part of the world where you have at most one friend? Her mother kept wanting her to invite all sorts of "people from school," but it wasn't as if "people from school" were a real category in Maya's life, except, of course, for Valko. So who was going to be there? Her family, and Valko, and her family's somewhat eccentric Cousin Louise, all of them pretending this was just as much fun as it would have been if it had been a real party, with lots of real friends, in California. Ugh.

She wrapped the egg up tenderly in her other sweater, hid it away in her closet, and (her mind full of birthday) resolved to hope for the best.

6

THE HAPPY BIRTHDAY
DANCE OF DEATH

But in the end, it turned out that as much as Maya had been worried about her birthday party, she hadn't been worried nearly *enough*.

The beginning wasn't so bad. Valko came at the end of the afternoon, and she unwrapped the gargoyles' egg to give him a look.

"They gave up and went away," she said. "They left it behind. It's beautiful, see?"

"You're sure you didn't draw on it yourself?" he said.

"I can't even draw stick figures," said Maya. "Look how pretty these pictures are! And they even kind of move when you look at them. At least, they did earlier."

"Hmm," said Valko. The egg looked like something a crazy old artist might make for a king, so densely covered with pictures and words that you could stare at it for hours and still be finding something new: little animals hiding in the grass, a kite soaring in the sky, trees and clouds. All frozen in place, Maya noticed, at the moment.

"There. See that writing? What is that? Is it Greek?"

Maya put her finger down on the words she could not quite read, and sure enough, at her touch the surface of the egg shimmered and came to life (a tiny sketch of a cat swiped a paw at an even tinier sketch of a bird).

"Hey, do that again," said Valko after he had poked at the egg with his own fingers to no effect at all.

Maya settled her whole hand on top of the egg for a moment, and it was almost like resting her palm on the head of a rabbit, the stone was so warm and so welcoming. And sure enough, when she lifted her hand, the design was shifting about and remaking itself.

"Oh!" said Valko. "That's your name!"

A word was spelling itself out in viney letters: *M . . . A . . .* something that looked like a backward *R*.

"And you're sure you're not writing on it yourself?" he said doubtfully.

"Why would I do that? *How* would I do that?"

She didn't even bother to keep the impatience out of her voice. But Valko, oblivious, was leaning even more closely over the egg now, working away at it as if it were a crossword puzzle.

"All those pictures, of course, but see the number forty there? And your name, lots of times—and look, more writing!" He pointed. "Look at that! All right, one thing's for sure: whoever made this for you was Bulgarian."

Bulgarian? Oh, blah!

Maya made a face.

"Honestly," she said, "I'm kind of hating Bulgaria these days."

For about one second Valko looked taken aback, and then he figured out what she meant by all that, and a slightly wistful version of the smiling crinkles came back into his face.

"I know," he said. "But it's not an awful country. I remember it being beautiful. It just contains some awfully stubborn grandmothers."

They were silent for a minute, thinking about that.

It's up to me, Maya told herself. *I have to find a way to save him from his horrible grandmother. I'm the stubborn one, and I won't let him go.*

Her hand was still resting on the gargoyles' egg, and the pictures were making and remaking themselves under her fingers. Maybe it was the warmth of the stone that brought her back to herself.

"If it's Bulgarian," said Maya, "then what does it say?"

"'Keep me secret, keep me safe.'"

They looked at each other.

"I don't know—," said Valko, but what he didn't know he didn't have time to say, because Maya's mother was calling them into the living room to "meet our guests."

Guests? (That was what Maya was thinking as she bundled the egg back into its hiding spot in the closet.) Where had her mother actually managed to come up with *guests?*

But it turned out to be as much her father's doing as her mother's. Assembled in the living room were more people than just Maya's father and mother and little brother, James, and the one guest Maya had been expecting to see, her mother's cousin Louise, looking quite elegant and mysterious in a tailored jacket.

She had been a highly forgettable person until quite recently, but then she had taken a large dose of a mysterious, magical substance (Henri de Fourcroy's *anbar*, distilled—oh, horror!—from the essence of charming children) and had become, overnight, astonishingly radiant and compelling.

The dose of *anbar* was slowly wearing off with the passage of time, of course, but for the moment Cousin Louise still outshone everyone else in the room. She was wearing the most extraordinary green jade earrings, and the reflected lights of the apartment flickered as if trapped in her eyes.

"*Bonjour*, Maya!" she said, coming forward to give Maya's hand an energetic shake. "*Joyeux anniversaire!*"

It was not just Cousin Louise wishing her a happy

birthday, either. On Louise's right were two people Maya hadn't quite noticed until that moment: an older Asian man in a slightly too elegant pin-striped suit jacket and, at the man's side, a young girl in a blue dress and wearing a half frown plastered on her odd, beautiful, and strangely familiar face.

Oh! It was the girl with the amazing hair! Maya had seen her many times in the school courtyard. It wasn't just her hair that made her stand out from the crowds (a profoundly frizzy brown-blond flood of hair, held back from her face by an industrial-strength black headband), it was the way she stood so tall and proud out there on the concrete of the yard, even though she must have been one of the shortest, youngest kids in the whole school.

You noticed that sort of thing when you yourself spent whole recesses hunkering down in the shadows, feeling very American and out of place, and trying not to be conspicuous.

"*Salut*, Pauline!" said Valko, who had already cheerfully shaken hands with Cousin Louise and the well-dressed old man during the time Maya had been thinking about courtyards and recesses. Sometimes Valko's embassy upbringing welled up in the most impressive ways. Now he was kissing the frowning girl's cheeks—left side, right side, the traditional French pattern. The girl's frown faded just a little.

"But I did not know you would be here, Valko," said the girl in French. "You've gone nowhere for vacation?"

"No, no, never vacations for us," said Valko with a smiling shrug, and to Maya he said, "This is the astonishing Pauline Vian. Have you two met yet?"

"Not yet," said the astonishing Pauline Vian, her frown becoming a shade friendlier as she reached out to shake Maya's hand. "You are the American girl. I am with Valko in many classes this year. Since he is actually quite clever."

It was all Maya could do to keep from gaping. She was not used to people in any country anywhere who talked as bluntly as this tiny, frowning Pauline Vian.

"It was in the cafeteria at work," said Maya's father, beaming proudly. "I found myself eating at a table with the head of the lab, Monsieur Pham here, and it turns out he has a granddaughter almost your age, Maya, and at your very school, too. Can you imagine? So of course I thought of your birthday."

No, she could not possibly be twelve or thirteen, not this tiny little girl with the amazing hair.

"What grade are you in, Pauline, dear?" asked Maya's mother from her chair in the corner of the living room.

"Same as us, Mrs. Davidson," said Valko. "You skipped a year, didn't you, Pauline?"

"Two years," said Pauline, and she added a crisp edge to her frown.

"Our little Pauline! Eleven years old, and the best student in the *collège!*"

So that was her grandfather. They did resemble each other just a little, around the eyes, though one was smiling as if pride might just burst right through his skin, and the other frowning just as hard.

"Physics, we think," said the proud old man. "She can already work equations like you would not believe, this one. Although she would also be a fine historian, wouldn't she? The talents of four continents, all combined in our Pauline!"

"But that's of absolutely no consequence, all that physics and history," said Pauline Vian, her frown so deep that whole textbooks could fall into it and never be seen again. "Since my vocation lies elsewhere."

A perplexed silence fell over the room for a moment, while those who were not native speakers of French tried to figure out what this little girl and her grandfather had actually been arguing about (or, in some cases, what the word *vocation* was supposed to mean). It was not a very long silence, because Maya's little brother, James, who was still only five and thus tended to produce loud noises when doing even quite ordinary things, went bounding over to Maya, one of his hands clutching something colorful and slightly grubby.

"Happy birthday, Maya! Can you open my present now? It's a real present! Open my present!"

Enough people laughed to break the general spell, Maya's father went into the kitchen to get some more glasses, and Maya sat down in the nearest chair to pay proper attention to the package James had just handed her.

"You didn't have to get me a present, you know that," said Maya.

James grinned at her.

"I found it," he said. "I actually found it this very morning. It's a really good present."

He leaned against her chair while she took extra time with the wrapping paper, just so James could savor every second of it.

"Is it maybe a *very large book* or a *helicopter?*" she asked, and he laughed.

Actually she was thinking it might be a few mints or— well, something small. But she kept working away at the layers of crumpled paper and the tape, until something round and gleaming dropped into the palm of her hand.

"Oh, James," said Maya, and then she was briefly speechless.

"Look, look. Do you see? It has a SALAMANDER on it! It's a real present!"

A *real present*! In fact (she couldn't help herself: she shivered), it was the very button she had thrown away, whenever that was. Yesterday morning. She had thrown it away, to show the gargoyles and the shadow and the Medusan stationery that they could not tell her she was bound to do anything. That she was free.

But here it had come back to her in the hands of her brother.

"Do you like it?"

"It's . . . a beautiful button, James. Where did you find it?"

He put his mouth to her ear: "In the courtyard! By the trash cans!"

And giggled.

"And it's not a button, anyway," he added. "It's lots specialer than that. It opens up, see?"

He took the button back from her and tapped some little latch on it that Maya had not seen before, and the top sprang open, like a locket.

"How strange!" said Maya. "Is it a watch, then?"

"Looks more like a compass," said Valko, who had come to look over Maya's shoulder. Maya remembered then, with a twinge of guilt, that she had never quite managed to mention it to Valko, this not-exactly-a-button that the ebony bird had spit out into her hands. "But the needle's not pointing north. Maybe it's malfunctioning."

It didn't want me to tell him, thought Maya. And felt trapped all over again, just *putt-putt-putt*ing her way down the clockwork path.

James, however, was beaming around at them all, happy his present was turning out to be so very interesting.

"There's writing on it, too," he said. "On the outside and the inside. It's hard to read. Maybe it's in code."

Maya was already holding the nonbutton up to the light to see what the words were, scratched into the inside of the metal cover: *forêt de Bière.*

The name of a forest. That didn't make any of this any clearer.

"Well, thank you, James," she said. "That's really sweet of you, to give me a present."

Inside Maya, it felt like a thin vein of ice had formed in her gut, though. She had wanted to be free!

Maya's mother broke the spell by giving Maya a kiss and slipping her a little box of her own.

"Something very old, darling girl," she said. "My mother gave this to me, when I was thirteen, and she had it from an aunt or great-aunt, who had no daughters of her own."

A bracelet, quite simple and lovely, with one milky stone set in it.

"That's an opal—can you see the colors hiding in it?"

said Maya's mother. "Our family stone, said my mother. More than one thing at once, you see: water, stone, and light, all mixed up together. Like a rainbow in the fog. Wear it, and be happy."

She fastened it on Maya's wrist, where the stone winked in the light, shy and mysterious. They watched it glimmer for a moment, Maya and her mother.

"Oh! And *it comes with a choice*—that's what she said when she gave it to me." And Maya's mother gave a surprised little laugh. "Isn't that funny? I'd forgotten that completely. It was so many years ago, you know."

"Choice?" said Maya. "What choice?"

A light flickered for a moment deep in Maya's mother's eyes—an old fire made of more than one thing at once, and seen from far away. The hint of a light, and then it faded again.

"No, I can't remember," she said. "Memories can be pretty shy creatures, can't they? Just the merest glimpse, and then they're gone."

On the other side of the room, Cousin Louise was talking very earnestly to Pauline Vian. And Maya's father was just now coming in with the cake:

"Happy birthday to you, happy birthday to you . . . !"

They sang it in English, they sang it in French; one of them even sang bits of it in Bulgarian. And then they ate slices of Maya's father's excellent chocolate cake, while

110

the various grown-ups made conversation with each other.

Meanwhile the astonishing Pauline Vian gave Maya long, appraising looks over her slice of cake.

"The adults, they want us to be friends," she said finally, in her blunt stare of a voice. "Papi is full of great enthusiasm about it."

"He is?" said Maya, figuring out only at the very last second that "Papi" must mean that well-dressed grandfather of hers.

"It's all *arrangé*," said Pauline with a shrug. "Because you do not have friends speaking French with you—"

"You apparently forget Maya's charming, loyal friend Valko," said Valko, leaning around Maya from the other side. He did not seem flustered by the astonishing Pauline at all, but that must be because he had gotten more or less used to her during all those advanced math and science classes they had together.

"But no," said Pauline. "I am not forgetting you, Valko, but you speak English to Maya all the time, and so her French cannot improve, can it? Whereas I will not speak English to her at all, because for one thing, I know only '*one, two, sree*' in English."

"You'll have to know more than that by the end of the year," said Valko. English was part of the big final exam.

"*Exactement*," said Pauline. "For preparing for the

exams, Maya's mother will teach me English; and in exchange I make Maya speak French. That is Papi's plan."

She set down her fork.

"But my plan is different!" she said, and for the first time a glint of something less frowny came into her eyes. "It is about the *violin*!"

For some reason—perhaps the remarkable shininess with which that one word, *violin*, stood out from everything else Pauline had said since entering the Davidsons' apartment—everyone in that whole room fell silent all at once and looked at her.

"Do you play the violin, dear?" said Maya's mother kindly.

"Yes, *madame*!" said Pauline Vian. She stood up when she said it, too, as if the very thought of the violin was something too elevating to discuss while seated at a table. "I play the violin! It is my true passion. And I know— I've heard—your cousin told me earlier—that you are an excellent violinist and could help me with my practice. Oh, *madame*, I hope you will."

Maya's mother's pale face looked quite taken aback.

"Oh, dear," she said. "It has been such a long time, Pauline. I'm afraid I hardly have the strength for it, these days. You must have a real teacher, don't you?"

"I've done a great deal of research online," said Pauline,

her chin somewhat higher in the air. "I have read a number of books."

"She is so busy, with her math and her science and her history," said Pauline's grandfather. For the first time, he looked distinctly uncomfortable. "And you know, *madame*, how children have these ideas, these passing enthusiasms."

"Papi is unhappy because I will be a violinist, and not a physicist," said Pauline. "Or even a historian. The talents of four continents, wasted. That's what he always says."

There was a slightly too loud whispering from the corner, while James asked his mother whether continents really have talents.

"No, they do not," said Pauline, not pretending not to have overheard. She gave James a long, serious stare. "Papi means my various grandparents come from many different places in the world, and that that must be better than having grandparents who come from one single place in the world, but of course that is not necessarily true. Perhaps I myself will marry a penguin from Antarctica and have little chick-children with *five* continents in their background, but that will not make them better or worse than anyone else."

Even when telling a joke (surely this was a joke?), Pauline did not crack a smile. Maya could not help being rather impressed.

But Pauline's grandfather looked, if that was possible, even more uncomfortable than he had looked ten seconds before.

"They might be really good swimmers," said James, filled with sudden enthusiasm for penguin/human offspring. "But they wouldn't be able to fly. What's in that black suitcase thing?"

Maya's mother followed James's pointing finger, and her face lit up.

"You brought your violin, Pauline. How thoughtful of you."

"So play us something, please!" said Maya's father in his cheerful, funny-sounding French. "A party like this should have lots of music!"

Pauline apparently did not require a lot of encouragement when it came to performing on the violin. She was already across the room, taking the instrument out of its case and tightening the bow, while her grandfather took a few tight-lipped sips from his wineglass.

"There is something I have just started," said Pauline, as she stood back up and tested the tuning of the strings. "It is not very like birthday music, I'm afraid. It is the beginning of a piece by the great French composer Saint-Saëns. His macabre dance."

"The *Danse macabre*," whispered Maya's mother. She seemed to recognize the title.

"What's a makabber?" asked James.

"Shh," said Maya. "It means something good for Halloween."

Then they really could not say anything at all, because Pauline had stopped messing with the violin pegs and was bringing her bow crashing down on the strings.

Makabber indeed! This had to be the most makabber thing Maya had ever heard.

She knew something was wrong even before the first notes came screeching out into the air. She had watched her mother play violin for many years, and she knew that your hand wasn't supposed to look stiff like that and that the violin shouldn't come shooting out from under your chin at that awkward angle. And then the sounds that Pauline's poor violin was producing! Her amazing face got all scrunched up with concentration, and the noises emerging from that violin were as scrunched up as her face. For the first two or three seconds, Maya felt the horrible sensation of laughter bubbling in her chest, but then she looked again at the girl's concentrated, passionate face, and that danger passed. You simply could not laugh at Pauline Vian.

But then Maya noticed something else: as the violin wailed and wobbled, the shadows were deepening in the corners of the room. She checked by looking away and looking back again, and it was really truly happening.

Darkness was seeping out of the walls and puddling at the edges of the room. There was something dreadful about it, too, as if a tide were rising, a tide of bleakness, and they might just all drown in it eventually. A moment ago she had been about to laugh, and now fear was rising up in her instead. She looked around quickly, trying to judge from everyone else's faces whether she was alone in losing her mind, but they all seemed to be feeling exactly what might be expected, under the circumstances: Pauline's grandfather looking uncomfortable and dis-contented, Maya's father politely amused, Cousin Louise sharp-eyed and inscrutable. Only Maya's mother put a thin hand to her mouth and widened her eyes in what might be alarm or distress or something even worse than that.

That was enough to make Maya jump to her feet (not that she had much of a plan, just that awful, quick-rising alarm, and wanting to make the darkness back away).

But it was at that very moment that the dreadful mak-abber music broke off in the middle of a jangling run.

"I don't yet know it all," said Pauline into the flabber-gasted silence that followed. "I just started."

The silence might have snowballed unpleasantly, if it hadn't been for James.

"Wow!" he said, plainly impressed. "That was SUPER Halloweeny!"

"Well, it does represent the Dance of the Dead," said Pauline. "Death comes and plays his wild song, and leads them all dancing away."

Maya shivered and stole another glance at her mother, from whose face the terrible sick-looking green was only just beginning to fade. The shadows had evaporated or soaked their way back into the walls or whatever shadows do when they fade, but Maya felt like someone who had swallowed an ice cube's worth of worry, whole.

"Physics!" said Pauline's grandfather sadly into his glass. "She is so brilliant with equations. And her textual analysis—so profound."

"*Papi!*" said Pauline, frowning again. "I started not so long ago, playing the violin. I *can't* be any good, not yet. How could I possibly yet be any good?"

All the grown-ups relaxed right away. At least she knew she was awful—that was what Maya could see them thinking. Adults (the reasonably nice ones anyway) do hate having to say discouraging things to visiting children. It looked like in this case they might not have to.

"It takes ten thousand hours to be really, really good," insisted Pauline. "They have done studies. Ten thousand hours to become an expert, a genius, a virtuoso. It cannot be done *overnight*."

Maya's mother gave Maya's father the tiniest little nod, and as he began collecting plates in a cheerful, noisy way, the party's attention flowed a little away from Pauline Vian and her violin. A few minutes later the enthusiastic, slightly plaintive voice of James rose up over the general hubbub:

"What I want to go see is a CASTLE!"

He was at the dining-room table, with Cousin Louise and Valko, all confabulating busily about something or other.

"Thoroughly possible," Cousin Louise was assuring him. "Why not? Your father will find the map for us now—"

"Found!" said Maya's father, coming in through the doorway with an armful of maps and guidebooks.

"An instructive outing," Cousin Louise explained, having caught Maya's eye. "With that nice young Pauline, whose French is so *correcte*. I have arranged it all with her grandfather."

A map was being spread across the table.

"So how does a compass even work?" James asked, leaning over the map. There was a little metallic jangle as Maya's button (or compass) slipped loose from his hands and hit the table. "Oops."

"Wait, pick that thing up a moment," said Valko. "I'll fix the map so north is more or less north. Okay, there. Now we'll see what it's up to."

Which was a good way of phrasing it, thought Maya,

still rattled after the way that music had started summoning dark shadows and making her mother turn so green. She scowled down at the slightly trembling needle of the whatever-it-was. Valko turned it around, and the needle stayed put, pointing stubbornly in some nonnorthern direction.

"Huh!" said Valko, his interest piqued. "So it *is* acting like a compass, isn't it? But since when is there a South-Southeast Pole?"

James looked down at the possible compass and then up through the living-room windows with their slightly wavy glass.

"It's pointing at the Laundromat!" he said.

"Or past the Laundromat," said Valko. "Look at the map. It could be pointing at a suburb, like Créteil. Or Fontainebleau, farther out. Or, I don't know, Lyon or Tunisia or somewhere else in Africa."

"I want to go to the one with a CASTLE," said James.

"That would be Fontainebleau, then," said Cousin Louise. "And why not? Tomorrow even, since it is vacation. I will take all of you young people: you, James, and Maya and Pauline and even Valko, too, if he wishes."

"There are very beautiful rocks in those woods," said Pauline, who had put her violin away and wandered over to the table. She was in a distinctly better mood, Maya noticed, after that long discussion with Maya's mother about how you should really hold a violin bow. "My class went on excursion there, last year. It will be very cold, I think, in October."

"*November*," said James. "It'll be November already, tomorrow. Halloween is the last day of the whole month."

"Even colder then," said Pauline Vian. "Makes no difference: I don't mind. Will we take the train?"

"No, no train," said Cousin Louise, and she lit up the room with her radiant, mysterious smile. "I will collect you. I have embraced mobility! That is, I have just recently bought myself a car."

That was when Pauline's grandfather came over to say it was time for him to take Pauline away.

"I'm afraid we have tired out your mother," he said, very politely, to Maya, who immediately craned her neck to see for herself: the chair her mother had been sitting in was empty. How had she not noticed? "She has been so very kind today, to Pauline. Give her our very, very best regards. And *joyeux anniversaire*."

"Yes," said Maya, distracted. "I mean, thank you."

Valko stayed long enough to fish a small, thin box and an envelope out of his backpack. The envelope was quite elegant, and had a great big shield embossed on it, a shield held up by lions.

"Coat of arms of the Republic of Bulgaria," said Valko. "Don't be too frightened: it's from my mother."

"Your mother!"

"No, no, don't look like that. She's inviting you to dinner at the embassy, some sort of cultural awards thingy, the week after next. Here, open the box."

It was a flashlight, little and sleek and cobalt blue.

"I figured you have enough shadows around you," said Valko, and his smile (since he of all people knew how much Maya worried about her mother) was kindness and sympathy, all the way down. "This is for scaring them off."

There was probably something eloquent a girl should say when a friend has just given her something as surprisingly perfect as that flashlight, but Maya just stood there and was happy. You could bask in that sort of happiness for quite a long time, before you'd want to turn the page and move on.

Then she noticed that Valko was letting the toe of his shoe trace out a little circle or two in the hallway floor, like someone with something else to say.

Her heart did a little tippety-tip.

"You know—," he said, and then stopped, and laughed at himself.

"What?" said Maya, though she jumped all over herself immediately for saying it. What kind of foolish person says "what?" like that? Really. You would not think she was someone who had just turned thirteen.

"Oh, it'll wait until tomorrow. Castles with James and Pauline! Hope she leaves the fiddle at home. Happy birthday, Maya!"

Left side, right side, left side.

Nicest boy in the world.

And off he went.

Her father was washing dishes in the kitchen, while James chattered at him about compasses.

Maya peeked into her parents' bedroom, and for a moment thought her mother must be asleep, she was lying so still on the bed. But the head on the pillow turned toward the door and smiled at her.

"Maya," said her mother. "I'm so sorry I wimped out. I got so tired and queasy, all of a sudden. Did you enjoy your party?"

Some questions cannot be properly answered at all. There was the little blue flashlight on the one hand and the shadows oozing out of the wall on the other. There was the fabulous chocolate cake, and there were the things you could not throw away, bossy compasses you could never escape. There was, above all, her mother, lying there smiling at her. Who was supposed to be getting better, finally. Right? Who should not be so exhausted that she had to go lie down.

"Look over there on the chair," said her mother. "Cousin Louise left it for you, when she came in to say good-bye. You know how odd she can be: she said it's for you, but it wasn't the sort of thing one should hand over with trumpets blaring over slices of cake, because it's not really a birthday present at all."

Maya's mother laughed weakly.

"That's what she said! You can just imagine."

Maya could indeed imagine. But she was quite puzzled, all the same.

It was a shoe-box-sized package, wrapped up in brown paper.

"She said it's the family archive—well, for the French side of our family, of course—and it came to her, and she finds she just is not interested in old family history, not anymore. But that it might be curious for you. I really have no idea what it is."

"Old, old, ancient letters," said Maya, taking a peek in the box. "She should have given them to you, really."

Nobody liked old letters more than Maya's mother.

"We'll look them over together, then, maybe," said Maya's mother. Her voice was hoarse. "When I'm feeling a little perkier."

"Mom—," Maya started, but it was hard to go on.

Her mother made a little gesture with her thin ghost of a hand.

"*Don't* you worry about me, Maya," she said fiercely. "I won't have you worrying about me. This is your birthday!"

"Almost not my birthday anymore," said Maya. It was

dark outside already. She couldn't really see her mother's face now, the night had so taken over that room. But the opal on Maya's wrist still murmured with its secret, inward light.

"I'll tell you one thing," said her mother's voice in the dark. "Thirteen years ago at about this hour I was feeling even more tuckered out than I am today. I was so tired I could hardly lift my head off the pillow, when my own mother came to meet you! And you know what she said?"

"What?"

"Such a funny thing: she said, 'Ah, now this one looks like our family, even if she wasn't born in the woods!' Your grandmother always had her own particular way of saying things, you know. When Daddy first met her, he used to actually twitch every time she opened her mouth, he was so nervous around her. But they got to be good friends eventually."

It's funny how you can hear a smile in a person's voice, even when the shadows in the room are already thick as blankets.

"Why the woods?" said Maya.

"Old family joke," said Maya's mother. "*The most magical children are born in the woods.* But then my mother would sniff and say the trees were all wrong in California, anyway, so what more harm could a hospital do? *She* was born in the woods, apparently! Can you imagine that? I can't."

Maya thought about her grandmother, with her raised eyebrows and her crisp French accent and her perfectly ironed blouses, and she couldn't imagine her setting one polished shoe in a forest, much less letting herself be *born* there.

"And now I'm truly tired out. Give me a kiss. And then go be happy, birthday girl."

There must be a trick to that, to *going and being happy* while your mother lies in her room like a pale question mark in the end-of-October dark. But it wasn't a trick Maya was very good at.

She carried the box back into her own room and sat on the floor with it for a while, wondering when her mother would be well enough to want to go through those old letters with her.

A small voice hiding out in the darkest corners of her brain said, *Maybe never.*

She took the top off the box.

All those old papers, some of them clumped together. She ran her fingers through them idly, taking little glances here and there. But the handwriting was hard to read.

Then she saw that at the back of the box was an envelope made of pale yellow silk, held closed by a loop of gold cord. More letters inside it—no, not letters. A little handmade book, its pages stitched together along the spine.

Oh, that made Maya's heart feel sore! Her mother used to make books for her, too, with pen-and-ink Mayas chasing pen-and-ink rabbits across the fields. This was like that. You could tell the person who had made this book had had an artist's hand, had made the pen swoop across the paper, calling forth the pictures quickly, quickly.

There was a tiny boy, trustingly holding the hand of a woman in long, old-fashioned skirts. They were walking along a forest path. There was a kite in his other hand. A little bird looked down from a branch. It was very well done.

She had to squint to make sense of the words:

At the end of every summer,
Henri and his mother walk together
into the old, old woods,
all the way back to the place where he was born.
Life is too short, but summers return.
They will leave their summer memories there,
hidden away in the Summer Box.

On the next page, the tiny boy and his mother had come to an enormous rock in their pen-and-ink forest, and the boy was digging in the earth at its base.

"So . . . what's a Summer Box?" said Maya to herself, full of curiosity and suspicion. More people being born in forests! And all these places memories could be hidden! Stones, letters, boxes.

It was all very well for that little boy Henri, wasn't it? He had his mother to hold him by the hand and walk with him into the old, old woods.

But here's the hard, true thing: some of us have to go into those woods alone.

7

THE ROCK OF THE SALAMANDER

She was supposed to meet Valko in the bakery closest to the Bulgarian embassy at 7:45 a.m. the next morning: that was the plan. To get picnic supplies for the trip to Fontainebleau and all that. But when Maya woke up—after having fallen asleep on the floor of her room, where she spent the night dreaming fitful dreams about mothers walking away into the woods—she felt slow and creaky and not at all in the mood to go on some castle-hunting expedition with Cousin Louise. It was that stupid compass, mostly, that was making her feel so grumpy. Because when you looked at the situation clearly, without covering your eyes with your hands or making up fancy explanations, it did not look good: Fourcroy's own writing desk spits out a compass, right into your own clumsy hands, and then you just let your baby brother and your friends talk you into following that little needle, wherever it points to? Pathetic, right?

But the really scary thing was she was pretty sure, deep inside, that there was nothing else she could be doing, right now. Even merely thinking about not going along on this little expedition made her heart rattle with worry: she *had* to go. She was *bound* to go. And then her brain just filled in all the blank places with excellent reasons why she *should* go: James really wanted to do this! Cousin Louise had made this nice offer, how could Maya back out? Maybe it would be helpful, to see where that compass wanted to take them. Brains are really good at finding reasons for things. That's pretty much the human brain's particular talent.

Well, there is nothing like feeling trapped to make a person want to do some groaning and grumbling and dragging of (trapped, bound, clockwork) feet. The foot dragging had worked so well that it was almost eight when she came racing into the bakery, where there was no Valko waiting, after all.

She caught her breath and said, *"Bonjour, madame,"* as politely as she could, and was about to order a bunch of croissants, when suddenly the world gave a sickening lurch, and Maya could feel the tingle-tangle of strangeness—of magic—spilling into the air. It was happening again! And oh, it was not a pleasant feeling. It was like being ever-so-slightly seasick, watching the waves of strangeness reach that glass case. Right there in front of her own pointing finger, the pastries began to twist and change.

"Five c-c-croissants," she managed to say somehow, nonetheless, and now the woman behind the counter stared at her with eyes that had fogged up completely, from one second to the next.

"Croissants?" the woman said vaguely. "Are those something you eat? What are those?"

Maya could not look away: the croissants on the tray before her were stretching out their arms, unfolding and remaking themselves, becoming something new. It would have been funny, in a video or a movie. It would have been like little lamps learning to walk or stuffed cats playing the piano—but in real life, it was awful.

"As you can see," said the vague bakery woman, "we have the *vines* and we have the *flowers*, but we have no—what did you call them?—*crescents*."

It's like it was that first time, thought Maya. *Like last Friday. Only this time it's worse.*

Maya emerged from the shop with a couple of baguettes, a bagful of *vines* and *flowers*, and a pounding heart. It was a relief to see Valko coming toward her, threading his way through a group of dazed businesswomen (again!), their abandoned briefcases around their feet, who were making the strange sounds of people about to break into song.

"Sorry I'm late!" said Maya and Valko at the very same moment. And then they tried to smile at each other, but Maya could see the tension in Valko's face and suspected he could see the same in hers.

"Look out!" he said.

Maya was about to back right into one of those singing women. She skittered to the side instead.

"Wait, don't tell me—they're not supposed to be acting that way, are they?" said Valko.

"No!" said Maya. At least Valko was doing a *little* better than the last time. At least he had *some* sense that something was wrong. "Can't you tell? It's happened again. Worse, even. Look what's going on with that car over there."

Several thin strips of metal had peeled themselves loose from the car's hood and were weaving themselves into a very complicated floral tangle.

"That's not normal," said Valko. It was still pretty close to being a question, though.

"No, it's not. Let's get out of here," said Maya.

"Okay," said Valko, but he was staring in the other direction, trying to figure something out about those singing women.

"Do you hear them singing? What do they think they're *doing*?" he said, the old investigative fire spiking up in his eyes, and he went zipping over to one of the nearest businesswomen before Maya could haul him away.

"Excuse me, *madame*," he said, waiting (since he was by nature polite as well as investigative) until the woman had paused in her shrill song to take a breath. "I can't help but notice you're singing in Bulgarian. Have you, perhaps, spent time studying that language?"

"Oh!" said the woman, pulling absentmindedly at the string of pearls around her neck. Striking hair, Maya noticed: one brilliant streak of white running through the carefully coiffed brown. "Bulgarian! Is that Bulgarian?"

And she giggled a little, which sounded strange coming from someone in the extremely buttoned-down wardrobe of a bank executive.

"But it is the *inspiration* that matters, is it not? We are, how do you call it, *samodivi*," she said, but in her very French accent the word sounded like this: *samodeeeeev*.

Maya raised her eyebrows in Valko's direction: What did that mean? Maybe she even said that out loud.

"Oh, well then," said Valko. "Thank you so very much. Come on, Maya."

"*Maya*," said the woman with the pearls. She rolled it around in her mouth as if it was a word she was not tasting for the first time. "*Maya.*"

The woman next to her turned around to look, too. But that was odd: her hair had that surprising streak in it as well.

"*Maya?*" she said. Something shadowy in her voice. And indeed over there in the thickest knot of singing, swaying ladies, the shadows were coalescing into a *shape*, and the shape was turning the top of its shadowy self in their direction—

"Oh, ugh," said Valko to Maya. "Ugh, ugh, ugh. *Gash!*"

Which was not as polite as Valko usually was. But by then they were around the corner and halfway down the next block.

"Blech," said Maya in an unhappy gasp when they stopped again to try to breathe. "Makes me never ever want to hear my name ever again."

"No kidding," said Valko, and then a different, more miserable expression came into his eyes. "Oh, rats, I forgot for a moment. The thing I have to tell you. It's a bit of a problem."

"What?" said Maya. What could be more of a problem than crazed women with streaks of lightning in their hair hissing your name?

"It's my grandmother-with-a-mole. She's threatening to come from Bulgaria and descend upon us in person. To see for herself how I'm doing and then probably drag me away by my hair."

There was a pause then, while Maya tried to remember how it had felt, a week ago, when it had just been beginning to be all right, being in Paris. But oh, if Valko *went away*—

That awful, awful thought was interrupted by an urgent murmur from Valko.

"Dang. That thing is still following us. Come on."

Her blurry eyes could hardly see the pavement before her, much less shadows half a block away. Valko was half dragging her along the sidewalk, and her numb feet complied.

"Look! Here's that bizarro edge in the air again," said Valko, pulling Maya right through it. "Farther away than last time, I think. I'll just mark it really fast. And did you see what's happening to that bench back there? Sheesh. Not to mention, we're pretty late for your Cousin Louise."

He paused, that interested look lighting up his eyes a bit as he studied the street behind them.

"It really can't get through," he said thoughtfully. "See that?"

Maya did see: the shadow leaning against that invisible wall in the air; trying, trying to writhe its way through. It made her feel a little sick.

"Like a fish tank for shadows," said Valko. "But let's go, or your Cousin Louise will pop us into an aquarium of her own."

Pauline Vian was already ensconced in the backseat of Cousin Louise's fluorescent-green Peugeot when it pulled up in front of the Davidsons' building. Cousin Louise leaped out of the driver's seat with all the showmanship of one of those people on old TV shows revealing the gorgeous dining set You Can Win.

"My goodness," said Maya's mother as she leaned a little against the nearest wall. She had come down to see them off, and to see for herself Cousin Louise's new and astonishing car. "What an extraordinary color."

"*Allons-y!*" said Cousin Louise, pleased as punch. "Packages and picnics into the trunk! Children into the car! Castles await!"

It was a bit of a squish in the backseat, and Maya ended up in the middle, so that Pauline and James could have windows to look out, which meant that Maya spent the next hour or so catching mere glimpses of tall buildings and busy intersections and edges of roadways, all while trying very hard not to think about the things going slightly wrong back there in the part of the universe nearest to the Bulgarian embassy—or about how carsick she was beginning to feel.

"Wow! The needle really jumps around when we turn corners," said James on her left. "Look."

Maya shook her head. Even opening her eyes was beginning to be a chore, but closing them wasn't good, either.

"Whatever is that?" said Pauline from Maya's other side. "Oh, the little compass toy!"

"We're going to find the—what pole did you say, Valko? It was fancier than the one where the penguins live."

"South-Southeast," said Valko, looking back from the front seat. "Maya, are you all right?"

"Fine," said Maya, spitting the word out as quickly as she could so that she could clamp her lips shut again.

"That sounds like a girl in urgent need of a *pastille au citron*," said Cousin Louise, as she veered left into traffic. "Be so kind, Valko, as to open the little compartment just in front of you—you'll see a small tin. Lemon drops. *Voilà*."

"Okay, Maya, try this," said Valko, pressing a small, round candy into Maya's hand.

It did help a little, the sour sweetness of the lemon. She could open her eyes after a minute or two. And as Cousin Louise's car whipped past the peripheries of Paris, the road became a huge, flowing highway, and that helped, too.

"Ooh, look at the needle now," said James, his eyes glued to the compass. He had clearly inherited his inner ear from some more robust side of the family. "It's pointing straight ahead. Are we going to get there soon? I've never seen a South-Southeast Pole."

"Let's be more precise: *nobody* has ever seen a South-Southeast Pole," said Pauline Vian. It was scary how much she could sound like an adult, sometimes. "Even the poles that do exist, nobody has ever seen them. They are a concept, not a thing like a stick for people to *see*."

"Scientists have seen poles," said James stubbornly. "They go there on big sleds. Right, Maya?"

"Ah, Pauline, what a lovely idea I've just had," said Cousin Louise. "You are excellent in *histoire*, are you not? Why don't you tell us a little about the history of the château de Fontainebleau while we drive. . . ."

Little stifled groans from various passengers in the car, and then Maya let herself fall into polite oblivion for a while (punctuated by lemon drops), while Pauline recited what must have been whole chapters from some history textbook called *Fontainebleau, the Renaissance Château*.

(King François I.
Artists from Italy.
Catherine de Médicis.
François II.
Charles IX.
Henri IV.
Sixteenth century.
Seventeenth century.
Eighteenth . . .)

Boy, these poor French kids sure had a lot of names and dates to memorize, thought Maya, her eyes shut again, the latest lemon drop melting tangily on the tip of her tongue.

And then they were there, piling creakily out of Cousin Louise's jewel-green machine, breathing the cold, cold air of a brand-new November, and being shepherded across acres of cobblestones to the entrance and the ticket office.

"Wow, look at this! It's a great big huge SIDEWAYS CASTLE," said James, looking at the staircases, the cobblestones, the long, long lines of windows everywhere. "I thought it would be going up in the air like the Disneyland one."

"But *non*," said Pauline. "Since the castle of Disneyland is not, as far as I know, originally from the Renaissance."

Maya was still having trouble telling whether Pauline had no sense of humor at all or some very dry, very French sense of humor that you had to be an excellent student and a native speaker of the language to appreciate properly. She thought probably the latter, but she was paying close attention until she knew for sure.

"Keep up, please, children," said Cousin Louise, who apparently believed in brisk visits. "I will be most displeased if anyone turns up lost. It is a vast place, Fontainebleau."

"I'm hungry," said James in an informative tone of voice, as they trotted up the entrance stairs.

He said it again in the long gallery of François I, but mostly he was counting carved and painted salamanders.

Salamanders! They were everywhere! Not to mention many, many golden *F*s.

"The emblem of *le roi François*," said Cousin Louise, whose sharp eyes did not miss a single flinch. "No need to look so concerned, Maya! An appropriate symbol for the Renaissance, in fact: the salamander is unscorched by the flames. Birth and rebirth."

Maya's hand had gone right to the Cabinet glass at her neck. There was an itty-bitty salamander in there, too—a tiny, magical echo of the bronze salamander guarding the Salamander House's door. Salamanders lived in more than one world at once. That was why they were the symbol of her mother's magical and amphibious family, the Lavirottes.

So. birth and rebirth. That was what *renaissance* meant: "rebirth." She shivered a little.

"Maybe our compass used to belong to the king," said James. "It has a salamander on it, too—see, there it is, sitting on a rock—and an *F*. You have to look close to see it, though."

"Different *F*," said Maya, biting her lip.

Why had they come here? That's what she was thinking. Why did the whole world seem to be conspiring to remind her of her troubles all the time?

"And NOW the South-Southeast Pole is THAT way," said James, looking up from the compass and pointing out the great windows.

Valko did that little shoulder-turning dance people do when they're trying to figure out which direction lies where.

"I don't think so," he said. "That's got to be west, not south. Let me see that thing."

He took the little compass from James and for a while kept looking at it and then up out those windows again, perplexed.

"That's definitely not south-southeast anymore," he said. "Strange."

"Keep moving, children! Did you see that statue of Diana? *Remarquable!*"

"Cousin Louise," said James, jogging a little to catch up with her. "We're going to find the pole, after the castle, right?"

"We're going to have our *pique-nique* in the local *forêt*," said Cousin Louise, pausing for a millisecond to admire another detailed painting of a mythological scene. "It's a cold day, but not damp. The woods will be refreshing. And you said you were hungry, I believe."

"We'll eat at the pole," said James.

"If your pole is in a pleasant place for a picnic, then certainly," said Cousin Louise. "Why not?"

They emerged from the castle after having seen only twenty or so of its fifteen hundred rooms, but they staggered out into the world rather stunned by the sheer castleness of the whole place: the height of the ceilings, the gilt decorations on the walls, the paintings and inlaid floors and tapestries and statues of goddesses and salamanders. It was all too much, somehow. It was a relief to be back out in the cold air and bickering pleasantly among themselves about the best place to eat their bread and cheese (and buttery, flaky *vines* and *flowers*).

Finally James put his foot down: Cousin Louise had promised they could have their picnic at the pole, and he wasn't budging until they all agreed.

"Very well," said Cousin Louise. "But you have to tell us how to get to this pole of yours, young man."

"We can just get in the car and follow the needle," said James.

"But not as far as Tunisia, please," said Pauline Vian.

"No," agreed Cousin Louise. "We follow your needle only in these woods here, and only for a little while. And when I say it is time for us to stop for our *pique-nique*, pole or no pole, then we cheerfully exit the car and eat our baguettes, yes?"

James accepted these terms quite graciously, for someone who was only five, but Maya could see he wasn't paying much attention. He was *sure* the compass would lead them right where they wanted to go. Probably (thought Maya) he did think the pole would turn out to be a long thin stick, stuck right into the ground.

The search for the Mysterious Pole turned out to be quite a lot of fun (for everyone with tougher stomachs than Maya's, anyway). Valko held the compass up in front of him, and as he pointed out the direction the needle was showing, Cousin Louise made daring swoops and turns. The riders in the backseat (the ones who weren't Maya) grinned and shrieked and held on tight, and Maya chomped down on lemon drop after lemon drop and was overwhelmed by a combination of excitement and worry.

Was it wise to be following the needle of old Fourcroy's own compass? Maya couldn't really see any way of answering that question that sounded anything like "yes!" It was not wise.

But on the other hand, she was curious—very curious—about as curious as a person can be without actually flushing red from eagerness—about what that compass needle had in mind. And if they were going to thwart that shadowy Fourcroy in his resurrection plans, they needed to know as much as possible about those plans, didn't they? Didn't they?

Even if finding these things out *was* part of his plan?

And why had the strangeness returned this morning,

anyway? (Remembering that brought the carsick feeling back.)

It was all dominoes falling, perhaps: she had *had* to find the writing desk, and now she *had* to follow the compass. But the trick was finding the—what had her mother called it?—wiggle room. She had left the letter behind in the writing desk, despite its important splotch of blood. Right? So that was what she would obviously have to keep doing. It meant being very clever and very careful. It was trying to fool the whole universe some-how, if the universe was really just a gazillion little rows of dominoes falling, one after the other after the other after the next.

Her mind got as far as this thought and froze a little.

She had another lemon drop.

Pauline Vian was tugging on her sleeve.

"Wherever did this compass toy come from?" she was asking.

An ebony bird gave it to me.

Maya squidged the lemon drop over to the side of her mouth.

"It's complicated," she said.

The car veered to the right.

"Wait," said Valko. "I think—keep going a little—yes!"

He turned around to the backseat passengers and waved the compass in the air.

"Okay! We must be almost there!"

"How do you know?" said Maya, while James made the whole backseat bounce up and down to mark his impatience.

"The needle's not stuck pointing in any one direction now. It moves a little every time we move. Let's get out. I'll show you."

Cousin Louise parked the car on the edge of the road and peered out through the glass. They were deep in the Fontainebleau woods: bare November trees as far as the eye could see and a low piney ridge dribbled with boulders.

"There should be good picnic places over that way, among the rocks," said Cousin Louise. "*Bon!* Out you all get! Bring the food!"

"So it is no pole at all, but a particular place," said Pauline Vian, as she scrambled out of the backseat and pulled her sweater closer around her. "From the perspective of magnetism, that makes no sense whatsoever. How can it possibly be working, this little mechanism? I don't understand it, not at all."

"Neither do I," said Valko with a grin. "This way!"

What Maya found herself understanding was that H de F's compass was like somebody running a large-scale game of hot-and-cold. The needle pointed, and they followed (hot!). When they swerved off course, the needle veered back in the other direction (cold!). It took them right up the piney hillside toward all those quite incredible clumps of boulder—toward one particular pile of boulders, in fact.

"You've been looking for a rock?" said Pauline. She put her hand on it, testingly. "But this is just sandstone. It couldn't be the least bit magnetic."

They stood in a semicircle looking up at one of the strangest of the boulders, the long end of which stuck right out in the air like the head of a huge and ancient turtle.

"It's magic," said James, who seemed quite satisfied. "It's a magic pole, and maybe before it was rock it used to be a dinosaur."

Valko laughed, but James was already out of sight again, circumnavigating the huge stone dinosaur that the South-Southeast Pole had so surprisingly turned out to be.

Maya was thinking, *I've seen this rock before. Where have I seen this rock?*

And Cousin Louise started looking through the bag of picnic provisions at her side.

"James—," she said, with the tone of someone about to start assigning small helpful tasks.

"I'm WAY UP HERE!" said James, from somewhere up above them.

Well, *way up there* was pretty much right—James was shinnying up the lizard-like head of the thing, too many feet above the ground for Maya's comfort. Cousin Louise had already leaped to her feet again.

"James!" said Cousin Louise. "Descend from there! Immediately!"

"My dinosaur has a name," said James as he scooted (reluctantly) back down. "Someone painted it right on his side."

"You mean graffiti?" said Maya. Sometimes it was a good thing that James couldn't read very well. Valko caught her eye, grinned, and ducked behind the boulder to see what awful thing might be scrawled there. He was back in a second, with surprise scrawled all over his face.

"You look," he said to Maya, so Maya and Pauline both followed him around the rock's corner, where in fairly neat lines of white paint someone had written *Rocher de la salamandre.*

"Ah," said Pauline. "The rock climbers. They like to name their rocks."

"So it's almost a dinosaur," called Valko to James. "But not quite: it says this is the Rock of the Salamander."

"Oh," said James. He was trying to decide whether or not he was disappointed. Dinosaurs are pretty cool, being so large and so extinct. But those sneaky salamanders kept turning up everywhere. And sneakiness is pretty cool, too.

"Well! Time for lunch," said Cousin Louise briskly. "Maya, you are looking rather perplexed."

"I'll be okay in a minute," said Maya. "Could I see that compass a moment? I'll catch up."

Cousin Louise gave her a look, but moved everyone a little distance away along the hillside, to a place where the rocks looked better for sitting.

Maya hardly noticed them leaving. She was looking at the compass again, at the funny salamander molded into its cover, standing on its tiny little metal rock. *To the Origin Point*—that's what it said on the back.

"Here?" she said to herself. "Really? Here?"

Because she had finally remembered where she had seen the Rock of the Salamander before. It had only been pen-and-ink, of course, only the sketchiest of sketches, but a pen-and-ink little boy had been peeking into a hollow of it, with his pen-and-ink mother watching, in her long, old-fashioned skirts, at his side.

She walked around the boulder, looking.

There was maybe more earth around the base of it, more debris gathered over time, or something. But she finally found what might once have been the top of a hollow. With a little loose rock, she started working away at the earth there. The dirt was packed pretty tight, but to her relief, right underneath that thin-packed layer, the ground gave way, and her hand was reaching into a small cave tucked away under the rock itself.

"What are you doing? What's in that gap?" said Valko.

She hadn't heard Valko come up behind her. Maya was almost flat on the ground now, stretching her hand into the cool darkness of that hidden hollow place. It was like the entire universe had just turned itself into some immensely complex lens, and all the world's attention was focused exactly *here*. She was no longer just Maya, but a part of that intensely focused attention.

"It was in the book," she said, while her fingers kept exploring the earth and rock of that hidden place, following the curves of the stone, the edge—the straight edge—cold and metallic—of a little box.

"It's really here," she said, surprise shivering right back up her arm. "It's here!"

"What's here?" said Valko. "What book?"

She shifted around, scrabbled a little, and finally found a piece of something to grab on to.

"This," she said, and out into the cold autumn air came her dusty, triumphant hand . . . and the hundred-year-old box of the Fourcroys.

8

THE SUMMER BOX

"I didn't think it really existed," said Maya.

She was sitting up now, leaning against the boulder with the old metal box cradled in her lap. The stone was cold against her back, and the box was cold in her hands, and the November air was cold in her lungs, but all her blood was flush with success, and nothing else quite mattered.

"What's in it?" said Valko. "Why didn't you tell me we were looking for a box?"

"I didn't know that was what we were doing," said Maya. "I didn't know until I recognized the rock, and I couldn't have told you any earlier, anyway, because I hadn't seen those letters until last night."

She tried to explain to him how that handmade story had made her feel, the mother and little Henri on their adventure together in the woods, the love that had been inked into those pictures, but she knew she wasn't making very much sense. And Valko was a thousand percent not interested in mushy stories written a hundred years ago.

"So it's Fourcroy's own box?" he said. "Um. Do you have a flamethrower or something we could zap it with?"

"From when he was a little kid," said Maya. "He came here with his mother. They used to put stuff in the box at the end of the summer."

"I don't care who he came here with," said Valko. "I'm just thinking *we* shouldn't have come here. You don't see that?"

"Oh," said Maya.

She did see that, actually. It looked bad, following compasses given to you by carved ravens belonging to shadows who had very sneakily bound you to bring them back to life. It looked like following instructions. It *was* following instructions.

But she couldn't help feeling curious, too.

It had all been so long ago. The little boy and his mother had stopped coming, but no one had found the box, it was hidden so cleverly, and now climbers had been clambering on the boulders above it for a hundred years, not even guessing there was treasure under them. If it was treasure at all, of course.

"Don't touch it!" said Valko. This made very little sense, because Maya had had the box in her hands for minutes and minutes already.

She looked at him.

"No, really," said Valko. "If it's part of his plan. I thought we were trying not to follow his plan. His stupid list from the stupid Salamander House."

They had been over that list a million times: some kind of *physical remnant* (that blood splotch Maya had managed to leave behind in the writing desk—the only wiggle-roomish thing she had pulled off so far, really); his *memories* (left in the stone wall, said the letter: all right, leave walls alone); and *Maya, the willing, self-sacrificing apprentice* (Maya scowled all over again), all brought to a *Suitable Magical Place*—

"And it said we would get there if we 'follow the guide'!" said Maya. Of course! The compass was the guide. And they had followed it. (*Clickety-clickety-clickety*: billions of little dominoes, toppling in obedient rows.)

So this must be what old Fourcroy thought of as a Suitable Magical Place. Well, yes, that made sense. The place he used to come with his mother, all those long years ago.

"Then what should we do with the box?" said Valko. "I can't believe you let us just go dancing off after that compass."

"Get it away from here," said Maya. She did feel that, very urgently. "If this is the Suitable Place, then we should keep everything away, right? Anything he might need."

Though she remembered the strange magic spilling through Paris that morning, the feeling in her outstretched hand as the croissants turned into Something Else, and for a sliver of a moment she felt all unsteady again.

"Or leave it alone," said Valko. "Or—I'm not kidding—find that flamethrower and melt it down."

That, however, was when Cousin Louise started calling Maya's name, and Cousin Louise, at that moment, sounded like someone whose nice picnic has been compromised by the rudeness of some young person who could not be bothered to sit down politely with her friends and family and spread some goat cheese on her baguette. She also sounded like she was coming their way, and at a clip.

"Quick," said Maya. "Your backpack."

She didn't give Valko time to protest. She stuffed the box into his bag, and they darted out from behind the Salamander Rock just in time to meet Cousin Louise and (in the case of Valko, who had particular talents of this sort) disarm her with extreme politeness before her full displeasure could be unleashed.

"We are all going to be icicles by the time you've finished your lunch" was all Cousin Louise had a chance to say before Valko's embassy manners had taken full effect. "And we've found some interesting things, too, so come along—with rapidity, please."

The others had found pebbles, and beetles, and a kind of stone hut built into the hillside, where climbers and walkers could hide themselves from a sudden rainstorm.

"How old is this place, do you think?" asked Maya, as she stuck her head into its musty shadows.

It felt ancient. She was glad to duck back out again.

Cousin Louise looked up at the slightly graying sky.

"Time to move on, *mes enfants*."

Daylight didn't last forever, especially not in November. And they had had their picnic quite late.

On the ride back into Paris, Maya sat in the front seat, where the ride would be easier on her stomach. In the backseat, Pauline told James a long, intense story about the violinist Paganini, whose fingers were longer and nimbler than anyone else's in the whole world, and who was rumored to have sold his soul to the devil in exchange for his talent.

"Which was a very ugly rumor," said Pauline, but she told the story with no small gusto, anyway.

James was listening with rapt attention. Maya could hear his breath catch when Pauline came to some particularly gruesome bit.

"Pauline, it's too scary," he said finally. "You wouldn't do that, would you?"

"Do what?"

"You know. Sell your soul to the devil, just to be able to—what you said—*trill* better. Or stuff. To play really fast on your violin."

There was a pause. The outskirts of Paris were flashing by outside, streetlamps and buildings against a backdrop of darkness.

"It's just a story," said Pauline Vian.

It wasn't just the scariness of Pauline's violin stories that made James slump back against the seat of the car: he was disappointed because the compass was broken.

Ever since the Rock of the Salamander, it didn't seem to work like a compass at all anymore. The needle flapped around, pointing this and that way, depending on who was holding it. Pointing in the general direction of Valko's feet, of course, where the backpack lay nestled, but Maya didn't think James had figured this out. Pauline was a different matter. She took the compass and looked at it and looked at Valko, and heaven knows what she was thinking.

"A strange little thing," she said finally. "Bizarre!"

"And now it's all broken," said James sadly. "I liked it better when it still worked."

They had to leave Pauline off at the quite elegant apartment house where she lived with her parents—"who are *hyper*-busy," she said with a frown. "They run great big important things, you see, like *banks*"—and then Cousin

Louise dropped the rest of them off at the Davidsons' building without coming up to say good night herself, because she was eager to get back to her own little apartment on the other side of Paris.

And what was in the Summer Box? Treasure?

"Not even one single pathetic little gold coin!" said Valko, after they had teased the latch open. He really did sound disappointed. "What's the point of that? A lot of random junk. Looks like my desk drawer."

What Maya was noticing, though, was that each piece of the "random junk" carried a tag, a slip of paper tied on with string. And on each tag was a year.

The envelope containing one little wisp of baby hair, tied up in a ribbon: 1901. And the envelope had his name on it, written in the same spidery, loving hand as that little story that had gotten mixed up in Maya's dreams the night before: *Henri de Fourcroy.*

Other things, as well: a silver rattle (1902). From other years, a toddler's cap, and pretty stones, and seashells, and even a miniature spyglass that turned out to make colorful patterns when you pointed it in the direction of the nearest window.

And the 1907 tag was tied to a bunch of long and ragged ribbons.

"Rags," said Valko. "Who would bother keeping that

in a treasure box for a hundred years?"

For a moment Maya was stumped, but only for a moment. Then she smiled.

"It's the tail of his kite," she said. "The whole of the kite wouldn't fit."

"Huh," said Valko. "Could be, I guess."

He was rummaging around in the box still.

"And that's the last year mentioned," he said. "No 1908 anywhere. I guess they stopped coming."

They were both silent for a moment, wondering about that. Then Maya went and got the gargoyles' egg from its hiding place in her closet. It warmed up at her touch, almost (she thought) as if it had been sleeping away the hours while she was off tromping through castles and forests.

"I like the idea of a Summer Box," said Maya. "Look how well the egg fits in here, too."

It looked quite cozy, the egg, dreaming away in the little nest of silk she made for it. There were forests spreading across its surface now, pine woods and trees.

Valko narrowed his eyes.

"I don't understand why you won't get rid of that thing," he said. "Why would someone leave a stone egg on your fire escape? Wish we knew how it *works*."

"Very Advanced Technology," suggested Maya. She was teasing him, but he didn't notice.

When Valko had left, Maya took the egg back out of

the box. She liked the feel of it in her hands. It needed her, she could tell. It appreciated being taken care of. (Did some part of her know she was being strangely foolish about this egg? Oh, yes. But still.) Those messages continued to scribble themselves across its surface, those numbers and words, but more and more it seemed to— how could she put this?—to *relax*, somehow, right the way out of language and into those flowing, changing pictures she loved.

The piney woods, the little ridges, the extraordinary boulders . . . The egg, warm in her hands, was echoing back at her the very places she had seen that day (but where Cousin Louise had parked her vivid green car, the egg showed an old-fashioned carriage, the horses patiently waiting).

Something had been nagging at her all day. What was it the story had said?

. . . back to the place where he was born.

Really?

It was like she had been sleepwalking, and now suddenly her mind was clear.

She tucked the egg away for the night in the Summer Box, and started more methodically through the oldest of those old letters, looking for the ones with dates around the turn of the century.

The writing was so hard to read.

There were love letters to "dearest little Yvonne," "my fairy-child Yvonne," "my wild girl of the woods," from 1899 and 1900; he had been a chemist or an engineer, hadn't he, that long-ago Fourcroy? He signed his notes with an illegible scrawl and a quickly sketched Eiffel Tower, so that was probably a clue.

"Fairy-child" was pretty over-the-top romantic lingo for an engineer, thought Maya, still scanning through the notes. It was not the sort of thing she could imagine her own father saying, adorable in his way as her own father undoubtedly was.

It was clear that that Fourcroy fellow had been head over heels in love with the girl from the magical woods.

And then, there it was: part of an ancient newspaper page, tucked in with all the letters. She held it very gingerly, but the edges still crumbled away at her touch.

It seemed to love dramatic stories, this paper, but Maya skipped the details of DREADFUL MURDER IN MALAKOFF!! and BRAZEN BURGLAR STEALS DIAMONDS WHILE ALL SLEEP! because her eyes had seen a third headline that set her heart beating fast:

HAPPY RESOLUTION TO FOURCROY AFFAIR!!

All Paris is agog at the harrowing story of Madame de Fourcroy, whose end-of-summer excursion to the forest of Fontainebleau became an unexpected and terrifying adventure—due to a coachman's sudden lapse into unconsciousness, an overturned carriage in the unpopulated depths of the woods, and the provocation, through fear and anxiety alone, of that most perilous Labor a woman must perform. "Frightened?" said the brave new paragon of Heroic Motherhood, whose rescue yesterday brought tears of joy to the most jaded Parisian eyes. "No! In our family the most talented and magical babies are always born in the woods—" But here her loving husband, the eminent engineer Gilles de Fourcroy, put an abrupt end to our interview and drew his beautiful wife and new infant most protectively to his side. . . .

Aha! thought Maya. There it was. The family joke, Maya's own mother had said. So the girl from the forest had run back to the woods to give birth to her possibly magical child. The little Henri!

There were fewer love letters after 1901, she noticed. Perhaps it was a blow to the ego of Gilles de Fourcroy to have become a scandal in the newspapers. People didn't like that, back in the old days. (Some people still didn't.)

A little card almost slipped through her fingers, but it turned out to be another piece of the puzzle: a birth announcement for a Robert de Fourcroy, dated February 14, 1908. The summers had gone differently from then on, she imagined. She hadn't been much older herself when baby James was born. You have a lot of years to get used to being the only child, when there's a gap like that. Not that she hadn't loved him right away! James had been the sweetest, most remarkable baby. He had laughed aloud when he was only four weeks old! But however special the little brother is that comes along when you're as old as six or seven, you know all too clearly what you've lost, too.

So that was definitely the Suitable Magical Place: the place where old Fourcroy had been born the first time, so very long ago.

Now he wanted to be born there again. And every step Maya took kept being exactly the step *he* wanted her to take. It was true. Valko was right.

I'm going to find a way, though, said Maya to herself. It was a promise: she was somehow going to find a way—no matter how bound the shadowy Fourcroy might think she was—to wiggle herself free.

9

ROSEMARY AND HONEY

The next day, however, as soon as James went off to brush his teeth, Maya's mother leaned across the breakfast table (not that she herself had eaten anything to speak of, Maya couldn't help noticing) and rested her hand on Maya's.

"Sweetheart," she said. "We need to talk."

Her eyes were dark and kind in her stretched-thin face. She really looked more like a tired, ghostly fairy than like somebody's flesh-and-blood mother.

Maya could feel her tongue becoming stupid.

"Now?" she said.

"Well, it was your birthday," said her mother. "And then yesterday you were gone all day. I'm sending James to the Luxembourg Gardens with your dad. He likes the carousel there, all those wooden horses and the grumpy man who lets the rings down for the kids to catch. That will give us some nice private time, before Pauline comes over to practice."

"Oh!" said Maya in alarm. She remembered the darkness seeping out of the walls. "Should you be doing that? That piece she played was so awful."

Maya's mother had one of those smiles that brought every inch of her face to life.

"Poor thing! She needs help, that's all. She really does. That's why I offered."

"But it made you so sick!" said Maya. "I saw your face. Didn't you notice? And the shadows started coming. . . ."

The smile faded.

"Oh, Maya, you should not have to worry so much about me. It's not right, the way you worry. That's why I didn't—but anyway, let me get James and your father packed off to the park, and then we can finally talk."

Here's what Maya felt then: panic. Her heart was racing and her ears were very cold or very hot—she couldn't tell which—and if she stayed sitting still at that table one more minute, something terrible was going to happen. She had wanted to know. She had kept asking her mother to be honest with her, to tell her the truth, but now the truth was too close, was waiting at the door, was almost right there in front of her, and she found she didn't so much want it, after all. Not this morning. Not right now. Right now she just wanted to hide.

The terrible hot/cold worry brought her right to her

feet, made her stand there trembling for a moment, on the verge of some kind of precipice, like a newly hatched chick on the terrible edge of its nest.

"What's wrong?" said her mother. "Maya!"

"I—I forgot," said Maya, bumbling all of it. "I have to go. Valko—"

"But you just saw him yesterday."

"Ice cream," said Maya. "Maybe we'll have ice cream."

"In November!" said her mother. She was settling back into her chair now, resigned. Maybe even—unless Maya's eyes were playing tricks on her—just the slightest bit relieved. It was probably pretty awful for a mother, too, having to have this kind of conversation with her own oldest child. "Well, dress warmly, then."

"It's just—they want to make him go back to horrible Bulgaria," said Maya, all of a sudden remembering. She wasn't being fair to Bulgaria, probably, but then again, Bulgaria wasn't being very fair to her, either, was it?

"Oh, Maya," said her mother. "Really? Not in the middle of the year."

She did look very distressed on Maya's behalf. It just made Maya feel worse about the panic in her ears and her head and her feet. A better daughter would not run away from her sick mother and from the truth. But here she was, already grabbing her jacket. She was saying goodbye. She was rushing out the door.

She walked around a couple of blocks' worth of Paris, shaking the tears out of her eyes and trying not to run into bundled-up little children and their errand-running parents on the rue Cler. The displays of lettuces and squashes and leeks in the market on the corner looked as jewel-like as ever. The women of the charcuterie were already grilling sandwich fillings outside their store and trading jokes with each other, and the outside tables of the corner café were all occupied, despite the chilliness of the air. It all looked so cheerful and normal.

But Maya didn't feel cheerful *or* normal.

One thing at a time, she told herself. That was the phrase she used to use to get through the bad days, back when her mother had first gotten sick. *One thing at a time.*

Only here, which *one thing* was she even supposed to tackle? They were all so huge and so shapeless; there weren't any helpful little angles to grab on to.

Her mother was sick again.

Valko was maybe being sent away.

Strangeness was warping the universe (at least the little corner of the universe near the Bulgarian embassy).

A shadow that had once been the purple-eyed Fourcroy wanted Maya to bring him back to life.

In fact, she might be caught up already in his instructions' clockwork spell.

She might. It was hard to know.

She was trying not to be clockwork, but how could she know for sure?

Because for one thing, she was certainly walking in circles. She had passed by the charcuterie three times by now. One of the women there actually gave her a sympathetic smile and tilt of the head on the third loop by—that was embarrassing. Maya turned around in some haste and went the other way, back to the sidewalk outside the ice-cream shop on the rue de Grenelle.

Where someone gave her a friendly tug on the elbow.

"Hey," said Valko. "Your mother said I'd probably find you here."

She was so surprised to see him there that for a moment she forgot how miserable she was.

"But I just made up that bit about ice cream!" she said.

"I figured," said Valko. "But here you are. And me, too. Let's pretend it's summer and get ice-cream cones anyway. Then we'll both have been telling the truth all along."

Valko chose the mint that had real little shreds of mint leaf sprinkled through it, and Maya went for a flavor she had passed by and wondered about a million times, but never tried: rosemary and honey.

"'There's rosemary; that's for remembrance,'" said the ice-cream woman with a smile as she dipped her scoop

165

into the bin. "That's your Shakespeare, *mademoiselle.* Rosemary for remembrance, and rosemary also for staying true. But the honey makes it sweet, *non?*"

It was so different from the usual vanilla or strawberry or chocolate! A powerful combination, herb and blossom: it tasted like summer, maybe even like magic.

She found herself, despite everything, feeling the tiniest bit encouraged.

Of course, it helped having Valko there, discussing the fruits of his latest research. (That's what he said, with one eyebrow raised: *the fruits of his research.*)

"Two important things," he said. "No, three. First of all, remember how I cleverly paused, despite those awful, crazy women kind of being after us, to leave a mark at the edge of the strangeness yesterday?"

Maya tried, but failed, to remember that particular detail, but she made a noncommittal sound from behind her ice cream, and Valko took that as a yes.

"So I went back last night on my way home and did some measuring. I mean, only approximate measuring, because I don't have one of those wheels they use to measure distance. Have you seen those?"

Maya shook her head.

"Well, they're pretty cool, but I never thought I would actually need to own one. Anyway, here's the thing: the first time we saw that shadow, the strangeness spread about a hundred meters out from, let's say, the hole in the wall. I think that's the center. I made a lot of marks that first time, so I'm pretty sure about that. But yesterday the radius was twice that. Two hundred meters."

Maya tried to remember how far they had run, to get to the place where the air was normal again. (She still wasn't very good at meters; a meter's a little bit more than a yard.)

"So that means it's either moving or growing," said Valko.

"You think it's going to happen again?"

"That's the second thing!" said Valko. He sounded oddly cheerful for someone talking about the world warping. "It was eight a.m. yesterday, right? Well, I started messing around with the calendar a little. The time before was four p.m. on Friday the twenty-sixth of October. And then I remembered that crazy Saturday night after that uncle of yours really crashed and burned—that was the night the transformer blew a hole in our wall. And you know when that was? *Eleven p.m.*"

He paused and gave Maya the sort of look that meant there was something significant in all of these numbers, and couldn't she see it?

"Go ahead and tell me," said Maya. "About once a week something goes seriously wrong around here. Is that it?"

"Almost!" said Valko. "You know how many hours there are between eleven p.m. Saturday and four p.m. Friday? One hundred thirty-seven. Okay. Now guess how many hours there are between four p.m. Friday and eight a.m. Thursday—if you remember that Daylight Savings Time ended that Sunday, which I did finally remember?"

"You're kidding," said Maya.

"No, not kidding: one hundred thirty-seven exactly," said Valko.

She looked at him.

"That's really random," she said.

Valko grinned.

"What's really random about it is that it's not random at all," he said. "Or maybe it isn't. We can test it, right? If it's every one hundred thirty-seven hours, then the next one will be—"

"Is it Wednesday?" said Maya.

"Wednesday at one a.m. Last day of vacation. I'm waiting up for it."

Maya took the last bite of her cone and frowned.

"It's such an unspecial number," she said. "Why would anything happen every *one hundred thirty-seven* hours?"

Valko shrugged.

"Would you prefer something else?"

"I'd prefer *never*," said Maya. "But that's not a number at all. What was your third thing?"

Valko looked puzzled for only a moment, and then smiled.

"It's the crazy women," he said. "I did some research. You know how they said they were *samodeeeeev*?"

Maya laughed. He mimicked their accent very well.

"Well, I looked into it. . . ."

He gave Maya a sly glance.

"That means I asked my mother. And *she* said that *samodivi* are, ahem, a key part of Bulgarian mythology."

"What do they do?" said Maya.

"Oh, the usual: they sing, they dance, they tear people apart. Like the whatsits in Greece. The ones who hung around Dionysus. Anyway, they're very dangerous, but especially to men."

"Didn't hear them hissing *your* name," said Maya.

"True. Anyway, I told her you had been asking, and she was very impressed."

"I didn't, though."

"Did so: they were coming after us, and they said they were *samodeeeeev*, and you said, and I approximately quote, 'What's that?' So that counts as asking, and now my mother's even more looking forward to meeting you, whenever that is. November twelfth. Just ask lots and lots of mythology questions, and everything will go smooth as silk."

Or I could come down with the flu, thought Maya, *and get out of the fancy embassy banquet altogether.* She filed that away under "Seriously Possible Options."

"So now can I ask you what's worrying you?" said Valko.

She told him. How a better daughter would have bravely stuck around to hear the truth. But not Maya!

"You can handle this," said Valko, after he'd heard a good chunk of her story. "Look at all the other things you've handled. Things are always worse when you don't know."

Maya looked at him with skepticism. She couldn't help wondering how much experience he'd had with really bad news. Because she wasn't sure, anymore, whether knowing everything was really the best way to go. She had been so hopeful, just a week or so ago!

That made her have to look away again.

"Go home and tell her you're sorry and you can handle absolutely anything the world throws at you. Tell her Valko told you so, and he's *always right*."

He had put his arm around her shoulders: a very comforting arm. It would have been pretty okay to stay exactly like that for a year or two, but time doesn't seem to work that way. A few minutes later she was heading back up the stairs to her own apartment, taking the steps steadily and with pretend courage.

Maya's mother came looking for her as soon as Maya was in through the doorway.

"Oh, Maya," said her mother. "I'm so sorry! It must have seemed like I was pouncing on you earlier. I'm so sorry."

"I'm the one who's sorry," said Maya. "I was awful. I don't even know why I bolted like that. I'm not a baby anymore. You can tell me any news you want. Go ahead."

Her mother looked at her a long time, and then smiled that private, sad, lovely smile of hers.

"Come here—come sit next to me on the couch—we'll be comfy together, even without the Blanket."

At home in California they had the coziest, fluffiest throw folded up on the couch in the living room: the Fuzzy Blanket. Snuggling up under it in times of trouble was traditional for the Davidsons.

For a few minutes Maya just enjoyed the old comfort of leaning against her mother, feeling her mother's kind hand smoothing her hair, that sense of being cared for, of not being the one who has to make everything all right. It was like glimpsing that wonderful just-next-door universe for a second, where mothers are never sick and bad things never happen. And that was that, of course: as soon as you start *thinking* again, the window into elsewhere whistles shut.

Maya couldn't help herself: she sighed.

"Oh, sweetie," said her mother, giving her a one-armed squeeze. "I try every trick in the book, just to get you not to worry. But it never works, does it?"

"First bad stuff has to stop happening," said Maya. "Then I wouldn't have to worry."

"Hmm," said her mother. "Well, let's try this. You know I haven't been feeling the greatest, not for a while."

"Yeah," said Maya. Actually, she whispered it: *yeah.*

"Remember when I had what I thought was the flu and ended up in the hospital, back in October?"

"Yeah," said Maya, or at any rate her lips moved the way they would move to say it. *Yeah.*

"And they ran all those tests, just to see what was up. Well"—her mother paused—"it wasn't exactly what we thought."

All right, thought Maya. *I can handle this. Whatever it is: step by step.*

"The thing is: I'm having a baby."

It was exactly like being clonked over the head with a saucepan.

"WHAT?" said Maya, her spine snapping straight again. "What? What did you say?"

"I'm pregnant," said her mother. "I know, it's a big surprise.

"You *can't* be!" said Maya. Maybe it was more like

being clonked over the head with an enormous, very cold icicle. Alarm was still zigzagging all through her, and her stomach was doing something funny with itself. "I thought the medicines—I thought that was something they did to you! You can't be *pregnant*!"

"It was unlikely," said Maya's mother. "But it was never impossible."

"And you didn't tell me!"

"Because you would just worry. And it was so early. There was no telling, you know, whether it would even stick around, the little bean. But it seems to be hanging in there, so far, and in a few days we'll be at three months, and—"

"It's not safe!" said Maya. "It can't be safe! You've been so sick. What if this—what if it—"

It couldn't be safe. All those cells growing and dividing. You didn't want that happening, if you'd had cancer. Did you? Maya felt the horror of it spreading through her. It wasn't *safe*.

"Oh, Maya!" said her mother, and her eyes were stubborn and full of sympathy, both at the same time. "Nothing is safe! Nothing in life is safe! But I thought about it, and I thought about it, and I have to go back to living, to moving forward. I can't just hide away somewhere, half alive, half not."

"I can't believe you did this," said Maya. It took her

aback a little, how angry she suddenly felt. "I can't believe it. What about James? He needs you to be okay! I need you to be okay! How could you do this?"

Maya's mother didn't respond for a minute. She just smoothed Maya's hair against her head, again and again. It was calming, even though part of Maya was mad enough not to want to be calmed.

"You've been through too much," said her mother finally. "That's the thing. I know it. And I'm so, so sorry about it. But I think this might end up all right. We have to let go. We can't control the future. Right? But sometimes things do go fine."

Not nearly often enough, in Maya's experience. But what could she say?

"Can you let go of this a little bit?" said Maya's mother. "This is your vacation still. You enjoy these free days of yours. Don't let worries weigh you down. Hmm, Maya? In fact, I know what we could do right now, before Pauline comes over to frighten our poor ears. You could show me that box of old letters. . . ."

And she tipped her head toward the table, where there was indeed a nice, clear spot, all ready for papers.

When Maya, still a bit shattered around the edges, was pulling the box of letters from under the bed in her room, her fingers knocked against the other box, the Summer Box, and she drew it out, too, more slowly. The egg wanted her to peek in on it as it slumbered there in its silks. It was so beautiful! Something that beautiful should not be hidden away in a dark box—at least, not always. Not all the time. Not when someone like Maya's mother was around, who was so precious and fragile and who so loved beautiful things.

Before she had thought much further, the egg was in one hand, the box of letters in the other, and Maya was heading back out to the dining table, where her mother was waiting.

"Oh!" said her mother, when Maya set the gargoyles' egg down on the table in front of her. "What is that?"

"It came on my birthday," said Maya. "It's so beautiful, I wanted to show you."

"Your birthday?" said her mother, taking the egg very gently into her own hands. "But it's amazing, Maya. Look how there are trees painted on it. No, not painted. How's that done? And writing, too. How interesting! What does it say, do you know?"

"I think it says, 'Keep me safe,'" said Maya. "'Keep me secret and keep me safe.' I figure showing you is still pretty secret. And that's my name there; look. It's all in Bulgarian."

"Oh!" said her mother again, and this time she really did seem startled. "Oh, Maya. *Valko* gave this to you?"

"It's a gargoyles' egg," said Maya, seeing she was going

to have to do some sidestepping.

"That's clever," said her mother, with a smile that went very quickly from amusement to worry. "But it must be awfully valuable, don't you think? I just wonder whether Valko's parents—"

She must have caught a glimpse of Maya's face, because she brought herself up short.

"No, there I'm being silly. Just because it's so lovely and so different. It's a wonderful present, Maya, really. I've never seen anything like it. I can see why it says to keep it safe. You will, won't you? You'll keep it very safe?"

"Yes," said Maya.

She wasn't sure about those gargoyles—they had had an agenda, sure, but then they had gone away.

And whatever the gargoyles were up to, their egg was beautiful, and it needed her help and her care.

Even her mother thought so, so that was that.

Maya Davidson made the promise deep in her heart: she would never let any kind of harm come to her mother, no matter what crazy thing her mother had fallen into. It was up to her to keep them all safe: her mother, the mysterious future new brother or sister (that her mind still rebelled against, to tell the truth), and the gargoyles' egg.

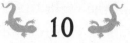

10

THINGS BEND— UNTIL THEY BREAK

Now, how does a person get permission from his or her parents to wander the streets of Paris at one a.m., checking the latest warpings of the laws of physics? Well, clearly, one doesn't. Permission is not there for the getting.

That had Valko, in particular, scratching his head. As he explained to Maya (who tried very hard to see the whole matter from his perspective, since it clearly meant so much to him), this was the first chance in his whole life to test an important scientific hypothesis (the Strangeness-Repeats-Every-137-Hours-and-the-Radius-of-the-Strangeness-Grows-by-100-Meters-Each-Time Hypothesis) in a scientific way. It was better than all those years watching the barometer.

"Well, if you stay up until one, you'll still know the main thing," said Maya. It was a drizzly, cold Tuesday, perfect for convincing you that winter was on its disheartening way. "You'll know the timing."

"But there's just no way I'm going to be able to sneak out in the middle of the night to see how far it spreads this time," said Valko. "There's *no way*. They've put in all this extra security at the embassy, since the wall exploded. Somebody probably thinks that was terrorism, right? Not that they tell me anything. So what do we do? I'm stuck."

"We glue five thousand little cameras to walls everywhere?" said Maya.

"Right," said Valko glumly. "Camera-equipped mini robots with night vision."

They were hiding out under the awning of the impossibly fancy chocolate shop on the rue Saint-Dominique: little tiny Parisian monuments in chocolate, chocolate deer, chocolate bunnies, chocolate hearts. Why was it that you could not look at chocolate, even on a chilly day, without thinking of it melting?

That gave Maya an idea.

"The strangeness changes things, right?" she said. "What if we put out markers along the streets, like a trail of chocolate chips or something, and then the next day see which ones have become all crazy and weird?"

Valko grinned.

"That's it!" he said. "You're brilliant. Only not chocolate chips, because the pigeons will get them."

That meant they had to pause to have a little argument about what objects (other than chocolate chips) were most likely to be changed by the strangeness, since it was so unpredictable: paper clips? pebbles? seeds?

"We won't make a mess, though, will we?" said Maya. "We'll have to pick up everything afterward."

"Obviously!" said Valko. "You can't leave data just lying around!"

Now that they had a plan, they had to work fast. They found a spool of plain white thread and a couple of needles in the Davidsons' cleaning closet and made a hundred tiny little loops, onto each of which they threaded a tiny piece of cabbage (this had been Valko's idea: something living, but tough) and a paper clip. Over and over and over: thread cabbage, cut string, tie loop, add paper clip.

It was very tedious work, which, said Valko, just made it all the more authentically scientific.

But Maya preferred it to the next stage, when they walked the streets of the neighborhood, trying to stay very inconspicuous as they sprinkled the sidewalks with little test loops every few meters. It worried her to be doing something so similar to littering, even if it was really experimental research.

The egg that night was more restless than usual. She sat with it a long, long time, watching the forest pictures give way to city streets, city buildings, all sketched in great haste and vanishing almost as soon as they had appeared. She caught a glimpse of the Eiffel Tower, of her own neighborhood as seen from hundreds of feet up in that tower; for a moment the Salamander House itself winked into view and then vanished. Carriages. Horses. Crowds in the streets.

"Go to sleep," she said to it finally, and put it away in the Summer Box to rest.

Then she couldn't get to sleep for the longest time, either. She was bracing herself for that unpleasant feeling of magic washing over her, she realized, as silly as that was, so far from where the strangeness was centered.

And to think that when she was little, she had spent every single possible wish (first stars, birthday candles, white horses, holding-breath-through-tunnels) on "please, oh please, let magic be real!" She had longed for there to be exceptions in the ordinary, boring old everyday rules. And now her long-ago wish was coming true, and here she was, all tense with worry and unable even to sleep!

The thing she hadn't realized, way back then, was that if the world is full of exceptions, then what can you depend on? We want to be able to fly, but we also really, really, really want to know that when we put our foot down on the ground, the ground will be there. Reliably. Boringly. Every single time. We don't want gravity working only when it's in the mood! And that made her smile, finally, because it was such a Valkoish way of thinking about things.

In the end she got stubborn with herself: if the egg could go to sleep, then she could, too. She closed her eyes and toughed her way right into oblivion, so successfully that when the alarm rang the next morning, she felt, first surprised, and then smug.

She had been dreaming about forests, spreading like green fire across a stone-gray world. The tingle of it still danced in her fingertips as she ate her breakfast. Funny how some dreams linger.

Out on the streets it was cold and clear, the drizzle having moved on to bother somebody else's day. Maya walked along her street, picking up unchanged loops of thread with specks of old cabbage on them and tossing them into a shopping bag. If she had been fifty years older, and a little more hunchbacked, she would probably have looked like a crazy old woman. But at the freshly minted age of thirteen, she was not very noticeable. And the few who did notice her gave approving little nods, thinking she was picking up litter for a youth-group project or something.

She must have been on her fortieth loop of thread when she first saw a paper clip that had rolled itself into a little cone. And the miniature bit of cabbage had sprouted roots. She was just sticking the tape on to label it when Valko appeared at the end of the block, inching his way along.

"So? What time was it?" she stage-whispered in his direction.

Valko gave her a thumbs-up: one o'clock, just as they'd thought! (said his hands).

"Let's see what your loops look like," he said aloud, as soon as he'd gotten closer.

She opened her bag.

"Normal, normal, normal, normal—except for this one right here."

She showed him the distorted loop in her hand, but at the same time Valko was holding up his formerly svelte scientific notebook, now as swollen as a python digesting its dinner. He had been more organized than Maya; he was taping each loop to a separate page (and probably keeping track of exactly where he'd found it, too). He flipped through those pages, and on every one was—well, now, how to describe *that*? That notebook would have felt right at home in an art gallery.

Threads of all colors. Threads frayed into a silky splash. Cabbage exploded into bloom or turned crystalline.

"So this is the edge right here," said Valko. "Four hundred meters, this time. That's my guess."

He took the loop in Maya's hand to tape into his note-book, and Maya could see him thinking. His face, before her eyes, was changing from scientific triumph to Dark Worries.

"You see what this means," said Valko.

"It's getting bigger?" said Maya. "We kind of knew that already."

"But we didn't know the rate," said Valko. "Of course, any getting bigger is pretty bad, but this is *doubling*. And if you notice, the effects are staying around longer, too."

Right behind them, the whole sidewalk now kind of lunged to the left, right out into the street. To avoid a stone turtle, whose head came peeking out from a wall. And all the pedestrians were hurrying along that warped bit of sidewalk, as if it had always been that way. The cars made their way carefully around the curve, too, and some of the cars had rubber-and-metal shooting stars or cobras where their windshield wipers used to be. Even though it was hours and hours already since the strange-ness had done these things to the city.

When you bend a piece of plastic the first time, it usu-ally bounces pretty much back. But after a few more bends, the crease will show—it won't fade away. And eventually the plastic breaks.

Then Maya did see what it all meant. After all, one of her favorite picture books when she was little had been about a brave girl who asks a king for a single grain of rice—merely doubled every day. She remembered those enormous, enormous mountains of rice. She stopped walking and looked at Valko, while inside she started doubling numbers and doubling numbers and doubling them again.

"It would be all right for a while," she said. "The first few weeks aren't so bad: four hundred meters, eight hundred meters, sixteen hundred meters. . . ."

"All of Paris in a month," said Valko. He went to a blank page in his notebook and kept doubling. "All of France in three months. How far away is New York? Six thousand kilometers? Anyway, it reaches New York two weeks later. San Francisco the next week. What's the farthest-away place from Paris, do you think? Australia?"

He did one last bit of scribbling, and then put his pencil away.

"Doesn't even matter where the farthest place is," he said. "The week after San Francisco, the strangeness covers the entire world."

"Unless it stops here," said Maya. It seemed like what her mother called *borrowing trouble*, to be worrying already about Australia.

"Unless we stop it here," said Valko. "Look!"

A column of dust and shadow had just turned the corner and was lurching along in their direction, larger and darker and more filled with purpose than it had ever been before. It could be heard faintly rasping something that sounded like her name.

And her fingertips were still tingling.

Already hours and hours after one a.m., and there was still enough hum left in the air for the shadow to be following them about like that!

So that was that: it was getting worse. The world was being bent and bent and bent again, and eventually maybe it would bend too far and be broken, and what does life look like, in a broken world?

They backed down the street to the place the strangeness could not yet reach.

In a month there would be nowhere in Paris to hide.

Valko and Maya looked at each other.

So. They had to stop it, then.

How?

11

NEVER TRUST GARGOYLES.
REALLY. DON'T.

Few things in life are as nerve-racking as heading off to meet (for the first time) the parents of someone who, although a boy, has become one of your best friends in the whole world. But the fates must have really had it in for Maya Davidson, because on top of the meeting-a-nice-boy's-parents-for-the-first-time worries, they had decided to toss in the following further complications:

His parents were Bulgarian.

They ran an embassy in Paris.

They had just announced they wanted to send Valko back to Bulgaria because he wasn't Bulgarian enough, and being friends with Maya was certainly not helping him be more Bulgarian.

The dinner was going to be a formal embassy banquet, probably involving hundreds of mysterious little forks and spoons that Maya would not know how to use.

And, finally, it just so happened that another 137

hours would be elapsing at six p.m. this evening, and that meant the laws of physics would be slightly suspended, in highly unpredictable ways, at more or less the same time as Maya was about to start reaching for the mysterious little forks she didn't know how to use.

Maya's mother didn't know about the spreading strangeness, of course, but because she knew or guessed most of the other items on this list—and because she was on an intense and obvious campaign to keep Maya from worrying so much about everything—she had been trying for several days to be especially kind and reassuring, and that, for some reason, had made Maya feel even more anxious.

Basically, thought Maya as she raced to get into her fancy clothes on Monday after school, no one in the long history of dinner invitations had ever been more full of twitchy, itchy nervousness than she was right now.

She pulled the comb through her nondescript brown hair and put on her party shoes, but when she dropped a barrette on the floor, she caught a glimpse of the Summer Box under her bed, and before she knew it, the gargoyles' egg was cradled in her hands. The warmth of it was so comforting.

There was a new word inscribed on it, she noticed. Now what did that say?

Valko would know.

She emptied all her school books out of her back-pack and popped the egg in instead, wrapped in an extra sweater just in case it got especially cold by the time they were walking back home.

"You look lovely," said her mother, as Maya spun around for a quick inspection in the living room. "Don't forget your scarf and gloves; it's cold tonight. Look, I've got some nice flowers right here, ready to go."

Somehow she made it out of that apartment. The sun was setting as she trotted across the avenue Bosquet, feeling foolish with the bouquet of flowers in her gloved hands. *Flowers (odd number only)—shake hands firmly—eye contact!* She was remembering all the rules for meeting parents from Bulgaria. Oh, and it was five p.m. already. One hundred and thirty-six hours gone; one to go. If the strangeness hadn't evaporated into nothing and spontaneously gone away.

The dinner invitation was for seven p.m., but Valko had said to come earlier, as early as she could manage, before anything odd had had time to happen. He was thinking of the shadow wandering the streets, Maya could tell. He didn't want her out there alone with the shadowy Fourcroy, if another wave of strangeness struck the neighborhood.

In fact, he was at the embassy entrance, waiting for her.

"You'll have to put those flowers through Ivan's

machine," he said with a grin. "I hope they fit."

It was one of those conveyor-belt X-ray machines, just like the airport versions, only smaller.

Ivan wasn't quite as beefy as you'd think a security guy would have to be, but he still would have looked pretty intimidating if he hadn't been joking the whole time with Valko in Bulgarian. Maya balanced on one foot and then another, waiting for the flowers and her backpack to emerge. The egg set off no alarms.

"Your coat's warm, right?" said Valko, and he swung a couple of sodas into sight, as temptation. "Want a nice view? Follow me!"

There were a couple of very grand flights of stairs and then some more stairs, less grand, and then a stairwell that looked like it wouldn't have been out of place in a tubing factory, and then Valko pushed open an old door, and they were on the roof.

"Oh!" said Maya. It was so beautiful. The sunset was still just enough in progress that the sky was the color of a ripe nectarine, and the Eiffel Tower loomed up over the buildings on the other side of the street.

The roof itself had a lot of wires and satellite dishes and who-knows-what sort of contraptions cluttering it up, but there was a low barrier around the edge, so it didn't seem completely perilous. The trees in the Bulgarians' private garden pushed up above the roofline of the building on

189

their left. And there, across the roof, were a couple of figures too small and too still to be human. Maya gripped Valko's arm.

"They're here!" she said, and her voice squeaked a little as she said it. "You didn't tell me they were back. Why didn't you tell me?"

The gargoyles stared stiffly ahead, right at them.

"I haven't been up here in ages," said Valko. "I wonder how those things got here."

"Flew, I guess," said Maya.

She did not like being stared at by stone creatures. Valko hesitated at her side. Neither of them seemed to know quite how frightened they should be, here under the gaze of those so-very-still eyes.

Finally Valko squared his shoulders and flashed a half smile in Maya's direction, his eyes catching fire just a little in the last remnants of the sunset. "They're only statues. Someone must have lugged them up the stairs. Come on. It's a chance to get a really good look, finally."

They picked their way across the rooftop, and the gargoyles stonily watched them come.

"So the question is, How'd someone get these here, without anyone noticing?" said Valko.

That wasn't the question at all, from Maya's perspective. What she wanted to know was what they were up to, and whether they were evil, and what the heck gargoyles had to do with Bulgaria, and why they seemed to do all their moving around in one high-speed burst in the middle of the night.

No, none of that was the first thing she wanted to know. The first thing she wanted to know was why exactly they had given her the beautiful egg. She really wanted to know that. But it's hard to get answers from a creature carved out of stone.

"I'm still curious about what they're made of, too," said Valko, dropping the sodas to fumble around in his pockets for a moment. "I could try scraping a little sample off with my knife. See if it's that fake plastery stuff they use for decorations sometimes—that would be easy to lug across Paris—"

"Wait—what are you doing?" said Maya. It made her nervous, seeing Valko walk right up close to those staring, staring gargoyles with his Swiss Army knife in his hand. In fact, it made her nervous in two ways at once: for Valko, whose little knife was really very small, compared to the statues watching him approach, and for the gargoyles, because . . . um, knives? Knives are sharp. Nobody wants somebody poking at them with knives. Maybe even a gargoyle made of stone wouldn't want knives coming his way.

"Valko, *don't!*" she said. Couldn't he feel it? That crackle in the air around the gargoyles' staring, monstrous, mishmashy heads? It was the smell of rocks beginning to lose their temper. It was the invisible sharpness in the air, right before a mountain gives way and becomes boulders and talus, screaming down the slope.

She was just reaching forward to haul him safely back when the world exploded. Din and dust! The harsh clatter of stone wings, rubble, pebbles, boulders, rocks! And there in the middle of all that noise, a human gasp— Valko. And then silence again. Instantly.

The mountain had fallen, and everything was different. Valko was staring up at her from the rooftop with wide, horrified eyes, but he could not move, because around his neck was folded a stony and inflexible wing. And a stone talon gripped Valko's right arm, and Valko's fingers splayed out a little, under the pressure of all that stone, and on the ground beside him, looking very weak and small and ridiculous, was his red pocketknife.

"Maya, go!" said Valko to Maya. He could only croak it, because the wing was too close around his throat. It was horrible, seeing that stone wing pinning him so tightly and so awkwardly to the ground and to the gargoyle behind him. The gargoyle was the one she had been calling Beak-Face; she could see that now. With its sharp, cruel stone nose. The other gargoyle was frozen just behind, a look of anger or horror or shock carved into the stone of its face.

It all made Maya very, very mad. She was instantly almost drowning in fury, to tell the truth. She jumped forward and pounded on the gargoyle's back (but being very careful not to pound on places that might jar Valko trapped beneath).

"LET HIM GO," she said, so mad that every word of hers was huge and wild and loud. "DON'T YOU EVEN KNOW WHO I AM? DON'T YOU KNOW WHAT I HAVE?"

She leaped back a pace, opened her backpack, and pulled it out—the gargoyles' beautiful, lovely, wonderful egg.

Another explosion! Rocks and wings and motion and noise!

And then that sudden stillness again. On the school playground, when Maya was very little, the kids used to play a game called red light/green light—run for green, freeze for red. This was a little like that. But no child on a playground ever froze as convincingly as these gargoyles froze. They were the world champion stars of Not Moving.

And now they were both using all of their incredible Not-Moving skills to gaze straight at Maya and at the stone egg (humming with warmth) in her hand. Valko was climbing to his feet again, over a little on Maya's left—he was trying to say something, and mostly all he could do was cough. But the gargoyles had let him go.

Good, thought Maya. But she didn't move her head to look at Valko. She was staring down those stone gargoyles with all the force she could muster. She jogged the egg up and down in her hand a little, just to give them something to think about.

"You listen to me," she said to the gargoyles. "See this pretty egg? If you want it to stay safe, you know what? You have to LEAVE US ALONE. Go home to whatever stupid cathedral you came from. Go away. Go home. Good-bye. Valko, are you okay?"

"It's like something fell on me," said Valko. Still stunned, it sounded like. "I think. Something heavy. Let's get out of here."

Good idea. Maya took a step backward, but she kept her eyes on those gargoyles.

"And don't keep exploding like that," Maya said to them. "You've got to slow down. Act normal. Okay. That's it."

"Did you just tell a couple of statues to *slow down*?" said Valko. That was more like his ordinary self, so that was good.

"When they move, they move too fast. Right? It's like they're movies playing themselves at the wrong speed. WHICH I DON'T LIKE." (That was for the gargoyles again.) "Now we're really leaving—come on, Valko.

194

REMEMBER I HAVE THE EGG AND LEAVE US ALONE."

They had gotten almost as far as the staircase door when there was another, slightly slower, eruption of stone and noise.

Valko gave a horrified yelp.

This time Maya could make more sense of what she was seeing: Beak-Face and Bonnet-Head leaning close together, *consulting*, some waving around of claws, then Beak-Face coming forward—all that took place in a second or two, but suddenly, as the gargoyle walked toward Maya, it was like a film running out of power: the speed dropped, dropped, kept dropping, until he was hardly moving at all.

"Mmmmmaaaaaaa—," said the gargoyle, in the rumbling, ghastly tones of a tape being run at the slowest possible speed.

Valko yanked on Maya's arm.

"Come *on*," he said.

He had a point, but Maya couldn't help herself: she was fantastically, overwhelmingly curious. (And a stone wing had not just been wrapped around *her* throat, which she could see might make a difference in how a person felt about stone gargoyles moving toward her and making almost word-like noises—wait . . . *word-like?*)

"Hang on a sec," she said. "I think it's trying to—"

"—yaa," said the gargoyle. Yes: it *said*. A stone gargoyle was *speaking* to them. "Maaayaa. Maya. Maya. *Zdrasti. Bonsoir.* Hello! Go away. Egg. Keep it safe. No. Aaaaah."

The creature turned his ugly face back to Bonnet-Head and made some clattering noises in its—no, *her*—direction. Bonnet-Head waddled forward a little, her wings sketching anxious little wringing gestures in the air.

"Deeeearrr," said Bonnet-Head. A sandy landslide of a word, all kind concern.

Maya felt an instant and surprising burst of affection for Bonnet-Head.

"But statues aren't *supposed* to talk," said Valko's faint voice behind her. "They don't *move*. They don't *talk*. They don't *grab people and strangle them*."

"He's rrright," said Beak-Face. "Sstone. Doesn't sspeak. Doesn't move. At all. No."

"Norrrrrmally," corrected the other one. Bonnet-Head. "But the bad man ruined us with his loophole. He did."

They seemed to be very quick learners, these gargoyles. Their words were already sounding much more like actual words (and much less like a mountain giving way under your feet).

"Yess," said Beak-Face. When he scowled, his whole

cobbled-together body seemed to twist in on itself. It looked painful.

"We need to get out of here," said Valko from somewhere behind Maya. "We really need to get out of here. Now."

"What do you mean, *ruined you with his loophole*?" said Maya. She put her free hand on her hips, to keep herself feeling tough.

Valko made a not-very-coherent protesting sound and tugged on her jacket.

"Bad man," said Beak-Face, still twisted into that whole-body scowl. "Digs into What Is and makes his big loophole so he can go on living."

"Loophole?" said Maya. It seemed a strange word for a gargoyle to use. "Like a way of cheating?"

"Cheating," said Beak-Face. "Yess! Also: hole in a wall. It can mean that, too. Bad hole that opens in a good stone wall. Things climb through loopholes: magic things, that should not be. Not just What Is, but everything that could be."

"Like us," said Bonnet-Head. "A block of stone, yess? May not just be a block of stone. May also possibly be a *box of gargoyles*. Ugh."

"*Ugh* is right," said Valko, from behind Maya's back. "Really, let's go."

Maya said, "You were made from the wall?"

197

"A trrrrranslation," said Bonnet-Head, with gusto.

Translation?

Maya must have looked puzzled.

"Nice sssilent sstone," Bonnet-Head explained, *"trrranslated* into gargoyles! Is it a word you don't know? It means changing things, yess? From one form to anotherr, you know. From sstone into gargoyles. And he got right into us, too, the bad man. Put his memories there and his sstrange words and his sspells—"

"We trranslated those, too, of course. Into what's-it-called. What you quick little people speak, back where we were quarried," said Beak-Face.

"Bulgarrrrian!" said Bonnet-Head, and she gave a great gargoylian shudder. "Maybe it changes his sspells somehow. Nothing stays exactly the same, when it's trranslated. Have you noticed that, dearr? It is the same and also not the same. *Au revoir* is not quite exactly the same as your English *good-bye*. No. So the bad man binds us to do what he says. He binds us in French. We trranslate his bad magic into something same-but-different, into Bulgarrian. We hope it will help, the same-but-different."

"Wiggle room!" said Maya. All three sets of eyes stared at her then: two pairs in brooding stone, one pair a puzzled, human gray. "Like finding little loopholes in his big loophole."

"Like that," said Bonnet-Head, rather fondly (it seemed to Maya). "For an example. He must consume someone to live again. He says! We trranslate into Bulgarian, and the magic shifts a little. Not just munch up some poor girl with magic in her blood! No, we trranslate that! To live he must feast on the heart of a— What do you call them in English? Magical beings, you know, like you and not like you. Powerful. Maybe wicked. Maybe good. Ah, it hurts, all this horrible thinking."

"Sstones should NEVER think," said Beak-Face. It was a gravelly grumble. "Now we have to think ALL the time. Think HIS thoughts. Speak HIS words. Do HIS work."

Maya's heart fell. This part sounded like very bad news.

"His work?" said Maya. "Fourcroy's? *His* work? So why should I trust you at all, then?"

The gargoyles looked at each other, looked at Maya, frowning with every square inch of their monstrous stone heads.

"You should NOT!" said Bonnet-Head.

("No kidding," said Valko.)

"No! Never trust us. We did sspit ourselves out of the wall, true—and sspit out the egg, the memory stone— always spitting out his memories, the poison of him. And trrrrranslating his rules and his magic wherever

199

we can—putting the little loopholes in—but it is never enough. And you, too, dearr. You also cannot be trussted, can you?"

Maya's heart was pounding like a drum. She backed up a step, and then another step.

"Believe us, quick-little warm-running child: he will eat you up, that bad man, for anotherr little blink of life. He alrready eats you up. Beware of him."

"Maya!" said Valko, interrupting. "Look!"

The sky had deepened way beyond nectarine by now. The sky was dark. But this being Paris, many other lights had come flickering on: lit windows in buildings across the way, the signs advertising cafés and restaurants along the street, the pulsating green neon sign of a pharmacy a block away. And above the crazy tumult of city life, the Eiffel Tower, which had been glowing all creamy and gold, had suddenly started to sparkle.

"But that means—," said Maya. She stretched her free hand out, out, out, toward the beauty of it. The Tower was programmed to sparkle every hour on the hour. Six o'clock already! She looked around. For less than a second she didn't feel anything; she even thought, *Maybe it has really just gone away.* That, of course, was the moment the wave of strangeness sloshed right over her, the tingle of it racing up and down her outstretched arm and making her feel just the slightest bit sick—an itchy, electric sort of queasiness, as if she were about to outgrow her ordinary, everyday skin.

Growing. Things growing.

Something was beginning to happen to the flowers in the bouquet. The gargoyles were clattering at each other. Valko had his hand clamped tight on her arm; the egg was huddled safely in that hand. The egg! She didn't want magic messing with that egg. It was strange enough on its own.

"Don't you change," she told it firmly. And she tried to hold on to her own self, too, so restless and twitchy inside her skin.

"Oh, no," said Valko, looking up over her head at the Eiffel Tower. Maya looked, too. The sparkles had started in the usual way, bright popping flashes, like manic fireflies or paparazzi. But something was happening now to the Tower itself. Dark blotches spread out from its usually crisp sides. The sparkling lights faltered, flickered, and then everything—neighborhood, embassy, neon signs, and Tower—went completely dark.

Maya could feel the ground trembling faintly, far below.

What did I just do? she thought. It was a peculiar sort of thought. She tried to shake it right back out of her head.

"Big loophole, getting bigger. Bad man," said a gargoyle sadly in the dark.

"You okay?" said Valko, not very far from Maya's ear.

"They'll have the generator going in a second."

"The Tower," she said. "The poor Tower. What's happening to it, do you think?"

(*Forest. Trees.* What was her mind doing, anyway? It was as bad as the gargoyles' egg, feeding her pictures like that.)

"Don't know," said Valko. "Look what I found in your backpack, though. Coming in handy already, huh?"

He had dug out that flashlight he'd given her. It had remained its old cobalt self, thank goodness. The little circle of brightness was ordinary and comforting.

Valko sent the patch of light flicking all around them: the flowers, the satellite dishes, the waiting gargoyles. Everything was there. Everything was still there. The flowers looked different, though. More complicated than they had been.

Maya shifted her outstretched arm around until she felt a gargoyle's stony shoulder—or wing?—under her fingers.

"Tell me, how can we stop this?" she said. They had called it a *loophole.* That was a funny way to describe a spreading tide of magic, wasn't it? But Fourcroy had needed a loophole to keep on living. That's what they had said. Maybe he hadn't known how awful that loophole would be, how it would grow and grow and grow.

The gargoyles sighed raspily and shifted from claw to claw.

"Harrd," said Beak-Face.

"Sstop the one who sstarted it," added Bonnet-Head, a bit farther away in the dark. "What more can you do?"

Valko made a very impatient noise. "Well, for starters," he said, "seems to me pretty obvious: you take the stupid *egg*, which is full of evil Fourcroy's evil downloaded memories, if I'm understanding what these walking, talking statues are saying—and I still don't see how they're doing it, the walking and talking, it doesn't make any sense at all—and you tumble that stupid egg over the edge of the roof here, and you let it go smash. That's the sensible thing to do."

There was some gravelly clamor from the gargoyles. "She HAS to keep it safe!" and "She MUST take care of it!"

Maya turned to look at Valko. "You don't understand," said Maya. He really didn't. "I can't do that. I have to keep it safe—I do."

"Because keeping a stone egg full of some bad guy's mind is a Good Idea? Or just because that's Fourcroy's master plan and he's got you totally trapped?"

Don't you see? Yes . . . and yes. She took a deep breath and said it aloud: "I'm pretty sure it's both."

"Yesss," said the gargoyles, off there in the gloom.

"Are you kidding me?" said Valko.

"It's not just *his* egg," said Maya. "It's theirs."

"Yesss," murmured the gargoyles.

"And that makes things better how?" said Valko. "They're monsters. They're working for him. They nearly strangled me. Oh, I know, don't tell me: they were scared of my very scary knife. Even though it's teeny-tiny, and they're made of stone."

There was a pause while Maya just stood there being stubborn and wishing she could find the words to describe how she felt about stone eggs and gargoyles. It was hard to explain to Valko because it wasn't totally logical. It was a *feeling*. It was a hunch. It was complicated. Maybe it was even another illusion, and the dominoes were still tumbling in their neat little clockwork rows, *clickety clickety click*.

Valko broke the silence with a laugh. He could do that: turn some easy corner and go from worry to laughter. Dark thoughts just couldn't stick to him.

"Oh, forget it. Let's go. We'll be late for dinner, and then my mother will be mad, and things will get *really* scary."

Maya had already rolled the egg up safe in her extra sweater and stuffed the thing back into her backpack. She was ready to follow the flashlight's nice ordinary light back toward the stairway door.

But first she did whisper good-bye in the direction of the gargoyles. Maybe they heard it, and maybe they didn't. They were being very still again, in the darkness.

They were back to behaving like stone. They made no sound.

Maya was thinking about gargoyles, and thinking about Valko.

Valko didn't understand about the egg, but that wasn't his fault. He wasn't used to things depending so much on him, probably.

But the way he glared at those gargoyles: it was the way other people sometimes glared into the mirror on a bad morning. *Yes,* thought Maya. *Into the mirror!*

Because think about it, right? Quarried in one place and hauled off to another! Part this, part that, part something else, always translating, always out of place! Maybe being a Valko—or, for that matter, even being a Maya—was not so entirely different, after all (thought Maya as she followed the flashlight's beam down the embassy stairs), from being a gargoyle.

12

VAMPIRES AND OTHER CULTURAL MISUNDERSTANDINGS

By the time Valko and Maya made their way down the stairs, the generator was rumbling away in the background, and the lights were back on. There were candlesticks set out hastily on all the surfaces, as well, just to be safe. Some of the mirrors above some of the chimneys had been warped by the strangeness into abstract whorls of glass, and at certain places in the paneling, bunches of wires had broken through the surface of the wall as they blossomed into wild designs. But in the grand drawing room of the embassy, the two Dr. Nikolovs—Valko's mother and father—were calmly waiting to greet their earliest guests. Had they even noticed the strangeness rolling through? The Nikolovs were diplomats, and thus by training unflappable, no matter what was going on at the time with the laws of physics.

Maya tightened her grip on her bouquet, which— after the excitement on the roof and a certain amount of molecular rearrangement—was somewhat the worse for wear, and surreptitiously wiped her nervous right hand on her skirt.

The lights were very bright. There were old paintings in frames on the walls, and the furniture was dark and elaborate, and there were flowers everywhere, as well as people standing by with trays in their hands, waiting for the real guests to arrive.

"Here we go, Maya," said Valko, with an encouraging smile. "Time to meet my absolutely terrifying parents. Mama! This is Maya."

Maya handed over the bouquet, shook Dr. Nikolova's hand firmly, said, *"Zdravejte"* with conviction, which was the proper Bulgarian way of saying hello, and looked straight into Valko's mother's brilliant dark eyes.

("Chessboard eyes," Valko had told her on the roof. "You'll see what I mean when you meet her. She was a chess champion when she was a girl, you know. Milena Todorova, queen of the checkered board. Her eyes are always at least seven moves ahead.")

"Lovely flowers, thank you," said Valko's mother. "I'm glad to meet you, at long last. Georgi, this is Valko's young friend from school, Maya Davidson. The scientist's child."

Valko's father shook her hand, too, and said something kind. His hair was gray at the temples, and he was in a suit that made him look like a movie star. Maya ran through all the polite phrases she could think of and tried very hard to keep smiling, but those sixty seconds before Valko rescued her by dragging her off to the drinks table made for a long, long minute indeed. The other guests had begun to arrive.

"Fine so far," said Valko. He seemed relieved, Maya thought, just to be off the embassy roof and away from the impossible talking statues. But a glittering dinner party with grown-ups you didn't even know had to be a thousand—a *million*—times worse than gargoyles! No, it wasn't fair: Maya was practically sweating bullets, and here was Valko sailing through the evening as if it were the most fun he'd had in ages. That was what being a diplomat's kid meant, Maya guessed. He hadn't even seemed all that nervous back when he first met Maya's parents, had he? Maya tried to remember. No, it seemed to her that even then, Valko had remained unreasonably cheerful and calm.

"So, this is the Bulgarian Cultural Foundation's annual award dinner," said Valko. "As you know. If you read the invitation all the way through. That means a lot of artists and doddering profs around the table tonight. Get ready!"

At least they were kind enough to seat her next to Valko at the huge dining table in the next room. She could keep an eye on which fork he was using, and she figured that might just save her etiquette-challenged neck.

On her other side was an older man, older than her father. He introduced himself, very politely, as a historian.

"What kind of history?" asked Maya, equally politely.

"At the moment, *mademoiselle*," said the old man, "I am completing a very important project on the history of yogurt."

"Yogurt!" said Maya. That surprised her, all right, but she kept her expression as much under wraps as possible.

"Yogurt, but yes, absolutely!" said the old man. "The crowning glory of Bulgarian, as it were, culture. That's a pun, my dear."

Maya blinked, not knowing what to say.

"Why, even the vaunted Greeks use *our* cultures! Read the labels on their cartons, if you don't believe me, child. Bulgarian cultures everywhere: *L. bulgaricus*, humble conqueror of the Western world. You, *mademoiselle*, I sense, are neither French nor Bulgarian."

"American," said Maya.

"Ah," said the historian of yogurt, making a very horrified face. "Where, I have heard, they serve yogurt *frozen*! And with—what do you call them?—*toppings*!"

Maya risked a quick glance at Valko on her other side. He was grinning from ear to ear.

"And now you have met our favorite crusty historian. But you are harmless, aren't you, Professor Stoyanov?"

The old man chuckled into his napkin.

"Oh, yes, yes, young Valko. Sad to say. Harmless, harmless. They need not hide me down here at the children's end of the table. I have given up breaking plates."

And that was when the dining-room doors flew open. All heads at the table looked up and around. A woman had paused with one foot through the doorway—almost, you might say, striking a pose under the elegant arch. She was wearing a tailored black skirt and a rather showy jacket (floral brocade with threads of gold!), but everything was slightly askew. Her blouse was untucked on one side. You could see that her hair had started off combed sleekly back into a ponytail, but had then rebelled. And down one side of that disobedient hair was a streak of surprising, blinding white.

"Madame Blakely!" exclaimed Valko's unflappable mother. "How pleased we all are that you have arrived!"

"I'm afraid I'm late," said Madame Blakely, in plainly American English, her face twitching into a foolish smile. "I am late, aren't I? I arrived just outside, and then the lights went off, and then . . ."

She moved her hands about hopelessly, describing something she was obviously in no condition to describe.

"The carnival downstairs," she said. "There's a

carnival, yes? And then suddenly, you know, I was singing!"

She laughed.

"Of all people: me, singing!"

Everyone else at the table sat as if stunned.

"Well, the adventure ends happily, *madame*," said Valko's mother, with professional courtesy. "You have found your way to our table, and before the soup! Please do take a seat. . . ."

Indeed, as the men at the table remembered their advanced manners and rose in greeting, members of the embassy staff were already guiding Madame Blakely to the empty chair across the table from Maya and Valko.

"Pernithia Jane Blakely is this year's winner of the Bulgarian Cultural Foundation's works-in-progress grant," said Valko's father to the table at large, "for artists whose works engage deeply and profoundly with Bulgarian culture. We are very happy Madame Blakely could attend our dinner this evening. It is an honor for us, I'm sure."

The soup had the tastiest little meatballs in it. Maya realized by the second spoonful that part of the funny feeling in her stomach had been plain, old-fashioned hunger. She was glad to have something to do with herself, too: she knew how to eat soup.

"Bulgarian culture!" said the historian of yogurt,

setting his spoon down in his empty bowl. "So your writing engages with Bulgarian culture, Madame Blakely? May I ask, what aspect of Bulgarian culture has attracted your interest?"

"Oh, *yes!*" said Pernithia Jane Blakely. "Vampires!"

Was it Maya's imagination, or did several people at that table stiffen slightly? Pernithia Jane Blakely, ignoring her soup, had jumped into a description of the book she was planning to write, *Love with Long Teeth*, in which, apparently, a beautiful girl was going to run her European rental car off the road and be rescued by a handsome and mysterious man with mechanical skills and a reluctance to share his name. Then they were going to go to his family mansion, in the hostile, barren Bulgarian hills, and one night the man would bare his sexy chest and reveal a set of surprisingly sharp eyeteeth, and she —

"Excuse me," said the historian. "But no. No!"

"Professor Stoyanov!" said Valko's mother, her voice chilly. But he waved her reproof away, while a crew of waiters replaced the soup bowls with plates containing little gourmet mounds of chopped salad, garnished with walnuts and—what was that? Maya's heart contracted. For a moment she thought the strangeness had affected the embassy's kitchen. Then she realized that what she was seeing was a radish carved—by hand, not by magic— to look exactly like a rose.

She relaxed again, but only for a second. Professor Stoyanov, historian of yogurt, was in the middle of a long lecture on the figure of the *vampir* in Bulgaria, and whenever he got to a particularly important point, he whacked his fork against his plate for emphasis.

"Not sexy!" (*Whack!*) "Not sexy *at all*! I am sorry, but I am fatigued by this nonsense." (*Whack!*) "Do you even know what creates them, *vampiri*? A bad death, someone dies and the funeral is not done properly. An evil man who dies badly—that can make the poor, unhappy *vampir*. And then, is it sexy, is it handsome? No!" (*Whack!*) "It is a hungry shadow—some say a bag of blood. The *opposite* of sexy!" (*Whack!*) "For forty days, the shadow wanders. If it can feast enough, *madame*, on the living, it can, on the fortieth day, return to life itself. That's what it hungers to do. Eat someone's heart, and live. That is all. No bare chests and romance. *No!* Not a *Bulgarian* vampire!"

A final couple of whacks for emphasis, and then the servers swooped in and took all their salad plates away. Professor Stoyanov, disarmed, glowered across the table at the American writer, who seemed to be taking the diatribe quite well.

"I am just simply asking you, *madame*," said the historian of yogurt. "Where you are getting your false information, about Bulgarian vampires?"

"It's not false information," said the writer in surprise. "It's fiction. I mean, I made it all up, of course. And anyway, vampires have to be sexy. Everyone knows that. Otherwise, what's even the point?"

The historian huffed with impatience, and, in any case, Maya was hardly listening anymore. The salad had been replaced by the gourmet version of stuffed peppers (tiny, beautiful peppers arranged on a plate and drizzled with bright swirls of some kind of sauce). But Maya looked at her plate and saw hungry shadows, wandering the streets for forty days.

"Forty days!"

That was Valko's quiet voice on her left side. So he had heard it, too. Of course he had.

"Valko—," she said.

He squeezed her hand quickly, under the table. They couldn't talk here. She knew that. This wasn't the place.

"Well, young lady, how do you like the *pulneni chushki*?" said the historian, on Maya's other side. "They've fancied it up, of course, for the French taste. And do American taste buds agree?"

"It's very good, thank you," said Maya, although to tell the truth, worry had taken most of the flavor away.

"That's a yogurt sauce there, on the side," he said. "That's traditional. Your hand is shaking, young lady. Have you had too much wine?"

Maya shook her head. She didn't drink wine! But when she raised her eyes a little, she was disconcerted to find Pernithia Blakely, the writer, staring squarely at her.

"You're an American girl," said the writer. "Where are you from? What's your name?"

Maya shook her head, and then realized that made no sense and nodded instead.

"I'm . . . I'm from California," she said. "I'm a friend of Valko's. That's why I'm here."

"What's your name?" said the writer. "I could send you a book, sometime. Are you a big reader?"

Maya nodded.

The writer was still waiting.

"I'm Maya Davidson," said Maya, almost under her breath.

The writer passed a hand over her eyes, and Maya saw something change in her face.

"Maya?" she said. "*Maya?*"

Oh, no.

That telltale stripe of white in her hair. She had been caught up in a "carnival" outside? She had found herself *singing?*

"Oh, Valko, help," Maya whispered again.

"I know, I know," murmured Valko, and, being the sort of person who takes direct action right away when direct action is needed, he knocked his water glass over immediately. Water rushed across the table and onto Maya's lap.

"I'm so sorry!" he said aloud, leaping to his feet and making a big show of dabbing at the table with napkins. "I've made an awful mess! You'll have to get all cleaned up."

His parents were half displeased (his mother) and half amused (his father).

"Oh, Valko!" said his mother. "Clumsy child—help the poor girl!"

"Excuse me," said Valko to everybody around that table, and he bowed his head for a second, took Maya by the elbow (she grabbed her backpack from under her chair), and guided her safely out.

She wasn't even that awfully drenched, when they surveyed the damage in the next room.

"You heard what that woman said," said Maya. "I mean, how she said it. And she's got that streak in her hair. She said she was *singing*!"

"It's not good," said Valko, shaking his head. "Not to mention her book sounds horrible."

"Well, it could be okay," said Maya, who was willing to read anything. "Just because she's been turned into a ravenous *samo*-whatsit doesn't mean she's a bad writer. Necessarily."

Valko made a face.

"We'll just have to hide out here until the dinner's over," he said with regret. "Too bad. I happen to know that dessert's going to be those warm chocolate cakes with melty middles."

They didn't go back in until the guests were saying their farewells and departing, and even then they were careful to hang back in the corners, while the writer, puzzled, kept looking around as if she had lost something and couldn't quite remember what that something was. Every time she caught sight of Maya, her eyes would light up again and she would lunge forward, but Maya and Valko were quicker on their feet. And finally even Pernithia Jane Blakely was ushered out the door by the Dr. Nikolovs and their efficient staff.

"And that leaves only the esteemed junior guests," said Valko's father, nodding to Maya and Valko.

"Poor girl," said Valko's mother. "Sometimes our son lives up to his name, I'm afraid. Wild wolfling, our Valko. Did you suffer very much?"

She had put a fond arm around Valko's shoulders while she said that, though. Maya found herself filled, suddenly, with determination; she shivered a little as she opened her mouth.

"It was so kind of you to invite me," she said (remembering to be very, very polite). "It was really kind. Thank you. I just wish—"

It was as if she had entered a fairy tale: you battle your way through to the castle where the king and queen of the fairies live, and you always end up (if you live) with the chance for a wish. Don't you?

"I just wish so much Valko could stay in Paris," she said.

There was a silence.

Valko's mother's eyes had snapped back into sharp focus; you could almost see the chess pieces being moved about in her mind as she raised her eyebrows at Maya.

"He has made a friend here, I see," said Dr. Nikolova finally, and with the faintest ghost of a smile. "That, of course, is a good thing—yes, even I know that. You'll see Maya safely home now, Valko? Without spilling anything more on her?"

And so, after tucking themselves into sweaters and jackets, Maya and Valko were dismissed into the cold, strange November night.

13

SAMODIVI AFTER DINNER

It was much colder now than it had been on the way in. Maya wrapped her scarf an extra time around her neck and hunched the backpack more securely onto her shoulder. Valko was looking at her, she could tell.

"All right, I'm sorry!" she said finally. She couldn't take it anymore. "I've messed everything up, of course. First I let the gargoyles tackle you, and then there your parents were, and I opened my mouth that way like a total idiot. I'm sorry."

"I wasn't thinking any of that," said Valko. "I'm not even sure what happened on the roof, but I think you rescued me from that . . . thing, whatever it was. And my mother—well, she almost *prefers* people to be unpredictable."

"But it's not going to help."

Valko shrugged.

"I am appreciative," he said. "Even if I'm packed up

and gagged and sent in a suitcase back to Bulgaria, I will always remember that you tried bravely to save me."

He was teasing her, but he was teasing her nicely. Maya shook her head at him, but just then she tripped over a rough spot in the sidewalk, and the backpack swung around and knocked the back of her elbow quite hard.

"You all right?" said Valko, and he looked down to see what it was she had tripped on. "Whoa, look at this."

Her first thought was that an old iron pipe had somehow broken through the pavement. But then she saw the roughness of the thing, the way it had thrust its way up through the sidewalk and slithered along for a while, before diving back down under the surface.

"Valko, what is this? It wasn't here before, was it?"

She backed up so hastily she ran right into a man passing by.

"I'm so sorry," she said. "I fell—the pipe—*what is it?*"

Valko was steadying her with one hand by now. The man smiled politely and dusted himself off where she had bowled into him.

"You are not from here, I see, *mademoiselle*," he said, and in the light of the streetlamps his eyes had the most unsettling sheen of vagueness to them. "They are, of course, the roots of the Tower, the *racines d'Eiffel*. In this neighborhood we know: the Tower's roots can be treacherous at night. *Attention!* Be careful! Beware!"

They watched him walk on down the sidewalk, his legs expertly dodging the *racines d'Eiffel* wherever they had lurched through the smooth surface of the sidewalk.

"That's not possible," said Valko finally. He dropped to his knees and rapped his knuckles on the thick length of iron that had tripped up Maya's toes. "It's not possible. What did he say? The roots of the Tower! Towers don't have *roots*."

"It's the strangeness again," said Maya, rubbing her elbow. "It's the loophole spreading. Only it's changing things *more* now. It's getting worse and worse, every time. You heard what the gargoyles said—the loophole thing. Stuff becoming what it possibly could be, instead of what it already is."

"And gargoyles don't talk, either," said Valko. For a moment he sounded a little lost. But then he shook his head and became himself again.

"Oh, well," he said. "What did you do to your elbow?"

"The egg whacked it when I tripped," said Maya. That turned some little light on in her head. "Oh, how stupid! The egg! I totally forgot!"

She unzipped the backpack to show him: the gargoyles' egg, a little chilly after all those hours of neglect, but still pockmarked with words she didn't recognize. It glittered a little under the streetlight.

"What's it saying there, Valko? Don't be mad at me

about this egg. The whole reason I brought it along was to ask you."

Valko studied the egg for a moment with distaste.

"There's that forty all over the place," he said. "Forty, forty, forty. Can't we throw this thing into the river?"

"No, we can't," said Maya. "But maybe it's like what the man said at the table: forty days for a Bulgarian vampire to—"

"There's no such thing as vampires," said Valko. "Oh, don't look at me that way! There's really not."

His breath was making little clouds in the air as he studied the egg.

"'Keep me safe'—we saw that before. And your name. That's in several places. And 'zmey.' I don't remember that being there. Here it is again: 'heart of a *zmey*. Life, life, in the heart of a *zmey*, Maya, *zmey*, Maya—'"

"Zzzzzmey," sang out another voice, not far away.

Maya and Valko jumped, and Maya's hands fumbled so badly that she very nearly dropped the egg right onto the iron root, which would surely have been the end of it. When the egg was back safe in the crook of her arm, she saw that Valko had frozen still, right beside her.

"Maya," he said quietly. "Behind us—look."

Maya looked up and around, and for a moment she, too, was unable to move or speak.

How had they not noticed them before? A group of

women in business suits had begun to gather on the side-walk behind them.

"Oh, no. Let's leave," she said, but when they turned to go the other way, they saw that another handful of women, swaying slightly and humming, had wandered around the corner ahead and were waiting there. And threading among them was a deeper column of shadow.

"Okay," said Valko. "This is where we move fast and stay calm. Here we go."

He put his arm around her, which did help, and they moved fast down the street. Fast and quiet, with their eyes on the ground, to avoid sudden iron roots. All around them, however, the humming grew and grew. And became shriller. And arms were now jostling them. Arms and shoulders and gracefully moving hands.

The *samodivi* were on every side of them now.

They were beginning to sing.

Maya caught a glimpse of shadow curling along on her left side. She had the distinct impression the shadow might actually be staring at her, from shadowy, formerly purple eyes. She clenched her hands more tightly around the gargoyles' egg and kept walking.

"Maya!" sang the *samodivi*. "Maya is a *zmey*, a *zmey*, a juicy-hearted *zmey*!"

"What's a *zmey*?" Maya whispered to Valko as they walked forward through the crowd, their heads still down as if fighting a strong wind. It was harder going now. The singing women were closing in.

"Means 'dragon,'" said Valko, pushing through the next swaying knot of *samodivi*. "I wish they'd leave us alone. Don't they have places they should be, at nine or ten p.m.? I wish they'd just leave."

"Hello, little girl from the party," said a voice Maya had heard somewhere before.

She looked up and felt slightly sick: it was the writer, Pernithia Jane Blakely, swaying with the others, her hair completely wild now, and that streak of white glittering coldly in the lamplight.

"Are you coming to sing with us?" said Pernithia Blakely.

"I can't," said Maya.

"You should leave," said Valko to the writer. "Go home and rest."

"But the shadow says this is *Maya*," said the writer. "The shadow says—something about you not really being a little girl at all, little girl. Apparently you are a—"

"—*Zzzzmey*," said the chorus of swaying women all around.

"Keep moving," whispered Valko. "Keep pushing your way through."

"I am *not* a dragon," said Maya. It was really beginning to tick her off. But it was harder and harder to move, with the *samodivi* gathered so closely around them.

"Dragon, dragon," said the writer, and she hummed a little tune to accompany the word. "The shadow needs you, you know. It needs a dragon like you—"

She leaned forward to whisper.

"It needs to eat up your heart for the magic. Hey, what's that you're carrying?"

Suddenly the gargoyles' egg seemed very naked in Maya's hands. The poor egg! She tried to tuck her coat around it. Trickles of ice were running down her spine. She didn't like being called a dragon, and she didn't like the sound of "juicy-hearted," either. If this was the gargoyles' helpful translation of the spell into Bulgarian, she didn't think much of it so far.

"Something you *care about*?" hissed Pernithia Blakely. The column of shadow was so close: it seemed to pass right through the writer, passed through and came closer to Maya, a colder darkness within the ordinarily cold dark. "Something you'd follow to the ends of the earth? Something you'd *give anything* to protect, maybe, little dragon girl?"

And then, in one terrible, sudden gesture, the crazy writer reached in and snatched the egg right out of Maya's hands. Took the egg and held it over her head and gave an entirely inhuman shriek of triumph, while Maya shouted and jumped at her (no use) and Valko shouted and jumped after Maya, pulling her away. The *samodivi* laughed and sang and flowed around Maya and Valko and away, moving faster than real people should be able to move, in any version of the universe that made any kind of possible sense.

Sooner than eyeblinks, the street was empty, the horrible singing women just a fading echo, Maya sobbing for breath and sobbing with rage, and Valko very still and helpless and miserable next to her.

She had sworn to protect the gargoyles' egg, the gargoyles' beautiful, lovely, precious egg. She had sworn to protect it—and now it was gone.

14

LOSERS WEEPERS

It's one thing to have failed miserably at something, but another thing entirely when disaster strikes you, and *nobody knows* the terrible thing that has happened, or how awful you feel.

Losing the gargoyles' egg was like that for Maya. She had promised to keep the egg safe, to keep it far away from the shadowy Fourcroy, and instead one of the wild women with the streaks of madness in their hair had run right off with it. That was really, no matter how you looked at it, the opposite of keeping something safe.

Maya's mother was horrified to hear the egg had been stolen "by some unstable homeless woman," which was how she interpreted the rest of the story, but after days went by and Maya was still slouching around after school, looking like all the beauty and hope had gone out of the world, her mother's sympathy began to mutate into the wrong kind of parental concern, and wasn't so helpful anymore.

"I know you feel terrible about losing that lovely egg, but Valko's been very good about it, hasn't he? It wasn't your fault, dear. Sometimes we just have to be brave and let things go."

That did not sound like bravery to Maya.

Valko knew more about what the gargoyles' egg meant to her, but of course he had also been the one who wanted to smash it to bits or throw it into the river. Mostly he just seemed relieved to have one bit of strangeness out of the picture. Maya had sent a reluctant Valko up to his roof right away the next day, to break the bad news to the gargoyles (from a safe distance) and maybe to ask their advice, but Valko came back saying the gargoyles were gone. And again, there was that clear strain of relief in his voice when he said it.

He still wasn't comfortable living in a universe in which a person could be trying to have a conversation with gargoyles.

"What are we going to do, then?" said Maya, knowing all too well she was sounding exasperated and unhappy. "I have to keep that egg away from Fourcroy's shadow. It's one of the things he most wants, right? You heard the gargoyles say it. I have to keep it safe."

"Keep it *safe*?" said Valko. "Phooey to that. We should have pitched it into the river—don't look at me that way!—when we had the chance. All right, sorry. But, anyway, the shadow doesn't have it. How could a shadow even hold anything that heavy? That awful writer has it. With the funny name."

"Pernithia," said Maya. "Pernithia Blakely."

"I have a *slightly* funny name myself," said Valko. They had walked across the river and into the cold, wintry Tuileries, where pigeons shivered on the manicured paths and the trees looked bare and severe. "Or so people tell me. But at least, thank goodness, mine's only two syllables. Hers sounds like a medicine or something."

"Don't duck the question," said Maya. "How do we get it back?"

"You're not making any sense, I hope you realize. If the egg is *his* memories, then it's bad. Seems simple to me. Rotten stone egg: not something to mess with."

"It's not simple at all," said Maya, feeling stubborn. Remembering how beautiful the poor stolen egg was, and how much it needed her help.

They were walking around the large round basin now, with the thin stream of its fountain playing in the middle and statues scattered around its edges. (The nearest statue was labeled MISERY. *Good choice*, thought Maya, considering how discouraged she felt.)

"It's the *gargoyles'* egg," she said. Her explanations weren't getting anywhere. "They're not what you think they are. They're not evil. No, really, I'm sure they're not.

Beak-Face thought you were coming at him with that knife, right? They're not bad. They're just trapped—like us, really. We're all trapped in Fourcroy's magic and trying to squirm out of it."

"I'm not," said Valko. "I have worse troubles. My grandmother-with-a-mole is coming to Paris any day now. So I'm just plain doomed."

"Convince her you need to stay," said Maya.

"Good luck to me with that," said Valko. "I'd say chances are slim to none, just at the moment. She's stubborn, my grandmother. You know what, though?"

"What?" said Maya.

"About your stolen egg . . . ," he said.

So he was at least thinking about it! That was comforting.

"Okay, here's the thing: maybe the crazy writer who ran off with the gargoyles' egg doesn't know exactly what it is. Doesn't know the shadowy guy needs it. Remember what she was saying when she grabbed it? Stuff about how important it probably was to *you*. How it could lure you anywhere, to rescue it. They want to use it as bait *for you*. Maybe they don't even realize the egg is something the shadow needs."

"All they have to do is read the stuff written all over it."

"They aren't all that smart, when they're being

230

samodivi. Haven't you noticed that? And the shadow thing isn't smart, either. They don't know much about anything—just scraps of stuff. Shadows don't have much room for brains, you know."

So maybe she and Valko were smarter than shadows. That was what Maya's mother called *clutching at straws*—but Maya reached out to that straw, and yes, she clutched. But she had heard what Valko had to say, about the egg being bait. Well, it was true: she had to rescue that egg. She admitted that. It was finding a way to do exactly what the shadow expected her to do, while still being able to wriggle out of the trap somehow at the last possible moment—*that* was the challenge for Maya.

Her mother was waiting for her when she got home. She had a perplexed expression.

"Maya," she said. "Guess who called to talk to me? The Bulgarian embassy."

Maya had a brief image of a building picking up a really enormous phone.

"I mean, your friend's mother. The diplomat. Dr. Milena Nikolova, who used to be Milena Todorova. Did you know she used to play chess?"

"She called? She told you about *playing chess*?"

Maya was taken aback.

"No, no," said Maya's mother, laughing. "I mean, yes, she called, but I was the one who asked her about the chess, when she told me her name. She was semifamous, you know, when I was young. My mother cut out an article from a magazine about girls doing remarkable things all around the world and put it up on our wall as inspiration. And one of those girls was Milena Todorova. There was a picture of her, the most intense child you ever saw, looking right into the camera with a knight in her hand. She married young; I remember that, too. Ha! Now I've spoken to her on the phone!"

Maya went from being taken aback to being slightly horrified.

"What did she say? What was she calling about? And Mom, what if she'd been the wrong Milena Todorova?"

Maya's mother laughed again.

"She would have said, 'No, I'm sorry, I never played chess,' and that would have been the end of it. Don't worry, Maya! I was polite and quite restrained. And she was perfectly friendly. I said you felt awful about what had happened, and she was very kind about it. She said no one had taken any offense, that these things happen, and they were simply glad Valko has found such a loyal friend here. I guess he didn't make so many close friends when they lived in New York."

"Wait," said Maya, that horrified feeling spreading very fast through all her limbs. "You said I felt awful? About what? What did you say I felt awful about? What were they not offended by? Mom, what exactly did you say to her?"

Maya's mother looked surprised.

"What do you think? That poor egg that was stolen, of course. I know how awful you've been feeling about it, such a lovely gift. And worried about what Valko's parents would think, too, that you'd been careless with it—don't look at me that way! I know it wasn't your fault! But anyway, as I said, she was very nice. I just said, 'My poor girl has been feeling so bad about what happened after the lovely dinner you gave,' and she jumped right in, very reassuring."

Oh!

"But that wasn't why she was calling, anyway. She called us because another guest at that party has been trying to contact you. The woman who writes books. Did you talk to her much, Maya? Anyway, apparently she was quite taken with you and was wondering whether you'd like to be a sort of advance reader or something for the book she's writing—"

"*What?*" said Maya.

"Don't look *so* shocked, Maya! I'd want you as a reader, if I wrote books for young people. You're a very good reader. So she needed our address, to send us whatever it is. The invitation or the book or something."

"Oh, Mom, you didn't give her our address."

"Of course I did. Why not? Dr. Nikolova did say this writer seems to be a little eccentric, but that seems par for the course for writers, doesn't it? Don't look so stricken! I think it's exciting."

"But she's the one who—"

Maya stopped herself midsentence, because she could see she needed to think. Now the crazy writer knew where she lived. All right, that wasn't ideal. But on the other hand, she, Maya, had to get that egg away from the writer. And so, when you thought about it a little, maybe Maya should have been the one asking Valko's mother for the writer's address, not the other way around. She looked at her mother and tried to be truthful, in a neutral, not-showing-any-cards sort of way.

"She was *very* interested in the gargoyles' egg," said Maya.

"Aha!" said her mother, relaxing again. "That explains it! A child who talks about gargoyles' eggs is for sure going to be an excellent reader. Don't be shy. Apparently the writer wants to invite us over or something. I know I'd like to meet her, if it comes to that."

It came to that sooner than Maya could have expected. By the time she got home from school the next day, her mother was grinning ear to ear: the writer had called and invited them to drop by her apartment that very Sunday! Just on the other side of the Seine! Brunch with the somewhat famous Pernithia Blakely!

"Have you read any of her books?" asked Maya's mother. "No? Neither have I. Well, all the same, it should be very interesting."

Yes, thought Maya. *Interesting, yes.*

By Sunday at ten a.m. she had to learn how to become a very sneaky thief.

She practiced on her family: she tried removing things from rooms they were sitting in, without them noticing. Mostly it did not go well.

"That's *my* fireman's hat!" James would squawk, as Maya tried to smuggle it out of the living room.

Or one of her parents would give her a most quizzical look and ask why she had that book tucked under her shirt like that.

It was beginning to look like Maya might be a total failure at filching.

Since clever thieves in films are always substituting a fake key for the real one, she scouted around after school in the Champ de Mars, eyeing the plantings and paths for a rock that might be about the size and shape of the gargoyles' egg, but the gravel was too small and the ornamental rocks too large, so that was a failure, too.

So far, then, her plan was to show up with her mother at the writer's apartment, let her mother distract Pernithia with lots of questions (this part of the plan was solid:

her mother could always be counted on to have a million questions), and then miraculously find the egg, snatch it, grab her mother's hand, and skedaddle.

Valko's opinion of this plan was pretty low. They were standing in the school yard, trying not to mind the faint spatter of rain that had driven most people to the more-protected edges of the place. In *Histoire-géographie* they were beginning to study the Second World War. It was that sort of day.

"You're going to go through this woman's closets and drawers, and she's not going to notice?" he said. "And have you counted to one hundred thirty-seven recently?"

There was a dreadful pause while Maya started adding up hours in her head.

"Eleven a.m. Sunday," said Valko. "Can you be out of there in an hour? Can you *promise* to be out of there?"

"Won't it be far enough away to be safe?" said Maya. The writer lived on some little street by the Trocadéro, on the far side of the Seine.

"Not this time," said Valko. "Doubling, remember. If the pattern holds, the strangeness will reach almost to the Arc de Triomphe. Think of the traffic jams then!"

Their dark thoughts were interrupted by the jangle of the bell.

That was Friday.

On Saturday, Maya's mother was in bed with a bad

stomach. She looked miserable.

"Don't worry. I'll be fine by tomorrow," she said, and turned her face to the wall to keep Maya from worrying.

That evening, though, she was no better.

Maya looked at that unhappy gray face, and all sorts of pieces of her heart that had been carefully glued back together over the past year or so fell apart again and were sharp and pointy in her chest. She could see that things were going very wrong.

"I'm so sorry," her mother said, reaching out to touch the opal on Maya's bracelet, a quick touch of a thin finger. "I know how much you wanted to go see this writer of yours."

Wanted! Ha. Not so much.

What Maya really *wanted* was to see her mother truly well and whole and safe again. No want went deeper than that.

She was responsible for that egg, though. She had to get it back somehow. She had promised to take care of it, and you can't take care of something a crazy writer has stolen from you and hidden away somewhere.

"I guess I'll call Valko," said Maya. "Maybe he can come with me instead. You rest and get better."

When she talked to Valko, however, his voice was a little strangled.

"All right," he said, in a half whisper. "Just, you should

know, the grandmother has landed. I will have to race back from your scary writer to pacify her. A quiet lunch in her room so she can grill me properly, that's my dreadful fate tomorrow. I can't be late, either."

"So you'll be leaving me alone with that writer?" said Maya. Worse and worse!

"Are you kidding? We'll both leave if time's running out. You have to be out of that place by eleven, anyway, or who knows what will happen. Just don't be late. I'll meet you downstairs here at nine thirty, right?"

It was a nicer day, that Sunday, than it had been for a week. Not anything even approaching warm for someone who used to live in California, but not raining, sleeting, hailing, or snowing, and the sun was doing its best, under the circumstances.

She made her way fairly cheerfully to Valko's imposing front door, but there was no Valko there. She ran her toe impatiently over a thin tendril of iron root running through the sidewalk outside the door and kept checking her watch: if they were late, then how was any of this going to work? That was when one of the guards—Ivan, she remembered—ducked his head through the doorway and waved her over.

"Note for you, *mademoiselle*," he said, and handed it over. It was sealed with staples. Maya tore it open as soon as the burly guy had turned his head.

238

Maya—go on ahead. Grandmother trapped me. I'll catch up. Ten minutes max. Valko.

Maya's heart sank like a stone. Valko was sending Maya off to the crazy writer *alone*? How could any grandmother possibly be as scary as Valko's grandmother seemed to be?

She thought about not going at all, about just giving up and going home, but that was not what a brave person would do. A brave person with responsibilities. She had *promised* those gargoyles. She *had* to keep that egg safe. She could handle ten minutes with a writer on her own, right?

The patchwork of iron roots became thicker as Maya came closer to the Eiffel Tower. She had not been directly under the Tower since the strangeness had changed it, and she had to stand there for a while and get used to the new version of it, with its iron vines and iron leaves sprouting out from that massive trunk.

"Eiffel Tower! Tree of the world!" said one of the young men waving the heavy loops of Eiffel Tower key chains he hoped to sell for a euro or so. The key chains showed the old untree-like Tower, but he didn't seem to notice. The not-noticing power of the strangeness was the strangest part of it, as far as Maya was concerned. It made her feel slightly ill, the way everybody kept not noticing everything changing all around them. "Take the Tower home with you! Souvenirs! Cheap!"

Maya shook her head and pulled herself away from the Tower, went fast under the noses of the enormous stone horses guarding the Pont d'Iéna, and crossed the Seine, wishing all the time and with all her heart she was not walking alone.

She was heading for the merry-go-round in the Trocadéro gardens. Those were the instructions her mother had passed on to her. A carousel at the foot of the great stairs up to the Palais de Chaillot (which was really just a few imposing museums and the plaza where tour buses stopped to let everyone get pictures of themselves in front of the Tower, to prove they had really come to Paris). She avoided the stairs, turned left at the carousel, and walked along the edge of the gardens. At the end of the park, there were supposed to be, according to Maya's mother, "secret stairs to a secret street."

Maya's mother had gotten the directions from the writer, but then, being Maya's mother, she had probably fancied them up a little.

There they were, though: stairs built into a dark brick wall, and a gate barring the way. Maya peered through, uncertain. Then she gave the gate a little push—it had been propped open.

The top of the stairs spilled her into a short street with

fancy buildings on the left and a cliff's-edge view of the Trocadéro park on the right. There were guards, too, because one of those buildings was flying a bright red flag with a star on it: another embassy, Maya figured. She walked by like someone who knew where she was going, which was almost all the way down the block, almost to the end, to number nine.

At the door, which was all elegant ironwork and glass except for the gleaming handles, Maya nearly lost her courage for a moment. It was the door handles that did it, because they were not ordinary handles; they were pairs of golden salamanders entwined. She put a hand on the disk of Cabinet glass around her neck and remembered dragging her brother through the halls of the Salamander House, and for a moment she considered turning around right there and walking away.

Some might say that, considering Maya's recent history, it was stupid to walk into a building with a salamander for a door handle. Or, for that matter, to go visiting someone with a streak of craziness running through her hair and her mind. But then again, there was the gargoyles' egg, waiting. And Valko was on his way. Ten minutes, tops, and then he would be there. So she sighed and rang the buzzer instead.

Pernithia Blakely turned out to live at the very, very top of the building, in one of those rooms that overworked maids had been housed in, long ago in other centuries. Maya trudged up the last bald flight of wooden stairs and concentrated on not thinking too far ahead.

Please be obvious, egg, she thought. *Please don't be hard to find.*

She stared at the door for a moment, gathering her courage together and waiting for some magical force to make this last little part of the decision for her, but no magic emerged. She was still on her own, in front of a plain wooden door with a crazy writer and a gargoyles' egg behind it.

She knocked.

The door opened; a shy head looked out.

"Oh, it's the American girl!" said Pernithia Blakely. "I was so afraid you might have changed your mind!"

Wait, thought Maya. *Did I just think the word* shy? *The crazy writer looks* shy?

"Come on in, please," said the writer. "Did all those steps wear you out? Sometimes I don't even want to go outside, thinking about the stairs waiting for me at the end of the day."

She seemed like the nicest person in the world. Dark hair twisted into a tame knot at the back of her head (the white streak of *samodiva* hair hardly even visible). Sensible clothes that looked like they would be perfect for typing in all day.

Still Maya hesitated for a second. *Don't be the fly that waltzes into the spider's parlor!* That was one of her mother's cautionary phrases. It was probably chiseled right into Maya's neurons by now.

But there wasn't anything spiderish about this shy, smiling woman at the door, was there? Nothing spiderish at all. And Maya wasn't a little kid like James anymore. At thirteen, you start having to make your own choices in life. And taking care of your own gargoyles' eggs. Et cetera.

"We have a lot of stairs at our place, too," said Maya, and, fly or not, she waltzed right in.

15

IN THE SPIDER'S PARLOR

Tucked away neatly under the whitewashed slope of the ceiling, the writer's room was filled with everything tiny, from the small table (set for three), to the doll-sized desk against the side wall and the extra-narrow inner door leading into a sliver of a kitchen. The wooden floors squeaked slightly underfoot; they were clean and old and as dark as the walls were white. But in fact Maya didn't even notice the floors or the kitchen or the desk for a minute or two: that was the window's fault.

"My one glory," said Pernithia Blakely, with a fleeting ghost of a smile. "The most beautiful view in Paris, I'm pretty sure. Well, one of them, anyway."

You could see the trees in the Trocadéro park, rounded rooftops and buildings glittering far away, and, to the right, the Eiffel Tower on the far side of the river. A person could get lost in a view like that. Maya leaned forward a little, just soaking in the spaciousness of it.

"You came alone?" said the writer after a moment. Not in a spiderish way. She actually sounded a little worried. "I thought your mother—well, never mind. I'll clear the extra plate away, then."

"She wasn't feeling well," said Maya. "So she thought you wouldn't mind if I brought Valko instead."

"Valko?" said Pernithia Blakely. She looked around in confusion for a second, as if she thought a Valko might be the kind of creature that could sneak into a room without being noticed.

"You know, he was at that Bulgarian dinner," said Maya. "His parents gave the party. He'll be here any minute."

"Oh," said the writer, and her face changed color. "The dinner! It's funny, I'm afraid I don't remember. . . ."

She started a nervous fiddling game with the salt-shaker, and very nearly dropped it.

"To be honest, I think I must have been a little ill that evening," she said. "Or the wine was too strong. I don't remember it very well. I may have had a fever, seems to me."

Maya studied the view with great intensity, to avoid having to respond to that. And the plates set so neatly on the tiny table—she studied them, too. She couldn't think of anything she could say to the writer that wouldn't be all bristly with horror: a *fever*!

"And my head hurt the next morning, too," said the writer with a grimace. "It was awful. So that's why I wanted so much to find a way to contact you, you see."

"Me?" said Maya cautiously.

"That lovely thing you gave me," said the writer. "The stone. I'm pretty sure I didn't thank you properly at the time. I mean . . ."

She looked at Maya with some distress in her eyes.

"It's all so hazy," she said. "I remembered your name, the next day. I knew it was you who had given me the pretty stone, but I couldn't recall—I still can't think—*why*, you see. And I did want to thank you. I knew I needed to look you up somehow, if I possibly could, to thank you and tell you how lovely it is—

"Oh, no, the quiche!"

She ducked through the narrow doorway to rescue breakfast, and while she was gone, Maya tried very hard to think fast, and think clearly. None of this was what she had braced herself for or expected, not at all. If only Valko would hurry up and get here! He would know the polite, comforting things one should say to delusional writers, and Maya would be freed up to scan the room for lonely stone eggs.

The writer came back in with a quiche, only slightly overbrown, balanced between a pair of enormous blue-and-yellow oven mitts.

"Not too charred, I hope," she said. "And I made coffee, too, but I suppose you don't drink much coffee? Oh, dear. I might have cocoa somewhere. I think maybe I do."

The quiche went down on the table, and Pernithia Blakely disappeared back into that thin slice of kitchen. Maya could hear sounds of rummaging.

"I'm fine without cocoa," she finally remembered to call out, but just at that moment Pernithia Blakely gave a triumphant shout and came back to the door brandishing a tin in her hand.

"Found it, look!" she said. "What did you say?"

"Water is fine," said Maya. "I don't need cocoa. Where did you say you put the stone?"

It was just like a police show on television: the writer flicked her eyes lickety-split over to a closet door on Maya's left and back again. But she didn't move to open the door or, for that matter, to answer Maya's question.

"I'm sure it must have a *fabulously* interesting story tied up with it," she said instead. "I'd love to hear more about it, Maya. I've never had a fan give me a rock before! Here, have some quiche. There's salad, too."

And there's a great start to the conversation, thought Maya. Since, for one thing, Maya was hardly a fan, and, for another, she hadn't *given* anyone the gargoyles' egg.

"I think maybe there was a misunderstanding," said Maya, pinching her own leg as hard as she could, just to wake herself up and keep herself brave. "Because you know you said you don't remember much. About that evening."

"I got the quiche at the store around the corner," said the writer, digging in with more gusto than Maya might have expected from someone so mild-mannered. "Pretty good, isn't it?"

"Ms.—um—Blakely," said Maya (uncertain how you were supposed to address a writer; "Pernithia" did seem like it would be going too far). "The thing is, I didn't actually *give* you the gar— the stone. Like I said, it was a misunderstanding. Maybe because you were so feverish? Anyway, you just took it."

Where was Valko? That was what every muscle, every cell, every neuron in Maya was fervently wondering just then.

The writer had gone very still, her eyes fixed on the next bite of quiche waiting on her fork.

"No," she said finally. "There's a lot I don't remember, but you definitely gave me the stone. I just forgot to thank you at the time."

She turned the fork this way and that, considering the bit of quiche, and then popped it into her mouth and looked up again at Maya.

"I'm sorry if I hurt your feelings," said Pernithia Blakely kindly. "You're not making very good progress on your breakfast, by the way."

Since at that moment she couldn't think of a single thing to say, Maya took a bite or two of quiche. It was actually pretty tasty, but her stomach was trembly with nerves.

"That's better," said the writer. "See, I had this sense about you, Maya. I remember that, too. I bet that sounds funny, but you know how writers are, always sensing deeper truths about people."

Ha-ha-ha, thought Maya. *Try the* deeper truth *that you turned into a crazy person a few nights ago!*

"Anyway, you're important somehow. To the story." She paused for dramatic emphasis, and then repeated herself. "Important to the story! That's right—I'm going to Write You In!"

The writer set down her fork and smiled very broadly and waited for Maya to respond in some appropriate way.

"You're going to do what?" said Maya.

"I mean, I don't usually have your demographic in my books—how old are you? Twelve or something?—but I knew right away you were more than meets the eye. Not just a child, but something else. A creature in human disguise. Something dangerous and wonderful."

"In the story you're writing," said Maya, wondering again where Valko was. It had been way, way longer than ten minutes.

The writer eyed her across the table, and Maya's stomach got tighter and tighter.

"I had it, before. I remember, I knew what you were. But then I woke up the next morning, and it was gone again. . . ."

Maya gathered all her courage into one golden heap and jumped in.

"Ms. Blakely," she said. "Will you listen to me, if I tell you something very, very important? I know it sounds hard to believe, but there's something going really wrong in Paris, and you got caught in it the night of the dinner. I can tell you're basically a nice person. . . ."

That was true, right? She was becoming a little scary, just now, but until then she had been fine.

"A nice person," said Maya again, with more definiteness the second time. "But the strangeness caught you and did something odd to your brain, and that's when you started, you know, changing and singing in Bulgarian. You can't trust your brain. You really can't. There's an evil shadow trying to take you over, and every one hundred thirty-seven hours—"

Every 137 hours! Maya gasped and looked at her watch. 10:57. No, 10:58. Oh, no. Where was Valko? Valko hadn't come, and Maya had completely lost track of the time.

Maya was pushing back her chair, and the writer

almost had tears in her eyes, she was so amused.

"You're a gem!" said the writer. "No, Maya, you totally are! Oh, my gosh, I sit up here writing all day, the well going all dry, and then you show up with your *evil shadows* and *singing in Bulgarian—*"

"Quick," said Maya, standing up. "You're a nice person, I know you are. Could you just show me that stone, the one I gave you, just for a moment? Pretty please?"

"You're going right into the story," said the writer. "And I'll even send you an advance copy, when the book's done."

"The *stone*?" said Maya, taking what she hoped was a subtle step closer to the door. "Just a quick peek?"

10:59.

The writer tapped her fingertips together, thinking something over.

"The stone, the stone," she said. "It was when you gave me the stone that I knew what you really were. It's on the tip of my tongue, what you are. Here, we'll do it again. Reenactment!"

Maya's heart was lodged so tightly in her throat that she could hardly breathe. The second hand on her watch was barreling past the six.

The writer went over to the closet and unlatched the door. Her hand reached up to a high shelf and came back, filled with something rocklike and roundish.

"Here it is," she said. "Come closer, now, so I'll remember. I had the stone in my hands, and I looked at you, and I knew what you really, truly were—"

A church bell began to chime. The hands on Maya's watch slid another notch ahead. Her fingertips were beginning to tingle, like the tips of trees in an electrical storm.

11:00.

"You'll see better if I'm holding it," said Maya, who had run out of cleverness and plans.

So this is what she did: she just reached out and took the gargoyles' egg right out of the palm of the writer's hand. It was so cold to the touch that for a millisecond Maya thought there might have been a mistake, that the writer's roundish rock might be some other random stone, after all. But almost as soon as her fingers touched it, a burst of warmth welled up to meet her.

It knows me, thought Maya. Then that comfortable thought was drowned in a wave of magic passing through them, through everything. You'd think you'd get used to it, eventually, the feeling of strange magic washing through the world, but Maya felt, if anything, sicker and wronger than ever before.

The door. She took a seasick step toward the door, and then another.

The writer, meanwhile, had gone completely still as

soon as the bell started chiming. She stood frozen for a moment, until a shiver rippled through her, and her eyes grew darker and fiercer, and she stared at Maya in deep, wild surprise—

"Oh, so *that's* what you are," she said, her voice raspier, deeper, wilder.

Another step, back toward the door, and another step; Maya's free hand had found the knob now, just there, behind the small of her back.

The writer threw back her head and laughed, while Maya wobbled the doorknob with her hidden hand.

Unlatch, unlatch, please unlatch—

"Yes, yes, I remember now! *Maya Davidson*, the girl who's a *dragon*—"

The latch gave, the door crashed open—and Maya ran.

16

BAD NEWS ABOUT DRAGONS

She slipped, stumbled, and flew down the stairs, the egg warming—no, scorching—her hands, flung herself through the heavy front doors, and then tucked her chin down and ran just as fast as she could for the river. She wasn't really thinking; she was just getting away from the suddenly dreadful writer with the wild *samodiva* streak running through her hair and her soul.

The magic still roiling through the air made her feel sick, but she hung on to the egg and kept running. She caught glimpses of things being made wrong by the strangeness—something peculiar going on with the trees in the park; the carousel spiraling up into the sky, as if some very powerful giant had snapped his fingers closed around the pretty flag at the top and *pulled*—but she had no time to stop and stare. Fear made her feet swift and powerful, all the way to the bridge, where a crowd of eager tourists leaning out over the bridge's stone railing got in her way and slowed her down.

That was when the lack of air caught up with her. She let her hands fall to her knees for a moment (the gargoyle's egg still very hot against her palm) and gasped a few times for breath.

Which was how she saw that little flowers were growing under her feet, stretching around the soles of her shoes to blossom—*ping!*—right there on the bridge. She was so itchy inside her skin! One moment more and she, too, would be *ping*ing into something completely new. It was the strangest feeling.

A child turned her way and smiled.

"They're doing tricks!"

"What?" said Maya. That was about all she could manage to say.

"You know: the big, big fish in the river. With their beautiful teeth!"

She stood up again and (on her toes) caught the merest glimpse of glittery creatures, almost too large to be fish, splashing about in the river.

Someone on the bridge threw a bright arc of sardines into the water, and the swimming things kicked up a deeper froth, and the fear came back into Maya's feet.

She was running along the banks of the river when she heard someone calling her name, not in a raspy, *samodiva* voice, but the way ordinary unmagicked humans call out names of people they're fond of: "Maya!"

She whirled around to look, the gargoyles' egg cradled in her arms and her eyes all blurry from exhaustion and worry, and a moment later, Valko was there.

Valko!

Her relief was so enormous that she forgot to be afraid or angry or worried. All those emotions just fell away in one great swoosh.

"You didn't come," she said with her last bit of gasping breath.

"My Baba Silva had me under lock and key," Valko said. "I'm so, so, so, so sorry. Are you okay? Some crazy stuff is happening out here. Did that writer try to eat you or something?"

"I ran away," said Maya, and she was so tired, all of a sudden, that she just sort of melted down onto the pavement. Her head was ringing, her face felt as hot as a gargoyles' egg, and little stars of light were prickling in her eyes.

She could feel Valko's hand on her shoulder, steadying her, but she couldn't find the energy to open her eyes.

"I'm so sorry," he said again. "Please don't faint. Huh, flowers. That's weird. Here—get your head lower and keep breathing. Any better?"

The roaring, starry heat was, in fact, beginning to fade.

Valko waited for a couple of minutes, giving her encouraging pats on the shoulder from time to time, and then he gave her a hand up—carefully, so as not to squash all those baby pink-and-yellow blossoms welling up all around ("The gardeners have been busy!" said Valko, but you could tell he was uncertain about it)—and Maya was on her feet again, feeling woozy and embarrassed.

"Guess I ran too fast," she said, and she gave Valko a shaky smile. "And you didn't ask me about the egg."

She held out her hands to show him. Valko whistled.

"Well, there you go," he said, but he eyed it with distaste. "You got it back. You have superpowers, know that?"

Maya almost managed to laugh. "If I had superpowers, I'd be a better runner," she said.

"Or you'd fly."

"That's more like it."

They crossed the road that ran along the river. Now they were only a few feet away from the Bulgarian embassy. Getting pretty close to Maya's own home—but apparently they weren't going directly there. Valko was steering her toward that imposing door.

"Come in and catch your breath," he said. "You're still shaky, I can tell."

That embassy had a lot of rooms she hadn't seen, back when she had come to dinner. There were the big fancy kitchens somewhere that did the cooking for parties and awards dinners, and there was a very ordinary, smallish kitchen upstairs, all yellow linoleum, that the Nikolovs could use when they didn't want to be fancy. There was a vine made of linoleum climbing up one of its walls, now, true, but that was just the strangeness making things fancy, not the Nikolovs. Her feet were behaving themselves, though (she took a quick look now and then just to check: no flowers). Valko poured her a glass of something very dark and sweet.

"It's cherry juice," he said. "I read somewhere that fruit juice is good when you've had a shock. Nothing's much fruitier than cherry. Okay. Tell me what happened at the writer's place."

She had just gotten to the part where the writer started rasping crazy stuff about Maya being a dragon when she realized there was someone standing in the doorway of the kitchen: a stout woman with an eagle's beak of a nose and the most extraordinary mole on her cheek. It was hard for Maya to take her eyes off that mole. It was mountainous.

The woman said something in Bulgarian to Valko, and Valko said a bunch of other things, also in Bulgarian.

Maya had scrambled to her feet very fast, but that made the room start spinning again, so that she had to grab the table with one hand.

"Watch out," said Valko's voice from Maya's right—and from the other side, a strong, stub-fingered hand settled firmly on Maya's arm.

"Sit down, sit down, child," said Valko's grandmother-with-a-mole. Her English had all sorts of jagged edges. "You fainted earlier, Valko says."

She made a disapproving sound with her tongue.

"Strange weather this day. Odd things going on. Stay sitting. See? I'll sit, too."

Boom. She had pulled another chair to the table and sat down, facing Maya.

"Make me tea, Valko."

Valko jumped up to fill the kettle.

"Now," said the grandmother-with-a-mole. "Maya. That's your name? Nice Bulgarian name."

"I thought it was more like a Hindi name," said Valko from the kitchen counter. "Or maybe Spanish."

"Valko, *tikho*," said the grandmother with a frown. You didn't have to know any Bulgarian at all to know she was hushing Valko up. "I said: Bulgarian name. Where's my tea?"

"Cooking, cooking," said Valko.

"So, Maya," said the grandmother-with-a-mole. "You are this American friend of my hooligan grandson."

Maya nodded.

"Well, he already lived too long in America. It's a

problem. All he cares about now is baseball and Mickey Mouse and Hollywood films with cars exploding like fireworks."

"Really?" said Maya. She had never heard Valko say anything about baseball.

"Yes, very bad," said his grandmother.

"No, not really," said Valko, leaning over to silence the teakettle.

"Am I talking to you?" said the grandmother-with-a-mole. "No. I am talking to this Maya here. So he is becoming practically an American boy. Then they move to France. I think, all right, something new. Variety. World travel. Then I hear: Valko has a new friend. From where? From America! So now we're back to baseball and that Mickey Mouse. I think, time for Valko to come home. Now you understand. You are a sweet, nice American girl, I'm sure. But this boy needs to be Bulgarian."

Valko made a growly sound and put a glass of very dark tea down in front of his grandmother.

"Sugar?" she said.

He brought a bowl of sugar and another little bowl of honey.

Maya was still trying to get her head around the news that it was because of her, the friend from America, that Valko's grandmother-with-a-mole had suddenly decided to drag him off to Bulgaria. That was not a very nice thought. In fact, it made her somewhat cranky.

"Excuse me, Mrs., um . . ." Whoops. This was Valko's mother's mother, right? So what was her name exactly? Maya tried to catch Valko's eye, but he was putting cups away in a cupboard behind them. Valko's grandmother took a sip of her tea, eyeing Maya over the top of her glass all the while.

"Never mind that. Baba Silva will do," she said finally, with a gruff little snort that made her mountainous mole tremble slightly. "Go ahead. Say what you want."

"I think you have the wrong impression of Valko," said Maya. "That's what I was wanting to say . . . Baba Silva."

"Oh! Well, do explain, then! He's only my grandson. I guess I know him quite as well as anybody."

Maya had that slightly sickening feeling she had often had in dreams, when there's a big crowd and a stage and someone wanting you to turn cartwheels or play piano concertos or make a big speech on a subject you know nothing about. What do you do? You open your mouth, and you do your best to start speaking.

"The thing is—Baba Silva, how could you think Valko's not very Bulgarian? That just seems like a mistake somehow. I mean, I've never heard him say anything, not the slightest thing ever, about baseball. Valko has been telling me about Bulgarian culture. He said to bring an odd number of flowers, and not chrysanthemums. I've learned a lot about the Bulgarianness of yogurt. . . ." (All right, that was a bit of a stretch, but sometimes in dreams you can get away with stuff like that.) "He's been teaching me Bulgarian words. He explained what the crazy woman meant when she called me a *zmey*—"

Thwomp! Maya jumped in her chair, but it was just Baba Silva letting one of her massive, stubby-fingered hands drop—like a brick, like a book, like the heavy tail of a dragon—onto the cheerful yellow-and-red of the tablecloth.

"Pause!" said the grandmother-with-a-mole. "Explain about the *zmey*!"

"Baba!" said Valko, giving her a slightly nervous smile as he sat down at the table. "We're trying to make her feel better, not frighten her to death."

"I'm not frightened," said Maya. Then she eyed the grandmother's narrowed eyes and truly mountainous mole. "Not too frightened, anyway. The woman said I was a *zmey* because she was crazy."

"Or because she's right, maybe. Hmm? You, Maya— are you a *zmey*?"

"Noooo," said Maya with some hesitation. It wasn't that she wasn't sure whether she was a dragon or not, but that she couldn't tell where Baba Silva was heading, asking questions like that.

"No? You *sure?*"

Baba Silva leaned closer to Maya. At that distance she really was a little frightening.

"Very sure?"

"Baba, *please* be nice!" said Valko from the other side of the table.

Maya was remembering: *eye contact!* She looked that grandmother-with-a-mole right in the eye.

"How could I be a dragon and not know it?" she said. "I'm definitely not a *zmey.*"

"Ha!" said Valko's grandmother, as if she'd just scored a major point. "Valko, explain to the girl about *zmey.*"

"I was going to ask you, actually," said Valko.

"Ha!" said Baba Silva again. She settled back in her chair. "Well, then. What you don't know about *zmey*: not like your silly-headed dragons, all simple like lizards. Bulgarian *zmey*—much more twisty and beautiful and complicated. Many things at once: flying bird and big snake, okay, and human being, too. Yes, Maya. A person can be a *zmey*. Why not? Changing shape all the time. Maybe your village has a secret cave nearby? Maybe the *zmey* lives there; maybe he's kind and protects you, maybe he eats you. Maybe he comes to you like a beautiful boy or girl, and you fall in love with the beautiful *zmey*. Sad, sad story, love with *zmey*. Sweet songs, but death at the end, oh, yes."

She looked like she got a good bit of satisfaction, that grandmother-with-a-mole, from the thought of sweet songs and death at the end.

"I'm still not a dragon, though," said Maya.

"Good for you," said Baba Silva. "Dangerous to love a *zmey*; dangerous to be a *zmey*. Human beings hunt them, you know. Not just old Saint Georgi with his horse and his sword. You know why they hunt the *zmey*?"

She leaned forward again.

"A man eats the heart of a *zmey*, and he gets strong, strong, strong. An already strong man becomes some great hero warrior. A sick, weak, dying man jumps up and lives again. You can see, Maya: not so good, huh, to be a *zmey*! Sweet songs are nice, but then death, and then someone cooks up your dragon heart all so tasty-delicious with garlic and rosemary—"

"Baba Silva!" said Valko reprovingly. It was true that for a moment there his grandmother-with-a-mole had just about been smacking her lips.

Maya looked at her own very human hands, which were pale and ordinary and so extremely undragon-like, and a tendril of fear sneaked itself down into her bones and took root. What had those gargoyles really done when they translated Fourcroy's evil plans into Bulgarian? It wasn't much good changing "Maya must sacrifice her life for mine" into "Life comes from eating the heart of the *zmey*" if crazy women were still going to come running after her, pointing with their crazy fingers and calling her *dragon dragon dragon*.

But that thought was enough to make Maya stubborn all over again. She was not a dragon. No. But she had a tough skin, didn't she? And a sharp-clawed brain. And, for that matter, a spine.

And my heart, said Maya firmly to herself, *is not tasty-delicious*.

So there!

17

BONES AND SHADOWS,
MISBEHAVING

"Honestly, though," said Valko. "If anyone's actually a dragon, it's my grandmother, not you."

They were sitting at Maya's dining-room table, which was covered at the moment with maps, pencils, and Valko's geometry paraphernalia (rulers, compasses). Dreadful, dreadful noises floated in from the other room: Pauline Vian had come over to practice her scales.

"No clenching!" Maya's mother called from the kitchen. "Gently, gently, Pauline! Big, lovely tone!"

Valko had put a red dot on the map of Paris, right where the awful Fourcroy had made the embassy wall explode, and now he was using the compass to draw a series of circles expanding outward from that center, each circle labeled neatly with date and time.

"You know what?" said Maya. "She's not actually as terrifying as I thought she was going to be, your Baba Silva."

"Ha-ha-ha," said Valko. "If you think she's not

terrifying, you just weren't paying attention. Look, that's the 3200-meter radius, coming up on Saturday."

It was a pretty big circle he had just drawn: it stretched halfway across Paris. Maya and Valko stared at it for a while, feeling grim.

"The next one's worse," said Maya, since stating the obvious can be satisfying when disaster confronts you. "Wait, let me look at my chart—November twenty-ninth at nine p.m. Draw that one."

Valko measured out a pretty impressive distance with the ruler and reached for the compass.

November 29.

There was something she should be noticing about that date. Maya was sure there was something about dates, about time. But what? The scritchy scales in the other room were making it hard for her to think.

Valko was tracing out a vast, vast circle now.

"And there goes Paris," he said, as his compass pencil made its enormous circle on the map. "Everything from the Bois de Boulogne to the Père-Lachaise cemetery."

"A cemetery," said Maya. "Ugh. How weird will that be?"

"Stay far away, that's my advice," said Valko. He put the compass down and stood up to get a better view of the map as a whole. "But you know what? We'll find out about cemeteries days before that. There are some other ones in the previous circle—see that there? That's the cimetière du Montparnasse. And hospitals and stuff. It's all bad."

Maya looked at those expanding circles, spreading like ripples across the Paris pond, and the thought she had been missing came zipping back into her mind so quickly she slapped the table with the palm of her hand.

"But it won't reach the Forest of Fontainebleau!" she said. It felt like a discovery.

"Will so," said Valko. "You know it will, eventually. Not for a few weeks, though. That's fifty kilometers away, at least."

Maya was shaking her head. She was feeling something she was hardly used to these days: a surge of real, actual hope.

"No, look! The strangeness won't get there in time," said Maya. "See? That shadow has *forty days* to get itself a body again. Think about it: if the strangeness reached the Salamander Rock, where Fourcroy was *born*, where the Summer Box was hidden—well, then I bet the shadow would be able to magick itself back to life, no problem. That's the Suitable Magical Place. But the shadow can't go outside the strangeness, can it? You know, like a fish needing water to swim in. And the strangeness isn't going to get there, not by November twenty-ninth! And November twenty-ninth is *the fortieth day*."

Maya looked up at Valko.

"I wonder what happens after that, if we keep him from getting what he wants. You know, like the memory stone and that splotch of blood he left on the paper. Which is pretty gross. And me. If he can't get me to sacrifice myself for him and we can just keep the things he needs out of his reach and somehow slow him down . . ."

Valko wiggled the compass back and forth, back and forth, as he considered the question.

"Well," he said, "if the forty-days thing is true, then getting safely to November thirtieth is, like, one of our goals, right? But then even if the shadow guy doesn't get his body, what about the strangeness spreading over the whole world? That's still very bad—"

Pauline Vian's head (that amazing hair!) poked through the doorway between the two rooms.

"Excuse me," she said. "But you are talking about what, in here? Why the maps, and what is 'strangeness'?"

Maya and Valko looked at each other. In fact, they had one of those rare mind-reading moments that happen from time to time. Each of them thought, at the very same time, *Could she understand? Why not? Let's try!*

"Have you noticed the strange things happening in the neighborhood, the last few weeks?" said Valko.

Pauline frowned.

"*Non*," she said.

"The explosion that took out a bit of the

Bulgarian-embassy wall?"

"Ah, well, then: *oui*."

"The changes in the trees and cars? The shift in the bakeries from croissants to *vines* and *flowers*? The remaking of the Eiffel Tower?"

"What's wrong with the Tour Eiffel?" said Pauline.

"You can't see how different it looks?" said Maya. "You really can't see that?"

"Different from what?" said Pauline.

"From the little Towers they sell for key chains, for instance? Wait, I think James has one in his room somewhere—"

Maya ducked for a moment into James's room, which was basically a mound of clutter with a bed in the middle, and looked around with quick eyes until a glint of fake bronze found her, a little Eiffel Tower souvenir that had been buried for a few days under dust and dirty socks.

"See?" she said as she came back into the living room. "Notice anything about this Eiffel Tower? It is not a tree. Right? It's just a nice, geometrical tower, with no leaves or roots."

Pauline looked at her as if Maya were the sort of unbalanced person who needed careful handling.

"The little toy Eiffels have never had leaves or roots," she said, explaining the universe to someone with very little sense and less experience or knowledge. "*Non!* It is *tradition* that the toy souvenirs look quite unlike the actual Eiffel Tower."

"No," said Maya. "Actually your brain is being fooled. See, this guy who was sort of related to me—"

"Henri de Fourcroy," said Valko. "He lived in the Salamander House, over near the elementary school."

"Anyway, he was close to dying, or actually dying, so he did this bad-magic stuff by the wall of the Bulgarian embassy—"

"That was October twentieth," said Valko. "The date becomes important later."

"And that caused the explosion, but what it really did was open this awful loophole in the laws of physics, so he could go on as a shadow until he could get his body back, which apparently he has forty days to do—"

"That part really does seem dubious to me," said Valko. "But we have evidence for the laws of physics being warped. It's a pattern, you see."

"Because one hundred thirty-seven hours after he did his loophole magic, I touched the wall he had left his memory in, the strangeness happened again, and that started this chain, and every one hundred thirty-seven hours everything gets strange—"

"We measured the radius of the affected area," said Valko. "It's doubling every time, so that's really bad."

"And we have to stop this from happening, but that's

hard, especially since I've been sort of trapped into helping him, like Oedipus Rex bound by fate, but still we just have to defeat the shadow, somehow, of that Henri de Fourcroy. Before the forty days are up—"

"Which is November twenty-ninth, at nine o'clock in the evening."

"Yes," said Maya. "That's it. We have to close his loophole. Even though we don't quite know how. Or else the whole world eventually becomes deformed and wrong and strange. Which would be awful."

Pauline Vian looked with incredulous and frowning eyes into each of their faces, first Maya's and then Valko's, and then she turned her lips down and gave a very Gallic shrug.

"But this is *impossible*," she said. "In fact, it's absurd."

"It does *seem* totally impossible," said Valko, looking just slightly embarrassed. "But some of it keeps turning out to be true."

"Pay attention on Saturday morning," said Maya. "The next round of strangeness happens at four in the morning. Saturday. Just see if anything looks changed to you, when you wake up. Try to pay attention."

"I am always paying attention," said Pauline. You could see that she was intrigued and suspicious, both at once. But then, she had been made fun of at school more than most, being so small, so out-of-the-ordinary, and so dreadfully, awfully smart. "Well. I will take care to pay *particular* attention on Saturday. *Au revoir,* you two." And she swung her violin case around and headed down the hall to the door.

Maya and Valko looked at each other; Valko shrugged.

"She's kind of right, after all," said Valko. "It's absurd."

"Yes, fine," said Maya. "Now focus. We have to figure out how to stop Henri de Fourcroy's shadow from getting itself reborn."

"And how to get the laws of physics behaving themselves again," said Valko. He smiled as he said it, though. "Don't forget that. At least it's good you don't have the letter with the bloodstain on it, right? You left that behind. He can't come back to life without a trace of himself, that's what you said."

"That's what that letter said. With the 'recipe.' Yeah. But what if sitting around and waiting is what the shadow wants me to do? What if *anything* I do or don't do turns out to be what he planned all along? What if that's what being bound means?"

It made a person restless around the edges, not knowing what the rules were. And not knowing whether there was any way she, Maya, could break those rules. You could drive yourself crazy, trying to figure it all out. How could Maya fight against Fourcroy's evil and shadowy plans if every step she took ended up being just the step he wanted her to take? That was awful. That was the *clockwork path*—and Maya absolutely hated it.

At least she had rescued the egg. Neither the crazy singing ladies nor the shadowy Fourcroy had the memory stone. So that was one good thing. Probably.

"Why's it good that *you* have it?" asked Valko. He was still grumpy about that egg.

"They wanted to use it to lure me to what they think is a Suitable Magical Place. Like where he was born! That was probably the best place for him to come back to life, right? But now we know he can't get there in time, not in forty days, because the strangeness won't reach that far by then, and the shadow can't go past the edges of his loophole. So now it's me luring them. We just have to find the right place. A sneaky place. Somewhere where *we* can bind *him*, you know—not that I've exactly figured out how—instead of him always binding me."

Where he won't get to eat my heart, after all, Maya added silently. *Even if the whole world thinks I'm actually a* zmey.

On Saturday morning Maya slept right through her alarm, she was so worn-out, and didn't open her eyes until her father came knocking at her door.

"There's a call for you, Maya," he said. "Pauline's on the vine."

What?

She opened the door more or less still in her sleep and

took the phone from her father's hands.

The vine!

The phone had sprouted during the night. Yes, and now she remembered: she had been dreaming of jungles. Long, dark tendrils hung down from every possible side, and it felt oddly squishy to Maya's fingers.

"Ugh," she said. "This is disgusting."

Her father gave her a puzzled look.

"Pardon? What is disgusting?" said Pauline, her voice managing somehow to claw its way through all that excessive vegetation.

"This phone," said Maya. "It wants to be a plant."

"Ah," said Pauline. She sounded uncertain. "It . . . changed?"

"Yes—oh, that's right. Did you notice?"

"I . . . I . . . but Maya, it is too bizarre, what has happened here. I woke up at four, to see. It was dark, of course. So I took out my violin and played, just to feel better, you see, about everything."

"Your neighbors!" said Maya, aghast. The Davidsons were regularly getting complaints from the people who lived below them in their building whenever James dropped a toy on the floor or Maya's father forgot and flushed a toilet after ten p.m. Practicing violin at four in the morning? Hard to imagine what Parisian neighbors might do.

"The neighbors, they are far away," said Pauline. "The

appartement is not small, you know. And I have this thing, a *sourdine*, I put on the bridge of the violin, that makes it very quiet. But Maya, I saw . . . I saw strange things. Is this what you were meaning? I saw the back of the chair curl into a roll like a pastry. I saw the pictures change on my walls. It was *horrible* and *bizarre*. And I opened my window and played my violin, you know, to stay calm—"

Oh, those poor neighbors! thought Maya again, but she tried not to let that thought show.

"Quietly, I played. My Saint-Saëns, you know, not scales. And Maya—it was frightening, truly. A shadow came crawling up the wall toward my window."

"A shadow," said Maya.

"It was a shadow in the shape of a man. It climbed up as I played, and it was . . . talking to itself. That is not typical, Maya, for shadows, is it?"

"No," agreed Maya.

"It seemed so angry, if shadows can be angry. It did not want to come, but it kept coming. It was following the *musique*—it said something like that. Angrily. And that is not the worst thing. The worst thing is, it was whispering your name, Maya. I became disconcerted, to be honest. I closed the window, and I put the violin away. There were other shadows out there, too. Dead things. Skeletons, even. I could feel them. Wanting to come climb up my wall. It was hideous!"

"So what happened?"

"The shadows went away, you see. When I stopped playing."

"Oh," said Maya. She was remembering the way the darkness had come seeping out of the walls on her birthday, when Pauline started playing. "Because you were playing that piece. The one about death."

"But yes, of course," said Pauline. She sounded a little defensive. "I like it. It's my best, most difficult piece."

The funny thing was, she played it so badly! When musicians in myths played their lyres or their pipes and made the wild beasts dance, wasn't it always because the music was so lovely, so exquisite, that not even a tiger could hear it without shedding a tear? Maya smiled into the tangled vinery of the telephone: the dead, it seemed, were not so picky. Or maybe they were picky, very picky, but what they picked, of all music, was the stiff scratchy wail produced by Pauline.

So apparently Pauline Vian did have a musical talent after all: unlike most people, even those with otherwise impressive musical skills, she could really, actually, raise the dead.

Because here is what happened next in Maya's apartment:

"You know what they said in the bakery this morning,

Maya?" said her father when she brought out the dreadfully changed telephone a couple of minutes later. "They said there's been some trouble with the old bones of the Montparnasse cemetery."

"What does that mean?"

"I guess they usually keep to themselves, pretty much. Quiet people, bones. But this morning they had some wild celebration and went rioting after. Madame Lasalle had it from her cousin, who's a baker over that way. Gang of bones broke right into his shop and made off with all his pastries, his *vines* and *flowers*. And then headed off this way, or so it seemed to him."

"Can bones eat?" puzzled James. "They don't have any tummies."

"No, they can't," said his mother. "So it was very rude and greedy for them to go troubling the poor baker."

Maya had listened to this much with distress growing like a weed (a vine?) in her.

"*Excuse me,*" she said finally, losing some of her cool. "But it's not just that bones can't *eat*! Bones can't walk, bones can't celebrate, bones can't break into shops—they can't do anything, because *bones are not alive.*"

Silence.

"Maya," said her mother. "Really, sweetie! That seems very harsh."

Maya hardly knew how to respond to that. "Harsh!"

"Yes, actually. This isn't California. It's not nice to come into a different culture and be so critical. It's intolerant, and I won't have it."

That in itself was more than surprising, the heat with which Maya's mother spoke. (She was so reliably calm and unflustered!) But to be reprimanded for not having paid enough attention to the feelings of *bones*—this was a bitter pill. It stuck in Maya's throat, that pill, and made it hard for her to say anything at all.

"Oh, dear," said Maya's mother, putting a hand to her brow. "I just snapped at you, Maya, didn't I? I'm so sorry. I'm not myself these days."

"All perfectly natural," said Maya's father. "We can handle worse snapping than that, can't we, Maya?"

Maya nodded, but her mind was tackling a new and even more dreadful thought: if her mother *wasn't herself*—how much of that was due to being pregnant, and how much, perhaps, to the waves of strangeness washing over their household every 137 hours? You weren't supposed to be exposed to chemicals when you were pregnant, were you? Or radiation or very high altitudes or kitty litter or even some kinds of cheese?

But what about being exposed to high doses of *magic*?

Maya shivered with worry.

It was another reason, on top of a whole mountain's worth of reasons, why she had to make sure that strangeness went away. To make the world safe for her mother (and the—what had she called it?—*little bean*), Maya absolutely had to slam all loopholes shut and seal the cracks and crevices and make the world leak-free and safe again. She had to. What's more, she vowed grimly, she *would*.

18

AN IMAGINARY COUNTRY

What happened on Monday afternoon was not entirely Maya's fault.

She had come home that day in a grisly mood because during her French class, the teacher had called on her (as he almost never did) just five minutes after it had started to rain so hard the water went streaking diagonally across the huge windows that looked out from the classroom into the bleakness of the courtyard. The rain had made her think dark thoughts about time passing and how the fateful fortieth day was now already this Thursday, and that had reminded her of how she still had no clue where in Paris might count as a Suitable Magical Place for summoning shadowy Fourcroys and defeating them, and that had made her wonder all over again how an ordinary human, even if very motivated and trying hard to be brave, actually goes about defeating a death-cheating shadow. And all of those thoughts (together with the grim, slanting rain) had distracted her enough that even though she had studied very hard the night before and had memorized the poem in question (which was by someone called Arthur Rimbaud, and as far as she could tell compared all the vowels in the alphabet to various colors, and had been quite difficult to understand)— anyway, even though she had studied and memorized and prepared, when the teacher asked her to explain to the class lines three and four, in which the letter *A* is likened to the black of "velvet-suited flies buzzing around cruel stenches"—which is, let's be honest, a peculiar turn of phrase—her mind and her French had failed her, and she had not been able to say anything that made the slightest bit of sense. So she would not be called on again for a month, probably. If ever. So much for hard work and fitting in!

Then when she came into the apartment after school, she found her mother sick in bed with a headache and nausea, and that made Maya herself feel sick inside with worry, and all those angry, anxious thoughts about how fragile and recently ill mothers should not be put through (or put themselves through) dangerous adventures like *being pregnant* battered against the glassy, brittle sides of her brain and were hard to keep hidden. She bottled her worries up and kissed her mother and promised to check on James, who, said her mother, had been "playing so quietly all afternoon."

And that was the third thing: James wasn't in his room. For a moment Maya panicked, remembering other awful times when she had looked for her baby brother and he hadn't been there, but that lasted only a moment. Because then she caught the sound of James humming, which meant he was busy with something fun and complicated and entrancing, and that sound was coming from behind her own bedroom door. And when she flung open that door, she found her little brother on the floor of her room, an old box open beside him, the box's ancient papers and letters strewn all around him, and several of his little toy people having battles on top of some very old and intricate illustrated sheet, which James had apparently dug out of the family-archive box and unfolded flat on the floor.

"*James!*" said Maya. (*Said* is kind: she actually shouted.) "*What are you doing in here with my things?*"

James went from prone to sitting up in less time than you would think possible. He didn't look guilty, but he did look very surprised.

"My little truck rolled in here by accident and got under your bed. Did you know there are boxes hiding under there? This box is mostly boring stuff, but I found this imaginary country in there, so my people needed to do some karate on it right away. It's a map."

"James!" said Maya. She could feel herself beginning to seethe, and that in itself was unsettling. All these years since James was a teeny baby, she had never felt as annoyed with him as she did now. He had always been so incredibly charming—he smiled at you with those soft brown eyes, and how could you be mad, really? But now she seethed. And maybe that was because she was especially stressed out and impatient, and maybe it was because James had fewer drops of charm running through his veins these days than he used to have: hard to say.

"You *cannot* come into my room and go through my stuff," said Maya. "That is one hundred percent NOT OKAY. Get up, take your people, and go back to your own room. Now I have to clean up this whole mess."

James gulped and looked around, as if he thought the nice sister he had known all these years must be hiding somewhere nearby. That just made Maya feel even grumpier, of course. She picked up his toys and stomped back across the hall to his room with them and left them in a topsy-turvy pile on his bed, while James trailed along sadly, and then she went back into her room and shut the door firmly and sat down on her bed and put her face in her hands.

That was a bad moment indeed.

So: on top of her mother feeling sick and the world-as-we-know-it maybe being about to end, she was having to look the possibility in the eye that she, Maya Davidson, was not always a very nice person. In fact, she, Maya, seemed to be turning out to be the sort of person who snaps at her beloved baby brother for almost no reason. It was discouraging and a disappointment.

After a short bout of misery, though, Maya's eyes started to wander around the room a bit, noticing the old letters everywhere and the general chaos, of course, but also, more and more, pulled in by that printed sheet of paper James had spread out across the floor as a world for his little people. It was indeed a map; she could see the roads and avenues wandering about across it, but what kind of town could that be? The artist had drawn in hundreds of little trees, cypresses for the most part, but also the wider, darker triangles of pine trees, and mixed into those trees were dozens and dozens of little houses, some with towers, some not. What was this place, and why did so many of the houses look like itty-bitty temples?

Maya moved the book aside that was holding the top of the map flat against the floor, and she couldn't help it—she gasped out loud.

Because under the book, it turned out, the map had been hiding a title: *Le Père-Lachaise*.

Of course! Those little temple-like houses weren't houses at all, but tombs.

Maya had never seen any map of any place quite like

this one, but now her mind had come quite fully to life and was racing ahead at full speed. Père-Lachaise cemetery! What was that map doing in the Fourcroy family archives? It was very, very old, she could see that. In the bottom right corner, in very small type, was the printer's date: 1887.

And all along the edges there were long lists of names. The little hairs on the back of her neck were standing up now; they knew what was coming, just as a tree knows trouble's on its way a split second before the bolt of lightning strikes it. She ran her tingling, slightly electrified fingers down the right edge of the paper: Flourens, Foignet, Fontaine . . . *Antoine François Fourcroy.*

The lightning whipped through her.

How about that? The Fourcroy family had a tomb in Père-Lachaise! Yes! *There was a Fourcroy tomb at Père-Lachaise!* Maya worked quickly now, matching the number after Fourcroy's name with the little numbers by the gravestones on the map, and there it was indeed. A tiny picture of a tiny funerary column, tucked into a paisley-shaped part of the map that was quite heavily dotted with graves and trees. Not far from Chopin! Well, she had heard of Chopin.

She sat for quite a while, thinking this all over, and then she telephoned Valko.

"I think I've found the Suitable Magical Place," she

said, little invisible sparks of wild electricity scattering all over the curling vines of that phone. "And you know what? I'm even almost beginning to have a plan."

Valko was not pleased, though, when she told him they would be spending Thursday night hiding out in a cemetery. In fact, he balked.

"I don't get it. If you think that's a place where he could come back to life, *why are you going anywhere near it?* You see how illogical that is, right? Plus I'm not a big fan of cemeteries," he said. "Are you?"

"Doesn't matter whether we like them," said Maya. "Listen. I *have* to find a Suitable Magical Place. I was bound, remember? I *have* to go near it."

"That's silly. Just stay at home. I'll lock your door or something to keep you there."

"Haven't you been paying attention? Every time I try to get rid of something I'm bound to keep or try not to go somewhere I'm bound to go, I end up doing *exactly* what that Fourcroy wanted anyway. I threw away the compass, and it came back. I dragged you away from the Salamander House, and then I went racing back to the writing desk myself! Because my brain came up with such wonderfully good reasons. If you locked my door, I'd probably find some really good reason to climb out the window. Seriously."

It was just facing facts, that was what she was doing.

Maya felt the tingle of it in her voice: it was all true. But she had figured out another true bit, too.

"So far the only time I've managed to wiggle out of doing something I'm bound to do is when I've *looked* like I'm doing what Fourcroy wanted and then kind of cheated right at the end—like when I went back to that writing desk and didn't take the letter. See? That's why the cemetery's so perfect."

Valko made a half-doubting, half-intrigued sort of sound.

"Because the Fourcroy family tomb *is* an in-between sort of place—with Fourcroy's name on it! It's *suitable*. And what he really needs is a dose of Eternal Rest, right? It's the opposite of the rock where he was born, out at Fontainebleau."

"Maybe shadows hate cemeteries, too," said Valko. "So maybe it's going to be kind of hard to get him to visit his family tomb. Because other than that, it's perfect, sure: you jump out from behind a grave and tell him you left that bloodstain of his in the Salamander House, so ha-ha! Ingredients missing! No new body for him! And then he cries wicked shadowy tears and we stick him to the Fourcroy tomb with superglue."

"Something like that, right," said Maya, not taking the bait. "Now we just have to figure out how to get him there."

Maya gave that question some serious thought, and then on Tuesday became anxious about the way time was passing and took a wild leap instead:

"Mom," she said. "Could you teach me a little emergency violin? Like, right away?"

Her mother laughed out loud.

"Excuse me? Violin? You? But remember how you hid under the bed when you were six—"

"I know, I know," said Maya. It was family legend. She had been under the bed for four hours. The police had almost been called. Maya's career as a musician had begun and ended, right there under that bed. "Because I didn't want you to show me how to play 'Twinkle, Twinkle, Little Star.' I know. But now it's kind of an emergency. That piece Pauline's always playing—I really need to learn to play some of it. By Thursday."

"*Bonjour!* And what is this about the violin of Pauline?" said Pauline herself, in her very correct French. Pauline! Maya's father must have let her in just now. Maya's spirits sank another inch or so into the mire. "What is it you are saying about the violin?"

"You are an inspiration to Maya, apparently," said Maya's mother. "She is suddenly asking for violin lessons. She wants to learn your Saint-Saëns piece, that *Danse macabre.*"

"Just a little of it," said Maya, feeling that dizzy-headed weakness that is a side effect of watching one's plans step out onto a patch of quicksand and be sucked down to their doom. "By Thursday."

Now both Pauline and her mother were looking at her with quizzical expressions.

"But Maya," said Pauline. "It is not *possible*."

"Even for you, my marvelous Maya!" said her mother.

And she went, laughing, to the kitchen to get some of those cookies she always brought out when Pauline came over to practice.

As soon as Maya's mother had left the room, Pauline whipped her head around and gave Maya a sharp-pointed, spear-shaped stare.

"What is this about you and the violin?" she said. "Why do you need the *Danse macabre*? Does this have to do with—with—the things changing? The shadow that climbed up my wall?"

That was part of the problem with Pauline, of course. She hadn't skipped two whole grades by being fuzzy headed or the slightest bit easy to mislead.

"Yes," said Maya.

Pauline waited.

Maya opened her mouth to explain, and then decided it would be helpful to have some props and dragged Pauline into her room to show her the map.

"There's an old Fourcroy tomb in Père-Lachaise, see? For an Antoine François Fourcroy."

"The scientist from the eighteenth century," said Pauline with a prim pursing of her lips. "Whose betrayal, some have said, cost the great Antoine Lavoisier, *father of modern chemistry*, his head during the Revolution."

Maya stared at her; Pauline surprised her by blushing.

"You mentioned the name Fourcroy the other day, you know," she said with a modest frown. "So naturally I did some little researches. So that old Fourcroy was the ancestor of this other one, the shadow?"

"Who comes following you when you play the violin," said Maya. "If I could just learn that piece, a little bit of it, maybe he would come following me. And I could lead him to his grave. And he could be finished. That's what I was thinking."

"This Thursday evening," said Pauline thoughtfully. "Because of the—the—"

She waved her hands about all loop-de-loop in the air. It was as good a way to describe the strangeness as any, thought Maya. There was a silence, while Pauline furrowed her brow.

"*Bon!*" said Pauline, and she nodded with such decision that her remarkable hair almost sizzled through the air. "It is clear. I will come with you to Père-Lachaise. I will play the *Danse macabre*, and you will lock the

291

shadow away in his family tomb. Good! Done!"

"Girls! James! Cookies!" called Maya's mother from the other room.

Done? thought Maya. *Done?*

It seemed quite far from done, to Maya. It was a plan without a plan—go to this enormous, probably very creepy cemetery, have Pauline play a bit of scritchy violin, and then what? Hope for the best? That was not "done." Come to think of it, that was perhaps even the opposite of done.

And that night, restlessness made her very uneasy in her skin, so she took the gargoyles' egg out from its hiding place in the Summer Box and watched the images ripple across its surface: fields of wildflowers playing in an invisible breeze, horses pulling old-fashioned carriages along a Paris street, a tangle of pine branches as if from the point of view of someone climbing a tree. A woman sitting in a park, turning her head, smiling with eyes full of love. Maya's heart did a little dance: she knew that face. She had seen it carved in stone above the door of the Salamander House. She saw an echo of it every day in the mirror, too, because the look of the Lavirottes had welled up all over again in her, along, apparently, with the Lavirotte magic, all these generations later. Light and dark rearranged themselves on the surface of the gargoyles' egg, and the woman, Henri's mother, raised a thin, nimble hand to brush the hair out of her eyes, and Maya saw the bracelet around that wrist, the delicate chain with the water stone embedded in it.

Oh! It was her own bracelet, or the shadow of it, preserved forever in the shifting pigments of the memory stone.

It comes with a choice—that was what her mother had said.

But what did that even mean? Really, what did that *mean*? Maya peered at the tiny image in the gargoyles' egg, but it was too small and too indistinct. No clues there, as far as she could see.

A *choice* would be an improvement over a world made up of billions of little dominoes. That much Maya knew. The problem with her life at the moment was the business of having no choice at all: of being on the clockwork path.

After all, what had she done so far that was what you might call anticlockwork? Not much. She had left the letter with the helpful bloodstain back in the Salamander House. That was good. So maybe the shadow could not get himself a body, exactly, if there was no physical trace of him mixed up in the spell. And she had taken the Summer Box away from the probably very suitable magical spot out in the woods where Fourcroy had been born. But whether what she was planning to do now was clockwork or anticlockwork, that was hard to say.

As she settled the gargoyles' egg back into the Summer Box, she found herself letting her fingers wander a bit through the little treasures there: the ribbons that had once been the tail of a kite, the envelope holding that lock of baby hair—

It was like being zapped by the most miniature bolt of lightning: a tiny shock that sprinted right through her, from fingertip to foot bones.

She had forgotten all about that lock of hair.

(So had Valko, by the way. He would not have been as excited about her leaving the bloodstained letter behind, if he had remembered the twist of silver-blond hair, tucked away in the Summer Box. A physical trace!)

Maya jumped up. How did you get rid of hair? She had tried throwing the compass-button out the window, and it had pretty much bounced right back into her hands. So this was a test. Was she still free enough to be able to destroy a lock of hair tied up in a narrow, old-fashioned ribbon?

I'll burn it, she thought, and she was already on her feet and heading to the apartment's little kitchen. *Burned things can't come back.*

There was a flaw in this plan, however. As Maya pounded into the kitchen, she practically ran down her mother, who was putting a carton of milk back into the miniature French refrigerator.

"Can't sleep?" said her mother. "Neither can I. Here, I'll heat up some milk for you, too."

Maya stared at the ring of blue flame on the stove, and her grip on the envelope from the Summer Box became instantly several notches more desperate.

"I'll watch the milk," she said with her newly tight-wound and desperate voice. "You go sit down."

And she clenched the envelope in her hand.

"Maya?" said her mother.

Could she do it? That was the clockwork question. Her muscles imagined flinging the little envelope onto the bright blue flames. She could imagine it. She could imagine it very clearly! But whether her hand could actually *move*—

"Maya!" said her mother. "What on earth are you doing?"

And she reached right over and plucked the envelope out of Maya's frozen and shuddering hand.

It was like being released from a trap made of a million rubber bands, all at once. Maya nearly lost her balance and fell over, the unpressure was such a sudden surprise.

"Oh!" said her mother, in a different sort of voice entirely—a delighted, wondering voice. "Look at this! That old lock of James's hair!"

"*James?*" said Maya.

"You brought this to Paris with you, Maya? But how sweet you are!"

"James?" said Maya.

"His first haircut! You had been reading some old-fashioned book, remember? And you said, 'I want a lock of his hair to keep forever and ever!' We laughed! But it was very adorable of you, actually. So I tied it up in a little bit of ribbon, and—"

"James?" said Maya a third time. Her mind had gotten itself completely stuck. This was not James's hair. This envelope had been in the Summer Box. Look at the name scrawled on it! The name was not James Davidson's name. The little ribbon actually had an *H de F* embroidered into it, with the tiniest of silk stitches. But her mother's eyes were soft and shining, caught up in that memory of young Maya, and baby James, and other locks of hair, and other ribbons. . . .

"You'll keep it very safe, won't you?" said her mother, and she tucked the loop of fine baby hair back into the little envelope and then tucked the envelope back into Maya's hand. "Babies are such temporary things! They grow up so fast, and there's so little to remember the babyness of them by. Promise me you'll take care of this."

"Even if it isn't from James at all?" said Maya. *Even if it's from somebody much, much less lovable than our*

James? "I think it's actually from someone who lived a long time ago."

Her mother laughed.

"No, sorry," she said. "Only our family's babies ever had hair quite that color. Moonlit babies, that's what my mother used to say. And only just at the start—look how lovely and brown you are now! Keep it safe, sweetheart. And now here's our milk, all steaming and ready. . . ."

So that was that, unfortunately. Maya could feel the little jolt and tug as the universe popped her right back onto the clockwork path. It is one thing to be bossed around by shadows and gargoyles, but once your mother has added her voice to theirs—especially if your mother is a Lavirotte, you understand, with just the faintest haze of magic still lingering about her, even if she doesn't quite know it herself—well, then you are well and truly bound. Stuck. And perhaps, in this case, doomed.

19

IN THE CITY OF THE DEAD

The main entrance to Père-Lachaise cemetery turned out to feature everything you might expect from a border between two worlds: a grand and arching semi-circle of marble wall, ornamental black chains strung from stubby stone post to stubby stone post on either side of the entrance path, massive gates between a pair of slightly tombstone-shaped plinths decorated with carved torches and carved wreaths and carved hourglasses and carved quotations in languages Maya vaguely recognized but could not read.

Maya and Valko and Pauline stood there for a moment, shivering a little in the fading sunlight, even though they had made special efforts to dress in layer upon layer of their warmest clothes.

"*Spes illorum immortalitate plena est*," said Pauline finally, with a frown. "Hmm."

Maya and Valko turned to stare at her, but she had

not just been possessed, slightly ahead of schedule, by demons. Pauline, of course, was in the track at school where the kids studied classical languages instead of "Trades and Technology": she was quoting the Latin from the gates.

"'Their hope is full of immortality,'" Pauline said again, in French, once she noticed the blank faces turned her way. "Well, our job is to dash those hopes, *non*? No immortality for your wicked and shadow-shaped Fourcroy, Maya. No! Ha-ha-*ha*!"

She could be a little frightening sometimes, that Pauline. She had her violin case strapped over her shoulder; her hair was squidging out fiercely from under her hood. Any person looking at her from afar would have thought this was a sweet little girl with an artistic soul, rather than the miniature Angel of Death she showed some signs of wanting to be.

"Only the kind of immortality you get from eating the hearts of my friends," said Valko, squaring his shoulders. "That's the kind I'm totally against."

"Let's go in," said Maya. If they stood here waiting one more minute, the last drops of her courage were going to seep out through the soles of her feet and be gone.

"You will destroy him," said Pauline cheerfully. "He will be squashed to smithereens by you. I look forward to it."

Maya lowered her head against the cold and led them in through the gates.

They were three kids sent by their *professeur de musique* to look for Chopin's tomb—that was their line. But the man in the little office to the left of the gates didn't ask them what they were up to, just handed them a map and tucked his chin back into his woolen muffler. It was a cold afternoon, and atmospheric wisps of mist had begun to gather in the tree branches farther away.

"Straight ahead," said Maya. She was checking the beautiful old map against the bright new one. "Along this main street here, and then there should be stairs, I think, up the hill on the right. . . ."

Her voice petered out, swallowed whole by the cold, still air. One of her mother's guidebooks had called Père-Lachaise cemetery a *necropolis*, which means a "city for the dead." And the path they were on really did feel like a street—a broad, empty boulevard through some town in a universe far away. The tombs stood like elegant small houses on either side, with cold-looking trees in between them.

They even had sidewalks. Why did the dead need sidewalks?

Valko was walking close enough by her side that his jacket kept rustling against her arm; he didn't like cemeteries, Maya suddenly remembered. It was inconsistent with his basically scientific view of the world, but inconsistency is what makes people people, and not just clever machines soaked in salt water.

"Good news is, Part One was a snap," he said to Maya under his breath.

Part One of Maya's plan was "get into Père-Lachaise before it closes." That had actually involved a lot of running through métro stations, because school got out pretty late on Thursdays, and of course they had to drop their schoolbooks and pick up supplies at Maya's apartment on the way—so having made Part One work was an achievement.

"Hope this map is still right," said Maya, wiggling her fingers in her gloves. "Hope he's still there."

Part Two was "find tomb and hide."

Once you left the main avenue, the topography of the place became more complicated. They kept stopping to look at the two maps, the bright and confident new one, and the lovely imaginary world of the old one. The paths up through the tombs on the old hillside were narrower and had more curves in them. Maya led them too far at first, to a grand circular intersection, the Rond-point Casimir Périer, where they turned their backs on the grand monument in the center and consulted the elegant metal street signs.

"Oh, I see where we are now," said Maya, turning the

map around. "Come this way. Eleventh Division—we just zigzag a little, and it's over here."

"Hiding's going to be easy," said Valko, looking around. "I was worried, down there by the entrance, but this is like a jungle, practically."

The graves in this section were old, their cupids and urns worn down by year after year of rain and snow and human neglect. And trees everywhere, a great tangle of plants and graves all up and down that hillside.

The whole cemetery had been so quiet, so hushed all this time, that when they turned a corner and saw a pair of flesh-and-blood old ladies gazing up reverently at the statue of a marble muse weeping into a lyre, Maya felt rather shocked.

She stopped in her tracks, but Pauline clapped her hands.

"And there it is!" said Pauline. "The resting place of the great Chopin!"

The old ladies turned around and smiled. Clearly they were mistaking Pauline for an angelic and sensitive child.

"Minus his heart," Pauline added.

The old ladies looked just the teeniest bit less certain about the angelic child.

"Shipped to Poland on its own," said Pauline. "I've always wondered exactly *how*. Ice? Or was it—"

The old ladies crossed themselves and moved farther away.

"Pauline!" said Maya, giving her sleeve a firm tug. "Come *on*!"

Sheesh! The whole point of Part Two of the plan was Not To Be Noticed, Not To Be Seen.

It was in this section somewhere, the tomb of Fourcroy. Maya took a deep breath. They would scour the crowded hillside and leave no little pathway untrodden—there was still time—surely they would find it eventually—

"Hey, Maya," called Valko from not so very far away. "Here's your guy!"

And there he was.

Antoine François Fourcroy, his bust looking out with a little half smile from within a hollowed-out square pillar. His gaze went over Maya's head, above the patch of browning weeds that had taken over his plot. The weeds suggested he was no Chopin. No little old ladies ever brought this statue bouquets of roses. Why, probably they themselves were the first people in years and years to come looking for Antoine François Fourcroy, tucked away in his neglected corner of Père-Lachaise.

"Good," said Maya. "We're here. Now we just need to find a place to hide."

Valko looked around and shrugged. He had a point. They could basically walk a few feet in any direction and sit down, and who would ever find them?

So they did what heroes on a life-and-death adventure so frequently do: they sat down with their backs against the imposing block of the next tomb over and started rummaging through their backpacks for encouraging snacks. Pauline, for instance, had brought long sections of baguette with chocolate stuffed deep into its innards.

"It's very traditional," she said. "For the children to nibble on after school."

Valko was happy enough about the chocolate, but Maya could feel his eyes scouting out the tombs all around them.

"Six o'clock," he said. "Cemetery's officially closed. Now we wait for three hours, right, General?"

"Right," said Maya.

"Without freezing to death?" he said.

"That's the idea."

Valko snorted quietly.

"What have you got in that backpack, anyway? Bricks?" he said. "It looks heavy. Is that a magazine?"

"Hey, excuse me, I was thinking ahead," said Maya. "That's got the description in it of the movie we're all supposedly out seeing."

"What else?"

Maya showed him: a big fleecy shawl borrowed from her mother, food, the Summer Box, the gargoyles' egg. . . .

It was dark already now, but she could feel Valko recoil.

"Are you *nuts*?" he said. "Are you *kidding*? Why'd

you bring that box? And the *stone*? Isn't that supposed to be the thing his brain's hiding out in? Are you even *thinking*?"

He reached for the egg, but Maya's hand got there first.

"Leave it alone," she said. "It wanted to come."

Pauline and Valko were both silent now, staring at Maya in the darkness. She had *had* to bring the egg, just as she had *had* to bring the Summer Box. There had been no choice about it. That was true. She admitted it. But Maya still hoped against hope there was some angle to the problem she wasn't seeing. Something that went beyond Fourcroy's plans and his bossy letter, beyond fate, beyond the clockwork path, beyond the *clickety-clack* of tumbling dominoes.

"Um, Maya," said Valko, frowning at the egg. "This is a problem."

"It's what, that thing?" said Pauline, from the deep shadows on the other side of Maya. "A rock? How can a rock want something or not want something?"

"It's not a rock," said Maya, and she could feel the stiffness in her own voice as she said it. "It's an egg. Actually, a gargoyles' egg."

"Look, Maya," said Valko. "It is so a rock. Even if it's a totally strange rock. Still."

"*Mon Dieu*, but this is bizarre. Gargoyles don't lay eggs," said Pauline Vian.

305

"Ordinarily they don't," said Maya. "But this time they did. They wanted a safe place for his old memories, see? So they made the egg. I promised I'd take care of it."

"And who is this 'they'?" said Pauline. "The gargoyles again?"

Valko and Maya were too busy glaring at each other in the dark to try to explain.

"They wanted the memories *kept away from the shadow guy*. And you are practically planning to *hand the memory stone right back over to him*!"

"No, I'm not," said Maya. "I promised I'd take care of it. It wanted to come along. You keep thinking of it as entirely, totally evil—that's unfair."

"You're bewitched," said Valko. "You are. You're under a spell, like the letter said. Whose side are you even on? Oh, gash, listen to me! We're all crazy. *Give me that rock!*"

And this time his hand got there before Maya's hand could intervene. He grabbed the egg right out of her backpack, put his arm back over his head, and, before Maya could move or squeak, he lobbed the egg right away from them, into the shadowy darkness of the cemetery.

Maya couldn't help it. She gasped aloud in horror, a gasp that was very close to being a shriek. And then clamped her hand over her mouth, because there was a bright light swinging along, suddenly, not that far away.

And the sound of someone humming.

She was so full of mad there was hardly room in her for fear, but the mad shoved over a little to make room, and her arms began to shiver.

The watchman had stopped, somewhere on the other side of the tomb. Had he heard the poor egg go flying through the air?

He would find them for sure. Oh, he would find them, right this minute, any second now, for absolute certain. He would shine that bright flashlight right into their faces, and shout at them and drag them away, and it would be awful. And then there would be no one left to stop the shadowy Fourcroy, or the strangeness he had let loose into the world. Everything would become stranger and stranger, and nobody would be safe anywhere anymore, nobody's mother or brother or tiny still-completely-unknown *little bean*—

The watchman started up his hum again; the light began moving farther away.

"*Bon*," said Pauline, very quietly. "He is going."

That was when the enormous awful thought hit Maya all over again:

Valko Nikolov—her friend Valko, the person she had thought of as her *true* friend Valko—had just gone and thrown her gargoyles' egg away.

The breath caught in her throat.

"How could you?" she said. The fury in her voice was startling. She had never heard herself sound like this, not in real life. And she was still trying to whisper, too. "I promised them I'd keep it safe. And you go and *smash* it!"

"Really," said Pauline. "I am confused. Who is this 'they' and 'them'? And Valko did not smash your rock, Maya."

"You saw him yourself!"

"But there was no sound of smashing, Maya. *Non.* Hard to believe, in this so-stony place, but it must have landed on grass somewhere. The rock must be all right."

It was true, Maya realized: there had been no great smithereening smack. If there had been, what's more, the watchman would surely have heard it.

Valko had meant to smash it, though. It was still a betrayal. It was still absolutely awful in every way.

"But Maya," said Valko, from quite close to her ear. His voice was miserable and loving and impatient—all those things at once. "You know I can't let the stupid shadow have you. What kind of friend would I be? I'm telling you: no way."

Maya was already crawling forward, however, feeling the ground with her hands. The egg had *trusted* her. And he had flung it off into the darkness.

"Bringing his memory here with you has got to be

what he *wants*," said Valko, still not very far away in the dark. "He thinks he's got you, Maya. He hasn't got you, has he?"

Maya opened the Summer Box, slipped some small thing from that box into her pocket, and stood up.

"No," she said. "He hasn't got me. I mean, I hope not. I mean, sort of he does, I know, all right, yes, but not all the way. I am doing my best. Help me find that egg, will you? I really did promise them I'd take care of it."

"Them?" said Pauline, from back in the shadows.

"The gargoyles," said Maya. "What time is it now?"

"Seven o'clock," said Pauline. "How often do you two talk to gargoyles? Because honestly, if you had told me these things a week ago, I don't think I would be here right now—"

"It's too dark, Maya. Listen, I promise: I'll come back tomorrow and find your egg. I promise I will. I just don't want it controlling you."

"Because honestly, the things you are saying now sound to me like the thoughts of lunatics—"

"All right," said Maya suddenly, and she plopped back down on the ground. "All right. It's too dark to go looking for it now. You're right. We'll have to come back."

The poor egg, alone in this cold cemetery! She had to push that thought out of her way in order to stay focused. She was in danger of losing her focus. She was forgetting the next steps in the Plan.

"So we wait a little while longer," said Maya, pulling herself together. "And then, around eight thirty or so, maybe a little after, you start to play that piece, right, Pauline? If your fingers can still move at all."

Pauline made a cold, but willing, sound.

"And here's the important thing," Maya went on. "As soon as the shadow appears, I want you over here behind this big tomb. You stay hidden, both of you. Got that? You guys stay safe. The Fourcroy business is up to me."

"Hm," said Valko.

"I'm serious," said Maya. "I'm the one he wants—that means I'm the one he'll have to listen to. Don't distract him. And Pauline's younger than we are—"

"Chronological age," said Pauline with a sniff.

"Exactly," said Maya, paying no attention whatsoever to the sniff. "We're responsible for keeping you safe, that's all. As much as possible, anyway."

It grew colder. The mist thickened. They huddled behind the tomb and regretted everything that had brought them to Père-Lachaise, at night at the end of November. When their misery became very large indeed, Valko checked his watch again and said it was well after eight.

Pauline popped the latches of her violin case.

"It's not going to sound very nice," she said, her voice

a little doubtful in the cold dark. "My fingers are stiff like icicles."

"It will be fine," said Maya.

Pauline was attaching the shoulder rest and fixing her bow.

"Too, too cold," she said. "Do you think it will still work if I do the playing with my gloves on?"

"Brr," said Valko. "I say go ahead and give it a try."

"And the *gardien*, will he come back?"

"He's hiding away in his warm office," said Maya. "Drinking cocoa, probably."

Pauline shot one of her spear-like gazes in Maya's direction.

"You know this is *folie*, what we are doing," she said. "Madness, and all that."

"I hope it's not," said Maya. "Let's see."

Pauline put the bow on the string to tune, but the violin was so cold it didn't want her messing around with its pegs.

"I can't tune it properly," said Pauline. "Impossible."

"Doesn't matter!" said Maya. She did not actually say aloud that Pauline was not likely to play in tune even on a well-tuned violin, but that thought did go through her mind.

Pauline narrowed her eyes and clenched her bow too tightly in her gloved right hand, and the bow went scraping across the strings. *A cry like a dying cat*, thought Maya. Not that she had ever heard a dying cat, and in any case, perhaps dying cats would find it insulting to be compared to Pauline Vian.

Maya had been worried about guards hearing the music and coming in droves to yell at them and snap handcuffs around their wrists, but the trees and the fog soaked up the sound of the violin like a chilly gray sponge.

If anything, the world around them became quieter as Pauline played.

It became more attentive.

Valko had come up and put his jacketed arms right around Maya, a friendly, comforting, comfortable hug that drowned out, for a long minute, all the cold and dark. Somewhere out there, beyond the tombs and the mist and the city of Paris, was a sky full of stars. Down here, where you could see no stars, Pauline's violin was trying its best, all the same, to dance: one small, brave, out-of-tune voice against the enormous silence of Père-Lachaise.

"If that shadow gives you any trouble," said Valko to Maya, "I'm jumping out and tackling him. Just so you know. And I'm sorry about your rock."

He said it quietly, so as not to interfere with the music, or maybe just so that the looming trees and stone tombs could not hear.

Maya was not sure shadows were things that could be *tackled*, exactly, but she felt a little better, all the same. Though on the other hand, Valko had thrown the gargoyles' egg into the darkness somewhere. He had wanted it broken.

Really, she didn't know how she felt, just at that moment.

"I'll be careful," she said. "You be careful, too. And we both have to make sure Pauline's okay."

Rum tumty-tumty! Rum tumty-tumty! That was Pauline's violin, sending its awkward signal out into the fog.

Valko was listening to it, too. He shook his head and smiled.

"That's not really going to lure anyone anywhere, you know? I think we're—"

And his mouth was just forming the word *safe* when the tide of strangeness came rolling over them, this time almost like a blow to the stomach, the sick-making tingle of magic was so strong—and the world around them folded itself away and began to change.

The sound of magic, it turned out, was a roaring sort of rumble: things growing and stretching under the ground, the sap running through surprised trees above the ground, the stone of all those cherubs and wreaths and weeping nymphs reshaping itself into shapes it wasn't used to. The ground beneath their feet rippled. The violin behind them faltered, but only for a moment, and then Pauline launched into her *Danse macabre* all over again, with extra gusto. Maya stole a look at Pauline's face in the misty gray light and was shaken to her core: nothing the strangeness was likely to do could be stranger than Pauline Vian, *smiling*.

"Are you all right?"

That was Valko, whose hand, Maya noticed now, was firmly on her arm, keeping her steady (or keeping himself steady—hard to say).

"It's happening again," Valko said. "Right? I can tell."

Maya forcibly restrained the part of herself that wanted to shriek or roll her eyes or both and nodded instead. *He has to state the obvious,* she reminded herself. Valko had to state the obvious for the simple reason that none of this, even after all this time, was all that obvious to *him*.

But there, the quality of the sound around them was already shifting again. Something new joined the rumbling, quake-like roar of change: a clattering sound, as if the universe had decided to roll a hundred thousand dice, just to see what numbers might come up.

"What's that?" she said. "Pauline?"

Pauline was playing and smiling, smiling and playing. Her smile was quite visible through the mist and the gloom.

"*Pauline?*" said Maya.

"I think it works!" cried the indeed quite scary, wildly smiling Pauline, while her gloved fingers flew up and down the neck of her instrument and her bow scraped tunelessly away. "Aha! Look: do you see? It's my *grand début*!"

The dice, or whatever they were, rattled. Valko made a distressed sound in the back of his throat. Up until now, Maya realized, he had been doing all right because the town of overgrown tombs had been, until this minute, so much like a town that the whole purpose of a cemetery had probably slipped to the side of his mind.

But here's the thing: a cemetery is a place full of people who once were alive, and now are not. There's another word for most of them, and that word is *bones.*

Suddenly they were gathering all around, the bones, gathering in little clattery heaps. They were swaying a little, those heaps, in rhythm with Pauline's vigorous, out-of-tune violin. You could hear them, in the dark and the gloom, more than you could see them, but you could tell they were there. And that was enough. That was enough to make even Maya feel colder than cold.

Until that moment, it had been dark, but not exceedingly so, because when mist settles in a place, the last of the daylight wanders around in the fog for a while and gets itself lost, and that makes everything dim without being pitch-black. A misty night is not dark the way a moonless night can be.

But true darkness was beginning to come seeping into the mist. It puddled at the feet of nearby monuments and thickened menacingly in the middle of those twitching, dancing bones. The little hairs on the back of Maya's neck told her first, and then her ears, picking up a still-faint leafy rustle, confirmed it.

"Quick," said Maya to Valko. "Back behind that tomb. We don't want him to know you're here."

Valko hesitated, but Maya was ready to be tough.

"Go, go, go!"

She gave him an urgent little push, just to get him moving.

"And you have to yank Pauline out of sight, as soon as the shadow's really here. Valko, go! You can't leap out and tackle him, can you, if he *already knows you're here.*"

Even if he had thrown the gargoyles' egg away, Valko was still one of the people in the world Maya most wanted kept safe. Oh, that was still true.

The cemetery felt larger and darker and colder, once Valko had crept back to the hiding spot behind Fourcroy's odd telephone booth of a tomb. The twitchy, clattering bones seemed to have found the pulse of the music now; they had leaped into the air; they were truly dancing. Pauline and her wild smile were obscured a little by the dancing bones, as if she'd been hidden in a cloud of chattering, clattering bees.

The air was full of the roar of the world being twisted, warped, remade, undone. And the roar wouldn't go away. It just got louder and deeper and more terrifying. Something very bad was happening down the slope from Fourcroy's tomb: there was an awful cracking, slurping sound, as if the earth had started swallowing up whole trees. And the ground was shaking under Maya's feet, shaking harder and harder and harder.

Something was coming, and as it came, the world fell into chaos all around it. Valko said something, but his voice was very, very far away.

Yes, there it was: shade and leaf meal picking its way up the hill. A more human shape to the shadow now, and two gleams of purple where his eyes should have been.

In fact, it could almost be said to be walking, that shadow. It was striding along the little path that wandered up from Chopin's weeping muse, and its footsteps were jerking along almost in rhythm, Maya noticed now, with the violin's untamed, rough-edged dance.

But with every step it took, the path behind it fell into darkness that was darker than any night had any right to be. And the earth around it bubbled and boiled, tombstones and all. Churned and boiled and gave itself over to darkness.

It was maybe the end of the world. That was one thing that Maya was thinking, as she stood tall (in the face of all that boiling, heaving dark) to meet the shadow approaching. The other thought, however, was *It actually worked!*

They had really managed to lure him here, to the family tomb of the Fourcroys. It had really, truly worked.

And then the shadow opened its own mouth, a small puddle of darker darkness in its shadowy face, and it said, in a raspy, shadowy, triumphant sort of voice, *"W e l l d o n e."*

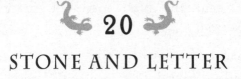

20

STONE AND LETTER

Maya was standing at the little break in the fence around the plot of the Fourcroys, the half-smiling bust of the original Fourcroy looking out over her shoulder from its marble telephone booth of a monument, and it was almost (she thought for a moment) like one of those sappy old movies her grandmother had used to watch all the time, where someone waits at the gate to welcome the tired soldier home. Only instead of a tired soldier, of course, it was a ghostly swirl of shadow and dust coming up the path toward her now, the echo of a person. That echo kept evolving, too—holding on to its human form for a second or two, and then, as a breath of air met it, losing its edges, rippling, fading, until it could pull itself together again, back into something resembling the shape of a man, striding proudly up the slope, while all around it trees and stones and earth were being unmade, melted, ruined. And that terrible roaring tearing sound everywhere, the sound of the world having been bent too far—the sound of the real world finally breaking.

"*Maya,*" said the man made of shadow. "*Maya. Apprentice. Well done.*"

The music had stopped: Valko must have remembered to drag Pauline back into safety with him. Good. Maya took a breath of cold, steadying air and tried not to be worried about the tremors rippling through the ground under her feet, the soft *whoosh whoosh* of trees losing their last hold on treeness and melting away into nothing, into nonsense.

I am a descendant of the Lavirottes, Maya told herself firmly. *And we walk in magic.*

She pulled herself as tall as she could manage.

"You have to stop this," said Maya. "You are ruining everything. Can't you see? Your loophole is eating up the world."

The shadowy figure shivered, became vague for a moment, shook itself back into focus.

"*You are Maya,*" it said. "*The one I bound. You will make me whole. You have brought it all with you. The—the—things.*"

"Yes," said Maya. "I have. It's all here."

The shadowy Fourcroy shuddered again and stepped nearer, while the earth writhed and darkened behind it.

"*Stone-Paper-Maya-Life—*"

Maya bit her lip to keep herself steady. When a shadow lurches toward you, its arms shimmering with greed, it is very hard not to turn and run away, or at least to take a hasty step back.

"*Life*—," it said, its dark arms reaching forward. "*From the heart of something—life, from the heart of a, of a*—"

"From the heart of a *zmey*," said Maya. "But the thing is, actually I am not a dragon."

The shadow became disorganized, remade itself, came so close that its shadowy violet eyes were looking directly into Maya's face: at her and through her at the same time.

"So what that means is, you can't have my heart," said Maya. Somewhere behind her back, Valko gave a faint whoop of approval. That gave her courage. "And it wouldn't do you any good, anyway."

The thing hissed in her face, a cold breath that smelled faintly of ashes.

"*Bound to make me whole*," it said again. "*Maya. Maya. Now!*"

And it reached out with one shadowy arm and actually wrapped something like fingers—icy, insubstantial wisps of fingers—around Maya's wrist. It was chanting something to itself now, as if the chant had been some way of holding on to what the shadow needed to know, all these weeks since it had stored its mind in the embassy wall and had had so few words of its own left: "*Stone-Paper-Maya-*Zmey: *Stone and letter, mind and body—life from the heart of the* zmey."

Maya pulled back her hand, but the shadow's fingers, wispy though they were, could not be shaken off. The cold in them sent little rootlets of ice into her skin and into her arm.

"*Give me my mind back*," said the shadow. It looked larger and darker now, and where its eyes should have been were two whirlpools of violet that looked, though that made no sense, even darker than the dark.

"You put it in the stone," said Maya. Her teeth stumbled a little over the words. The cold had run up her arm and into her shoulder now. She had never in her whole life been this cold. "Let go."

"*Give me my mind back now*," it said. "*My mind and my body. Stone and letter. Or I swallow you.*"

That was what it was doing, she suddenly understood, with its icy hand on her wrist: it was swallowing her. There was something she had to do. Oh, Maya was trying to think, but the cold running through her made thinking very hard. The hum of magic, the distant clattering of little bones, the more human rustling and whispering going on somewhere behind her—all of that seemed very far away. The cold was climbing up her neck; the cold was already fingering her brain. You go very still when a shadow is swallowing you.

A number of things happened then, all at once:

"Hey!" shouted someone, infinitely far away. "I got it!"

A light was shining, she noticed. Where had the light come from? It came up from her nearly frozen wrist; it seemed almost like part of herself, that light. It was bright, like a star.

The shadow made a strange sound, the ghost of a sob. The icy pressure on her wrist let up just a little. She was about to be able to think again—it was like a mist pulling back from her, pushed away, perhaps, by that inexplicable star.

An arm that was no shadow went around her shoulders, interrupting her not-quite-thoughts. Why was Valko there? He was holding something out in his other hand; he was saying something, but not to her.

What he was saying was this: "Here it is—your stupid memory stone. I found it. Let her go, and you can have it. But I'll smash it to bits if you don't let her go. And by the way, she never even touched the letter with the blood-stain on it, so you lose."

And there in his hand was the gargoyles' egg.

"No!" said Maya, though she was still so cold that no sound came out of her mouth when she said it. She put her other hand out, the unfrozen hand, to touch it. The gargoyles' egg. She had promised to keep it safe.

The starlight was very bright now; it spilled and splintered across the surface of the egg, sending the pictures dancing. The field, the trees, the face that looked like Maya's own. The images brightened and grew and fell apart. Oh, it was the egg itself that was changing, that was trembling under her hand.

"*Mine*," said the shadow.

"Let her go," said Valko.

I promised, I promised, to keep it safe, thought Maya.

And the egg shook itself into a million million pieces of light.

It was broken, broken—no, not broken. Changed. Utterly changed!

The gargoyles' egg had finally done what eggs are meant to do, that's all: it had hatched.

A spray of stone was organizing itself now, in the confused starlit air. An immense whiplash of a body, with the most enormous wings.

Craaack!

The stone tail collided with the bust of the old Fourcroy, and sent a fountain of sparks spinning into the air.

"*But what is that?*" cried Pauline from not very far away. "What is THAT?"

To tell the truth, Maya had completely forgotten, back when the cold was still swallowing her, about Pauline Vian.

Now she shouted back, pleased to have a voice again for shouting with, "A gargoyle!"

But as soon as she said it, she knew she was wrong.

This creature twisting itself into being in the air looked nothing like Beak-Face or Bonnet-Head, with their solid, funny stone faces: it was really almost more like fireworks than stone, and the shape was so familiar, somehow, the wings and the long, long tail. . . .

Maya caught her breath with a quick, cold gasp.

No, this was no gargoyle—it was a *dragon*. An amazingly salamander-like dragon. An amphibious dragon. A dragon that could live in many more worlds than one.

The dragon opened its long, miraculous jaw and let out a great and ancient cry, the sort of thing that must have made people stumble out of their caves, millennia ago, and look up, astonished, into the sky.

The shadowy Fourcroy let go of Maya's wrist entirely. Those violet whirlpools-for-eyes turned toward the creature that had emerged from the gargoyles' egg.

"*Zmey!*"

That was what the shadow said, as it staggered forward toward the creature circling there in the air.

"Wow," said Valko, still right at Maya's side. "Wow, look at that! Is that really a *zmey*? How could two gargoyles have a baby *dragon*? Is that even possible, genetically speaking?"

But he was laughing an amazed sort of laugh as he said it.

Not far in front of them, the shadow of Fourcroy was reaching up for the salamander-dragon, which danced in tight circles in the air, tumbling end over end, stretching its surprising and brand-new wings, crying out with the sheer pleasure of no longer being merely an egg. The shadow leaped up; the dragon darted away; the shadow made a swipe with one of its icy arms, and the dragon slithered around Fourcroy's back and climbed another foot into the air.

"Watch out!" Maya called to the dragon, but it showed no sign of hearing her. Why didn't it fly itself farther away from the shadow? It spun around and around the darkness—so close to the shadow that it seemed unbelievable that that ghost of Fourcroy had not grabbed it yet.

"It's like it can't quite get away from him," said Valko, not laughing anymore.

"*See how they dance!*" cried Pauline Vian from farther away.

She was right, thought Maya. That was what they were doing: dancing. And the circles of the dance were growing tighter and tighter, the shadow's fingers brushing now against the dragon's tail. In a moment the beautiful, bright, stone-and-fire *zmey* would be caught for real. Swallowed up by the cold of the shadow, just as Maya had almost been swallowed up. But the *zmey* was too lovely; it didn't deserve to be lost in the dark and the cold.

She heard herself shouting something, but didn't know what it was. There was a flicker in that deadly dance, the briefest of pauses, and she felt the eyes turned toward her for a moment, the dark-violet eyes of the shadow and the glittering stone-and-fire eyes of the *zmey*. They looked at her and considered something.

"*Maya*," said the shadow; her name was one of the few words it had left.

The *zmey* looked deep into her eyes and also knew who she was. A flash of images went splashing across the glittering fiery lacework of its belly—forest, rocks, a field in summer.

"Oh, watch out," said Maya to the dragon. "He wants to swallow you—"

And at that very instant, the shadow of Fourcroy reached out with one of its terrible arms and grabbed the dragon just like that—*thwap!*—around its bright and narrow throat.

The dragon screamed.

A ripple went through both of them, the lacy stone of the *zmey* and the shadow-man, and the shadow became one jot denser and deeper, just like that. It turned its head back to Maya, and the eyes were brighter now. Brighter and clearer. It was beginning to remember bits of itself, with its hand clamped to old Fourcroy's memory stone (now become this oh-so-improbable dragon).

"Maya!" it said. The voice was already about three awful steps closer to being human. It was smoother, somehow. More certain of itself.

Maya shuddered. She was caught in the echo of the poor dragon's scream; she saw the spreading ice crackling up and down its throat, radiating outward from the shadow's cruel hand, and in her own bones she felt the cold spreading and the horror of it.

"Quick," said the shadowy Fourcroy, more confident now. "It is time. What a mess you seem to have made of the world! Well, never mind. Now we will mend me."

For a moment Maya was flabbergasted, and then she was pretty much spitting mad.

"Me making a mess! That's your own selfish loophole ruining everything."

The shadow made the strangest noise: it scoffed.

"You blind, blind child!" it hissed at her. "Haven't you learned a thing about *anything*, all this time? It's *you* it feeds off of. It's your *own* magic, your *own* power, that's undoing the world. Have you really not noticed that?"

It was a shock running through her: the tingle in her fingers flared up, subsided, flared up again. She had pointed at the Tower, yes, the night it changed. The magic had started undoing the world when she first touched the stone of the wall—the alarm had gone off—the count-down had started. Something had been triggered in her at that moment. Why? Was it because she was getting older? Was that what happened to Lavirottes at some point, as they grew into their magic? But it was terrible what had been started then: the universe had begun to bend.

"Liar," said Valko, with total conviction.

And every time the strangeness had come back, the way she had felt it so strongly, like an electric shock to the gut—feeding off her? Feeding off *her*? Could it be? But that meant she was not keeping anyone safe, she was not saving anybody, she was not making anything right.

She, Maya, was what was wrong with the world.

21

HEART OF A DRAGON

"Oh, no," she said, almost under her breath, her voice as small as the disaster was huge. "What do we do now?"

The shadowy Fourcroy snapped shadowy fingers under Maya's nose.

"We do what I have bound you to do, little cousin-niece. The trace of the old me—you will give it here. Now! Then you will make me whole. As you are also bound to do. As your magic, your power, makes possible now. I think you begin to understand me. Do you?"

From beside her, Valko's voice, a little shaken, but trying not to let it show: "Didn't you hear what I said? She never took the letter with the bloodstain. She left it in the Salamander House. There *is* no trace of you!"

The shadow ignored him.

"*Now, Maya!*" said the dark remnant of Fourcroy. It tipped its head, almost as if amused. "You have done it all, everything you were bound to do, yes? The trace—"

"Yes," said Maya, her heart sinking into some kind of hollow. She had wanted to find a way off the clockwork path, and all of her best efforts were coming to nothing. It had been her own self, feeding the strangeness as it swallowed her world. And now there was no way left to make things right! Oh, why hadn't the poor, captured *zmey* been more careful! But it had been looking at her; it had been distracted by her; she had tripped it up, and it had not paid close enough attention, and now the terrible cold was marching up and down its stone body.

Her hand—like a puppet's hand, like the hand of a machine run by wires and radio waves and cogs—was already pulling a little envelope out of her jacket pocket. Dominoes were falling all around: *clickety clickety clack.* She was bound to do this, she was completely trapped and bound, but the binding didn't prevent her from turning her face to look at the horrified Valko standing there beside her.

"I'm so sorry," she said to him, and suddenly she was so sad about all of this—about having wanted to save the world and make everything all right again for everybody, and yet having utterly, stupidly failed to do so—that she couldn't even quite see his face clearly. "I'm sorry about the poor world, about everything. And there was a lock of his hair in the Summer Box. I'm so sorry. I tried to burn it, but I couldn't. I did try."

"Oh, Maya," said Valko. "Why didn't you tell me—"

The shadow broke into Valko's sentence with a shout, a strange and unsettling sound, half human and half something else, unclassifiable, but surprised. Its bright violet eyes were fixed now on the starlight dancing around Maya's wrist as she held out that little envelope, the envelope that had come from the Summer Box, the one that held the lock of Fourcroy's baby hair.

"Aaaah! And you've even brought my *bracelet* with you!"

"Excuse me!" said Maya, angrily swiping the back of her left hand across her leaky eyes. "Not yours. Leave it alone. My mother got it from her mother. And then it came down to me."

The shadowy Fourcroy laughed (but did not lose its grip on the poor dragon's neck).

"Don't speak nonsense, girl," it said. "It *should* have been mine. It was always *supposed* to be mine. There it is, in a tiny nutshell's worth of stone: our magic and our power! Oh, she made a mistake, my poor mother, when she let it go—"

"She sent it far away from you. She sent it to my grandmother. That was the opposite of a mistake," said Maya, but her mind was already circling around that one particular word: *power*. It was true, the opal on her wrist was alive with light. She looked at it more closely and saw how complicated that light was, how many colors were winking in and out of its tangled dance. Maybe there was a better sort of magic in that opal than the dangerous stuff that had kept bubbling up in Maya herself the last few weeks. And if there was magic there to be tapped into, now was the moment for that *tapping-into* to happen, wasn't it? She gave the stone a pleading, impatient look and shook her wrist a little, but the light just brightened another notch, and Fourcroy kept laughing.

"Maya, watch out!" said Valko from not very far away. "What *is* that thing?"

"I think you must maybe throw it right at him!" said Pauline from much, much farther away than Valko. "*Ka-boom!*"

And then the stone of that bracelet did sort of explode, in its own strange way. They were standing in front of a tree: Maya with the radiant wrist held up before her face, and the ever more substantial Fourcroy with one hand clasped like a ring of shadow around the neck of the poor, struggling *zmey*, ice still spreading farther and farther down its neck and back. The tree stood behind them all, its branches spread wide and quiet in the mist. But as the light from Maya's opal grew brighter and brighter and brighter, the tree trembled and split—not down the middle, though, not as trees split when an ax or lightning strikes them. Instead the image of the tree wavered and split, left and right, into two images, of two trees. Like an old-fashioned stereoscope card, where almost-identical scenes on the left and right wait to be brought together in a viewer to make one three-dimensional picture—with depth. Or the way tired eyes sometimes wander to the side and the thing you're staring at doubles. Yes, like that.

There was the tree, and there was the double of the tree, and the two trees now stood before Maya's eyes, one more or less to the left and the other more or less to the right. She turned her head, back and forth, looking at them. They were not, after all, exactly the same. The world seemed to have split in two with them: so strange. On the left-hand side the tree was dark and grand and mysterious, and underneath it stood a very powerful-looking Fourcroy, with his hand still so cruelly around the neck of the stone dragon; and Valko was there, looking appalled and concerned, his mouth open as he said something that seemed to be fierce; and Pauline was there, farther away, with a fist in the air; and even Maya herself was there, holding out her wrist with the star on it; and none of the people (or dragons) were moving. The split-apart world seemed also to have frozen.

It made Maya feel very strange, to be looking in on herself from—from—where was she? Outside. She tried to spin around, to see where she was, but she could not move that way. Or maybe there was nothing whatsoever to see. She could look only to the left, where everything, including herself, was frozen as it had just this moment been—and to the right, where again there was a tree, mist wreathing around its branches.

Under that other tree, the right-hand tree, a girl was walking. Maya thought at first it was herself again she was seeing, which still felt wrong, but when the girl raised her eyes to look at her, Maya saw that there was something odd about her edges. They flickered, somehow, like a candle flame. And the eyes did the same thing. Many eyes, many colors, flickering. It wasn't restlessness, exactly. But it wasn't until the girl opened her mouth and spoke that Maya finally understood.

"We told you: it comes with a choice," said the girl, holding out her hand. Here was the thing about that voice: it wasn't just one voice; it was a chorus of voices. The girl, Maya saw now, was not one girl at all, but many, many people, all at once and overlapping somehow, all holding out their one many-layered hand together, in which was one single opal, glittering.

Maya glanced back to the left, where the shadow of Fourcroy still had the dragon by the neck, and Valko was caught, mouth open in midshout. (What was he trying to say?) Valko's lips moved just a hair; Maya jumped. The world over there wasn't *frozen*, after all:

it was just moving very slowly. Like molasses, as her mother might say.

She turned back to the flickering girl, standing there under the (now she saw it) flickering tree, which was also many trees, all at once.

"How does it work?" she said. "Quick. Tell me how to use it. He's breaking the world. Or maybe I am—oh! The world's breaking, can't you see that? I have to stop him. I have to destroy him."

The girl who was many people at once looked at her.

"*That is one choice,*" she said. "*It is very powerful, our family's magic, when used. You have it in you to be powerful. We can see that in you.*"

To reach out with a brilliantly starlit fist and crush the shadow! To crush him to nothing and make him finally, finally go away! It made Maya gasp, to feel how much she longed to do that—but the girl's eyes flickered in front of her, watching her. Maya found herself twitching a little, under the pressure of so many layers of flickering eyes.

"What other choice do I have?" said Maya.

"*Ah,*" said all the voices in that one girl. They said it all together, and the leaves of all the many trees that were in that one tree spun a little in the breeze. "*The choice is that: to use it, or to pass it on. We all reach this age, Maya, this age when the magic in us wells up and wants to be heard. It is being at a place where the path splits in two:*

where we can walk on in magic, under the trees, or take the other way, the bracelet's way, and use our power to remake the world. We all choose. And one day that power will need to be used, we think. The choice is real: is it that day?"

Maya, impatient, turned to look again over at the world on her left, where she saw that something very strange was happening, inch by inch by inch. The Maya there had begun to lean sideways, had already begun to crumple, one inch's worth so far, to the ground. Valko was still caught in midshout—but she couldn't look at his face anymore: he was staring at the just-beginning-to-crumple Maya, and there was hopelessness in his eyes, and Valko was never, ever hopeless.

The purple-eyed shadow was already taller than when she had looked the last time. His violet eyes were triumphant and bright—one hand of his still clenched the dragon's neck, and the other was now filled with the brightest starlight, leaking out in brilliant glimpses from between the dark, dark fingers of his hand.

"What's going on?" cried Maya. It was horrible, all of it. "What's that? Why does he have the bracelet? When did he get my bracelet?"

"Soon," said all the many versions of that girl, and they leaned closer, urgently, like a forest of trees (in one tree) bending in the wind. *"Soon! Don't you see? Don't*

you see? You are bound. . . ."

That was when Maya finally did see. She was still bound to make him whole. Apparently choosing power did not unbind a person. She could become the most powerful magician in the world, and still be bound to use all that power simply to do whatever that awful Fourcroy commanded. Like one of those genies in fairy tales: an all-powerful slave, trapped in a stupid clay jar or something. Oh! She took a step back deeper into the Nowhere where she was standing, full of horror at how close she had come to destroying, finally, everything.

She had been about to choose to use that power that was bound up, somehow, in her family's old magic, and all that power would have flowed from her right to that awful, selfish, hungry Fourcroy, and there would have been no hope left, then, for any of them—for her, for Valko, or for her mother and the *little bean*. No hope at all.

"*Maya!*" said the girl-who-was-many-people, in warning. Maya knew them now, some of those faces that were in that girl's flickering face. Even her own mother was there in those faces.

And that was when the two worlds came slamming together again, and Maya was on her feet in front of the shadowy Fourcroy, and the poor *zmey* had just screamed, and Fourcroy was gloating, gloating, gloating, and holding out his free hand for the lock of his baby hair and the bracelet, because of course what other choice could you make, when the world was breaking all around you? Of course, you would choose to fight with whatever power you had! And then, if you were bound—

"No," said Maya, drawing back her wrist.

The shadowy Fourcroy shrieked, which was an awful sound.

"That's it. I won't. I choose to *pass it on*," she said, gasping as she said so. Which had been her mother's choice, and her grandmother's choice, and long ago the choice of Henri's mother, too.

"To *me*," said Fourcroy, but he was already a bit shorter than he had been, and he sounded a little petulant. "Pass it to me—it is *mine*."

"Never to you," said Maya. "No way. To my sister."

That was when the poor dragon trapped in Fourcroy's hands cried out again, a cry that began as a clear trumpet call of a note (everything that dragon did was too beautiful for this everyday world of ours) and ended in the crashing din of a rockslide.

Wings! Beaks! Claws! And there they were: gargoyles.

For a minute the shadow of Fourcroy was buried in a stony blur. The gargoyles were not moving at merely human speed tonight, that was for sure. They nipped and pulled and poked, and it was a great racket they made as they harried the shadow. How they got the upper hand, Maya could not see, it was all happening so fast, but a minute later, there they were, Beak-Face with his claws deeply embedded in one side of the shadow, and Bonnet-Head grimly hanging on to his back—and the dragon had shaken itself loose and was twining itself around a branch of the nearest big tree, whimpering a little as it pawed at the dark frozen spot on its neck.

There was a moment of silence as the gargoyles caught their rocky breaths and Maya tried to steady hers.

Then Bonnet-Head looked over at Maya and said, "How bright your bracelet is tonight! Do it quickly, dearr. We cannot hold him forever."

"Do what?" said Maya.

"Your magic," said Beak-Face more sharply (but in his defense, his hold on the shadow's side did not look all that secure). "Quick, girrl."

But what magic did Maya have left? She had just chosen not to use it. She had just chosen to pass it on.

"*Bound to make me whole*," said the shadow. After all this time and all this trouble, the shadow of Fourcroy was still hungry. She could see that however much it managed to swallow, it would always be hungry.

She tried hard to ignore the ground, still rippling underneath. She was a Lavirotte, and they really did walk in more worlds than one. Even if she had no magic left of her own, none of the powerful kind, that was still true.

"*Bound*," repeated the shadow.

"Yes," said Maya.

So she walked right up to the shadowy Fourcroy, there where the gargoyles held him so tightly between them, their stone eyes thoughtful as they watched her come, and she put her hand on the patch of darkness that was his arm. Valko protested, somewhere behind her, but she ignored him. It was not the same as being swallowed, not when you chose it yourself. She rested her hand on his arm as she had rested it so many times on the gargoyles' egg in the weeks gone by, and it seemed to her the shadow became just slightly warmer under her hand.

"You bound me to make you whole," said Maya.

"*Yes*," said the shadow.

"I think I can still do that," she said. "Even without my magic. But I've decided it doesn't mean what you thought it meant, when you opened that awful emergency loophole in the wall. Just going on and on and on forever isn't being *whole*."

She could feel the shadow's uncertainty like a chill wave under her hand, but she held on and thought warm thoughts, and the cold backed off again and quieted.

"You are hungry because you're so empty," said Maya. "But what could possibly fill someone like you? That's the puzzle."

341

She leaned her head closer to him.

"There's a lot you've forgotten," she said.

Maya turned to look up at the dragon, watching her so intently from its tree limb.

"Come down here to me, Egg, will you?" she said. She was almost shy, in front of that amazing, glittering creature. But it had recognized her a moment ago, she was quite sure of it.

"*Egg!*" said Beak-Face, shifting his wings around to see better. "Is that the besst she could do, naming our poor child?"

"Husssh," said Bonnet-Head. "I rather like it."

They did not loosen their grips on the shadow, though, not one tiny bit.

The dragon unwrapped itself from the tree and flew down to Maya with all the grace and loveliness of water flowing over a cliff somewhere, or ivy growing down some old rock wall, and tucked itself under her left arm, so that her hand was comfortably resting on the lacy stonework of its side.

"Look, you—Henri," she said to the shadow. "Do you see what this is? The gargoyles' egg was also your memory stone, you know. That means this dragon holds a lot of summer in it, deep inside. I liked the you I saw in the stone."

Under her hand she could feel the amazing skin of the

zmey, stone as fragile as eggshell, knit together with light. It warmed to her touch as the egg used to. The dragon looked extraordinary and new, but it felt familiar, and that was comforting.

One hand on the *zmey*, one hand on the shadow's still fairly chilly arm, Maya asked for the memories back, and they came, forest and field, sailboat, kite, and whistle.

The dragon's skin rippled with images: Henri's mother, smiling that wise smile of hers, her hands quickly folding paper, shaping and sewing some child-sized marvel.

"I went back to the Summer Box, Henri," said Maya. "Look what I found there."

She had put that in her pocket, too: not just the baby's lock of silvery hair, but the colorful, raggle-taggle ribbons. She brought them out now (keeping her arm always close to that *zmey*).

"Do you remember what this was? It was a dragon once, you know—another kind of dragon."

The *zmey* gave a little shimmy of pleasure (a meadow, all grass and wildflowers, and the mother unfurling a long spool of thread).

"She made it for you. I think maybe there was magic in it, the way it could fly. . . ."

A magical dragon of wind and fire and paper, a kite sailing fierce and wonderful above the meadow.

The shadow's arm was changing under Maya's hand.

It felt smaller and sweeter now, the arm of a child who has wrapped himself in cold darkness only because otherwise he is so very alone facing the world.

And the dragon was glowing like a paper lantern, a knot of brightness deep within it and spilling out through the delicate tracery of its skin.

A shiver of longing went through the shadow's small and tender arm.

"There!" said Maya. "That's it, I'm pretty sure. That memory there: *that's* the heart of the *zmey*. And you can have it. It's yours. Only—"

The shadow was leaning against her now, small and trusting. For a moment Maya was reminded of James, but that thought wrenched her heart, so she had to take another breath before she could go on.

"Only you can't just eat it up, you know," she said. "Things get ruined when you eat them up. Your mother knew that. But you forgot."

She thought about it.

"So what you have to do is, I think, you have to let the memory swallow *you*. If you want to be whole."

Total silence for a minute. The dragon was very still under her left arm, the child-shadow very still under her other hand. The gargoyles were as still as only stone knows how to be. The mist was lifting, and the air was quiet, still, and cold. Somewhere deep inside the *zmey*, it glowed with all the light of summer, and a little boy was flying the dragon kite that his mother had made for him with scissors and paper and so much love.

The tiniest shadowy finger traced the edges of that picture on the dragon's side.

"Again!" said the shadow.

And the images came rising up from inside the *zmey*, flowed right up the shadow-child's finger, flowed golden and warm into all that waiting darkness, until the shadow was hardly shadow at all, was a shining glowing ball of light balanced in the gargoyles' paws. You could see the boy running through the grass; his head was thrown back, and he was laughing, and the sphere in which he ran was only the size of an orange now—it was shrinking, it was shrinking, it was traveling away—it was a spark hidden in the gargoyles' paws, which had come together as the shadow shrank. The gargoyles, paws clasped, looked at each other and then up at Maya again.

"How odd you quick-living people are," said Bonnet-Head, with a great stone yawn. "How tiring everything always is! But well done, dearr. An effective translation. Yes. And now we really must have a nice rest."

"Yess," said Beak-Face. "To be stone again, finally."

They turned their faces to the *zmey* and said something rockslidish to it, and the dragon slithered lovingly in and around them, a bright figure eight of living rock, before springing into the air and flying off with another one of its beautiful trumpeting cries. All that lasted only a moment: the gargoyles, their paws still clasped together around the glowing kernel of memory that had once been the shadow of Henri de Fourcroy, gave Maya a last nod and somehow leaped, all at once, right into the stone monument of Antoine François Fourcroy, dived right into the stone as if it were a vertical pool of water and disappeared.

Silence. Followed by the odd clatter of something small and metallic rolling across the stones. A happy shout from Valko: it was his long-lost barometer.

"You do realize," he said (but he was giving Maya an enormous triumphant bear hug as he said it), "that we're going to be in the worst trouble ever, when we finally get home. We're locked in the Père-Lachaise cemetery, and it's four whole hours after closing time."

But Pauline Vian just shook her head with wonder as she packed her violin carefully away.

"They danced to my music!" she said, her frown not quite back to its regular strength. "And, *mon Dieu*, how beautiful that dragon was. But what you did with that awful shadow, that I could not entirely understand."

The night was ordinary again. Ordinarily dark and ordinarily cold. It was almost unsettling, how unstrange everything was—the tombs just tombs, the trees just trees, the heaps of chaos left in the shadow's wake already on their way back to being earth and stone and grass. The world unbreaking.

I will not cry, said Maya sternly to herself. It had been her choice. She had chosen to pass the magic on. (And then she thought: to my *sister*?)

Well, salamanders live in more worlds than one, and every time they leave one world for the next, their hearts must break a little. But they are strong, salamanders, and they keep moving, all the same.

"Ha! Look at his nose," said Valko, pointing to the old bust of Antoine François Fourcroy. "That's what happened when the *zmey* swung its tail."

Maya took a closer look. A chunk of marble had been knocked off one side of his nose, it was true. But the bust kept smiling its half smile over their heads, nonetheless.

As Maya's mother might have said, "the merest scratch."

The thought of her mother did the trick: Maya shook herself and woke up. It was late, right?

Time for all salamanders to gather up their things and go home.

22

INTO THE REGULAR OLD UNKNOWN

When the bells of Saint-Peter-of-the-Big-Pebble rang the hour of two the following Wednesday, a girl and a boy stopped in their tracks on the avenue Rapp and raised their capped and mufflered heads to look at each other. They remained standing that way for five minutes or so, despite the discouraging iciness of the weather, despite having places they were really supposed to be, despite everything. Passersby with their heads more sensibly lowered against the wind kept not seeing them until the last possible minute and then having to swerve so as not to plow into them: it was not the sort of afternoon when normal people would ever stand stock-still on the sidewalk, just staring at each other, almost as if they were bracing themselves for an explosion or a shock. But once some significant length of time had passed, the boy checked his watch again and grinned.

"Aaaaaaand we're good!" he said. "One hundred

348

thirty-seven hours, come and gone."

The girl cheered; the boy squeezed the girl's hands, and then, because that wasn't nearly enough, they hugged each other and twirled about for a while like fools.

"What's happened, you young people?" said an old man passing by.

"Nothing!" they sang out. "Nothing! Nothing! *Rien!*"

"*Bon!*" said the old man, and he stopped and tapped the sidewalk with his cane. "Then, *mes enfants*, may your lives be always as happy for as little reason as they are at this minute!"

It was a very good blessing.

Maya carried her happiness right over to the embassy wall, where a hole in the stone (now mostly forgotten by everyone in the neighborhood) had been plugged by a salamander-like dragon of stone and light—a *zmey*— that had come plummeting out of the sky. You could see its long, sinuous form in the wall, if you looked very hard. Maya put her hand on the stones and said a silent hello and thank-you, the way she always did when she walked by.

All those awful loopholes, closed. That was truly something to be glad about. There were still places where the roots of the Eiffel Tower had broken up the sidewalk, and Maya had seen a few *vines* and *flowers* for sale in the bakery the other day, but for the most part, all the strange business of the last few weeks was fading, not just from the streets of Paris, but from all memories and all minds. Human brains were just not built to register strangeness; really, they weren't. That sort of memory was unlikely, in the end, to stick.

"Too bad and unfair," said Valko. "They'll never know what a hero you are, Maya Davidson!"

"Ha-ha-ha," said Maya. "Without Pauline, that shadow might never have even shown up. Not to mention it was you guys who got us out of the cemetery afterward. That was pretty heroic."

It had involved waking up the night watchman and telling him some sad story about having missed the shutting of the gates by half an hour and then having wandered and wandered without ever seeing a soul. Pauline had surpassed herself by looking very young and weeping the most amazingly realistic crocodile tears; the tears had disarmed the *gardien* and saved them all a lecture.

She might have no talent for music, but that Pauline Vian was astonishingly competent at absolutely everything else.

"No, Maya," said Valko. "You can't dodge this one. You saved Paris, and, what's more, you saved me, and everyone else may have forgotten it all, but I never, ever will."

He did a diplomat's bow, very fancy, and pinned an invisible medal on Maya's jacket.

"It's the Cross of Saint George. For defeating my grandmother, who is much worse than any dragon."

"No, she's not," said Maya. "She's just a little crusty, that's all. I like your grandmother."

Here's what had happened with Valko's grandmother-with-the-mole: once she had heard their accounts of *samodivi, vampiri,* and the *zmey,* she had packed up her bags in very good humor and gone back home—without her grandson—to Bulgaria. "He seems to be pretty sufficiently Bulgarian," as she said to Valko's parents at the airport, "even without much help from me. Though if that nice girl Maya starts forcing baseball on him? Then I'll be coming back quick-step."

So that was all right, too. At least for this year, Maya was not going to be left in Paris alone. It almost surprised her, how happy she was about that, how happy and glad and relieved.

"Oh, Maya, what sweet little pictures she drew!" said Maya's mother. "This is a treasure, this story. And it's really some grandmother of ours who made this?"

She and Maya were huddled comfortably under a quilt on the sofa, turning the pages of Henri's little book.

"Not a grandmother," said Maya. "A great-great-

great-aunt—well, I'm not sure exactly how many *greats*. A couple. You know what? I think she must be the same one who sent your mother the opal bracelet. She was a Lavirotte, and she didn't have any daughters of her own to give it to."

And I said, "my sister"! thought Maya, letting her fingers rest, for a moment, on that mysterious bracelet. Someday, those girls had said, its magic would have to be used. . . . It was a comfortable sort of wondering, though, so warm and so cozy, with her mother right there beside her, studying that other mother's drawings from so long ago.

"Just this sweet little Henri here, with his wide eyes and his sailor suit. You can tell from the pictures how much she must have doted on him, can't you? Cute boy. Reminds me a little of James."

Maya winced.

"Ugh, don't say that! That Henri didn't turn out to be a very nice person."

Maya's mother shook her head.

"Really? I don't believe it. Look at his face! That face could not possibly belong to someone who wasn't a nice person. Unless something absolutely awful happened to him at some point, poor boy."

"Something did happen," said Maya. "His mother had another baby."

As soon as Maya said that, she realized how terrible it sounded, but before she could get all knotted up inside about it, her mother surprised her by breaking into an outright laugh.

"Oh, Maya!" she said, actually dabbing at tears of laughter in the corners of her eyes. "Am I about to ruin James's life with this baby, is that what you think? No, no, don't get offended. I remember when James was born, how guilty I felt about you. You'd had all our attention for all those years! It didn't seem very fair, bringing this demanding little new person into the picture. But you came to like him pretty well, eventually."

"I love James," said Maya, slightly indignant.

"Of course you do," said her mother. "James is remarkably lovable. But that doesn't mean it wasn't hard for you when he first appeared."

Maya wasn't sure how to respond, so she just turned the next page of Henri's little book.

"'Life is too short,'" said her mother thoughtfully, her finger running very gently over the words. "Isn't that funny—my mother used to say that, too. And then she would let me have more ice cream, or take me to the lake to feed the ducks."

"But it's such a gloomy thing to say," said Maya. She thought of Henri de Fourcroy, his hungry shadow, so greedy and so cold. Life had always been too short for him. He had wanted more and more and more. Until the very end, he had been willing to mess up the whole world, just to grab himself some more life.

"Really?" said her mother, shifting a little on the couch to make her belly more comfortable. "I don't know—doesn't seem so gloomy to me. Life seems too short, because it's just so interesting and so mysterious. There's so much to do! There's so much we don't know!"

"Oh, Mom," said Maya. That was one thing she had in common with that little Henri, after all: she loved her crazy, wonderful mother so much that sometimes it hurt. "Just promise me you'll be okay. You'll be okay, right? And the baby, too? No matter what?"

"Maya, sweetheart," said her mother, wrapping her arms right around Maya as if she were as little as the boy in the pictures. "I haven't got any of this figured out. One thing I'm pretty sure of, though: as long as there are people in this world who love each other as much as I love you and James or you love me, *everything*—no matter what happens—is okay. Deeply, deeply okay. A thousand miles deep."

That wasn't exactly the promise Maya wanted, but in the great uncertain universes there are little havens here and there, where a person can relax for a moment and be at home, and this was one of those.

Maya closed her eyes and curled up next to her mother

like a comfortable question mark—like a salamander—and outside the window, where so much was so unknown, all of Paris hushed: the sky became white and tingly, a sky made of fog and opal (because magic, like love, passes on and on and on), and it began, for the first time that year, to snow.

ACKNOWLEDGMENTS

As I keep learning again and again from Rosemary Brosnan, it takes plenty of science and magic to turn a story into a real book. Thank you so much, Rosemary! Heartfelt gratitude also to Andrea Martin and the whole HarperCollins team. I am in awe of the talents of Iacopo Bruno. Andrea Brown and Taryn Fagerness keep things humming on the West Coast.

I am lucky to have true friends who are also good writers. Roo Hooke, Sharon Inkelas, and Will Waters kept me cheerful and afloat. Jayne Williams and Isa Helfgott hauled me over the rough patches. Linda Williams and Leslie Reagan supplied encouragement. Mark Sandberg shared great stories while walking uphill. Marguerite Holloway made everything seem possible.

The Apocalypsies, the members of SCBWI, and the writers who congregate at the Enchanted Inkpot taught me everything I might ever need to know, and then some. Special thanks to Lena Goldfinch, Pedro de Alcantara,

Tioka Tokedira, Ann Jacobus Kordahl, Regan Orillac, and Rachel Grinti for being such thoughtful early readers. My writer-neighbors Mike Jung and Malinda Lo inspire me. So do Cindy Pon and Sarah Prineas, who live slightly farther away.

I traveled up and down the West Coast with a wonderful bunch of writers in 2012—Marissa Burt, J. Anderson Coats, Jenny Lundquist, Jenn Reese, and Laurisa Reyes. Jenn and Jillian made Los Angeles and Seattle feel like home. Thank you!

My gratitude and affection also go out to the Archer-Axelson clan, to the incredible Berkeley Marina Dog-Walking Society, and to the kind people of Berkeley Friends Meeting; particular thanks to Biliana Stremska, for her infectious enthusiasm about all things Bulgarian.

I am truly grateful for the love and support of my very extended family. The New York nieces and nephew wow me with their talents; so do Caroline in Florida and Ruby and David in Wyoming! Bob Naiman traipsed around French forests. Kathryn Anderson made granola. Lenny Helfgott, whose heart is bigger than any banjo, led the bluegrass jams.

Thera Naiman, Eleanor Naiman, and Ada Naiman are the best readers anyone could have. And this book is dedicated, with love, to Eric Naiman, who wanted a story about East Berlin, but was forced, again, to settle for Paris.

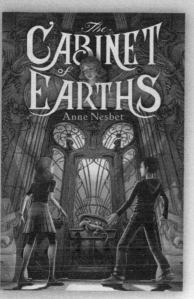